Leaving's Not the Only Way to Go

About the Author

Kay Acker grew up in northern Alabama and lives in southern Vermont. She and her wife play tabletop games with friends and enjoy the daily antics of two cats. The first queer romance novel Kay read was found in a public library and hidden in her room until well after the due date. She now borrows, reads, and writes them openly. This is her first novel.

Leaving's Not the Only Way to Go

KAY ACKER

BELLA
BOOKS
2021

Bella Books, Inc.
P.O. Box 10543
Tallahassee, FL 32302

Printed in the United States of America on acid-free paper.

First Bella Books Edition 2021

Editor: Medora MacDougall
Cover Designer: Judith Fellows

ISBN: 978-1-64247-186-1

Acknowledgments

Thank you to my dad and both of my grandmothers, who always did their best for me and, most importantly, read to me. Thank you to my wife, Ray, for so many things I can't possibly list them. Thank you to my dear friends, who talked me through problems, soothed my anxieties, praised my successes, and even bought me sushi. Thank you to my local librarian, who went above and beyond to find resources for me and provide encouragement when I needed it. Thank you especially to everyone who read this book and helped me make it the best it can be. Some of you are friends, some are kind mentors, and all of you are people I admire and am endlessly grateful to.

Dedication

For Ray, always.

CHAPTER ONE

When the bus pulled up at the last station, ten blocks from Prysliak and Associates Architecture Company, Lauren handed the driver five quarters. The bus fare was only twenty-five cents, but Lauren always tipped a dollar because Frank was a good driver who didn't talk to her much. That was a comfort when she was too exhausted to get around in her car safely.

"You have a good morning, Ms. Ashburn," Frank said, pocketing the change.

Lauren rubbed her eyes under her glasses and failed to smile. "Not a chance."

The snow piled up on the curb crunched when she jumped down from the bus. She bowed her head against the cutting breeze and tucked her bare hands deep in her coat pockets, regretting that she hadn't taken the time to put on gloves. It was bitterly cold, and the sun was a cruel joke in the gray sky. Vermont could be beautiful, but its current winter misery set a perfect tone for the day Lauren was about to have.

Today, Lauren was presenting the untested, unacceptable crock of crap that was the Green Mountain Architecture

Suite. Volunteering for this had been an intentional choice, a professional study in how to handle customers when things go wrong, because there was no way things were going to go right. They'd had nine months to build this software from scratch. Other companies would have spent a year or more, and those companies would have been specialized, not a freelance free-for-all like Green Mountain Software. Len, the CEO, had refused to admit there might be a problem with this timeline, and under the management of Felix, the problems had multiplied exponentially. No one would have run a software company like this back in Philly.

Then again, things hadn't been going as well as Lauren had planned in Philly, either. Who was the common denominator, the most likely cause of her underwhelming career?

Lauren scraped her boots off on the mat in front of Prysliak and Associates and entered at nine twenty sharp, ten minutes early. The restored colonial house the architects worked in was almost blindingly bright, all clean white paint and hardwood flooring. The receptionist behind the wide front desk signaled for Lauren to wait a moment while she wrapped up a phone call.

"Hello," someone else called. "Are you one of the trainers?"

A tall woman with waves of honey-blond hair was descending the stairs. The way her skirt swished allowed a glimpse of the pink Band-Aid on her right knee before Lauren averted her eyes. The woman didn't smile or extend her hand, but her voice was cheerful when she said, "I'm Georgia Solomon, one of the architects. Welcome!"

"Lauren Ashburn. My coworker isn't here yet."

"It'll take a few minutes for everyone to pull their noses out of their work and get to the meeting, anyway. Don't worry about it. Can I show you to the conference room?"

"That conference room?" Lauren said, pointing to the clearly marked double doors.

"Yes," Georgia said.

She headed in that direction, nodding when the receptionist waved gratefully. Her stride was long, her shoulders and hips were broad, and she didn't try to reduce the amount of space she took up. Lauren admired that kind of presence. She kicked herself for not being more professional in front of a woman with such poise.

The conference room was paneled with natural cuts of wood, and the wide gaps were filled with chunks of white marble. Lauren instantly classified it as strange, but Georgia said, "Most of the materials we use are reclaimed or recycled, and I love the effect of the broken pieces in here. It looks like a snowy forest."

Lauren gave the design a second look while she hung her coat on a stand by the door. She decided she agreed.

Georgia pointed out a series of photos framed on the wall. "These are from some of our previous projects."

The pride she felt for her work shone in her eyes and the way her fingers fluttered at her sides, so Lauren looked at the photos closely. She was surprised to spot a site she recognized.

"You renovated First Congo," she said, tapping on the framed picture of the First Congregational Church. "My parents got married there, and my dad threw a fit when they gutted it. He came around when he saw the arched doorways, though."

Lauren realized too late that she'd revealed her lack of familiarity with the company's work. Georgia didn't seem to notice, or at least she didn't mind.

"I do make a good arch," she said. Then she latched onto another detail Lauren hadn't meant to admit. "So you grew up in Holderness?"

Lauren nodded and moved on to the next photo without looking at Georgia. She got enough unimpressed looks from the locals who knew her; she didn't need judgment or pity about being stuck in her hometown from a stranger.

"Is this the crew I'm gonna be working with?" she asked, pointing at a group photo. She could see Georgia among the people gathered around a solar panel array.

"Pretty much," Georgia said. "Bev, the interior designer, is new, and Kyle is...not here."

"He got a new job?"

"He died."

That drew Lauren's eyes back to Georgia. The woman's face was blank, but her fingers had strayed to the ends of her hair, toying nervously. Lauren knew one was supposed to say something in these situations, but the usual platitudes made her roll her eyes at the best of times. After a month of gritting her teeth through people's banal condolences for the recent death of her father, she might actually gag on any kind words she tried to say.

Georgia spared her the effort by muttering, "I probably shouldn't have brought that up."

Lauren shrugged. "I've said less appropriate things."

At first she thought that was the wrong thing to say, because Georgia still didn't smile, but then her hands relaxed and drifted back to her sides. She met Lauren's eyes briefly. They stood together for a long, lovely moment.

It was a damn shame, because this woman was going to hate Lauren within the hour.

Georgia broke the silence between them by pointing out the environmentally friendly light fixtures in the conference room. She was explaining, with detailed hand gestures, how they worked when a tall, bear-shaped man in an L.L. Bean fleece blustered in.

"The Madisons are at it again, George," he said, "and I think the mister is an idiot, so can you put your eye to this issue real quick before I take his head off?"

"Excuse me," Georgia said to Lauren before telling the man, "You'd never take anyone's head off. Describe the problem?"

It was reassuring to know that man wasn't really a head taker-offer, because Lauren was pretty sure he was Gerald Prysliak, the man who had paid for Green Mountain's doomed software. She watched him and Georgia walk away, deep in a jargon-filled conversation that made Gerald fume but didn't seem to fluster Georgia at all.

Pretty and professional. Such a damn shame.

Her phone buzzed in her pocket, and she checked it, even though she knew what she'd read.

Good luck surviving your presentation! her little sister Tracy had texted. *Don't forget about the group tonight.*

Lauren didn't bother to answer. She'd already lost the argument about whether or not she should go to a bereavement group, and Tracy had worked hard to find one that was run by a queer woman after Lauren objected to the alienating spiritual approach of the group Tracy and their mother had joined. Tonight, Lauren was going to the Healing House, to sit in a circle and talk about dead people.

She turned her attention back to the light fixtures, still in awe of Georgia's grasp of the various concepts involved. Behind her, Felix clattered into the conference room like a goon. The employees of Prysliak and Associates gathered soon after, while Lauren and Felix queued up the architecture program to project on a large screen. When all eight trainees were assembled, Lauren began.

"So, the software we've prepared—"

Felix's voice boomed over hers, and Georgia visibly flinched. "Ladies and gentlemen, we're proud to bring you the Green Mountain Architecture Suite!"

He clicked the icon on the desktop with a flourish. For five long, dreadful seconds, nothing happened, but then the program booted. Slowly. The user interface looked decent, if maybe not quite what Lauren would have made if she'd been working on that area. Each drawing tool Felix demonstrated moved smoothly, although his lines were shaky from using a track pad—not the best method, according to Lauren's ignored research.

Georgia raised her hand and waited while Felix talked more, not noticing her. Lauren broke in and pointed to her when she had a chance.

"Are there other ways to draw on the interface? We've been using a tablet most of the time with our current system."

Felix was going to show off his vast knowledge, so Lauren leapt in and answered the question simply. "Yes, there are other ways to draw, such as mouse and touch screen on applicable devices, but it's not currently compatible with tablets."

A few minutes later, another woman raised her hand. She introduced herself as Bev and asked where the interior design example options were. Felix had to admit there weren't any. They were making a separate program for that, which would be available later in the year. Given that interior design was a new part of Prysliak and Associates' offerings, and therefore a burden on the programmers that was added later, Lauren considered this delay fair. Apparently Gerald didn't agree.

"That's not what we were told when Len showed us the demo," he said. Georgia nodded in confirmation.

"It became problematic when we started making the other requested changes," Lauren said. There had been a lot of requested changes, all of which Len had told the customers would be simple to make. They hadn't been.

"Is that the Bezier curve function?" Georgia asked, no longer waiting to be acknowledged before speaking up.

"Yes," Lauren said. She clicked on the button with a parabola on it, relieved that this was something she'd made and could count on. The Bezier curve created smooth arches that could be scaled almost infinitely. Lauren loved the simple elegance of the concept, and it had been a joy to program.

Nothing happened onscreen.

The deep breath Lauren took was subtle, unlike the calming breaths her father used to take, which had done more to signal his anger to others than to calm it. She'd been taking a lot of these deep breaths lately.

She clicked the Bezier curve button again. Nothing.

"What features *does* this program have?" Gerald asked.

"It transfers and converts files of different types, as requested!" Felix said.

He was going to continue, but Georgia spoke up with a voice that was suddenly loud with tension.

"Show us."

Dread made Lauren's knees weak.

One of the architects went upstairs for a flash drive with a file on it. Felix continued listing the program features that definitely worked, though the program got slower and less responsive as he went on. Lauren tried not to think the worst, but the idea loomed ever larger as the speed of the program decreased. When the flash drive was delivered, Felix plugged it in and opened the file.

And then the worst happened. The entire program froze, and when Felix tried to close it, it didn't respond. Neither did Task Manager, or anything else. He tried to pass it off as a problem with the computer, not the program, but Lauren knew better.

"It's a memory leak," she hissed at Felix. "Damn program's taken up the entire computer's RAM. Turn it off and start it up again. Or don't."

Felix shut down the computer, but he didn't restart it.

Lauren turned to the architects, the unhappiest clients she'd ever seen. Georgia in particular was turning red, and her smile was twisted and forced like a dented fender.

"Clearly," Felix squeaked, "there are some problems we were not previously aware of. We'll attend to them and start over next week. Thank you for your patience."

It was obvious to Lauren that the program wouldn't be fixed by next week. She suspected the clients knew that too. She left the building at a dignified pace, feeling Georgia's wrathful stare as she went.

Felix didn't offer her a ride back to town, and she wouldn't have taken it if he had. She slumped down at the bus stop and waited for Frank. What had she learned today?

One: Don't get optimistic about what you can accomplish. Lauren had quickly banged out a couple successful programs for Green Mountain Software in her early days, and Len had overshot the team's ability to keep up that pace.

Two: Don't rely on the manager to manage problems, especially when that manager is Felix.

Three: Lowering your standards does not improve your outcome.

Her father had told her this last bit of wisdom the day she applied at Green Mountain. Len's enthusiasm had charmed her, like it charmed all the people he lied to, and the low stakes of a small-town independent operation beat the constant stress of her corporate job in Philly, where she ground herself down to earn less money than she deserved and didn't even have time to spend it. Len paid even less, but he had promised much more.

He'd told her the workload would be manageable, especially for someone who had moved home to help care for her ailing father. He'd assured her she'd be filling her portfolio with work she could be proud of. He was a car salesman, and Lauren was the sucker who'd bought the lemon.

Her father had warned her. How could she ever make it big in Philly or somewhere better if she thought a place like Green Mountain Software was worth her time? Of course, maybe they'd both been too optimistic about what Lauren could accomplish.

On the ride home, Tracy texted her again.

You are going to the Healing House, right? You already missed the first week, and you promised you'd try. I love you.

Yes, I'm going! Jeezum crow, Lauren replied while she stomped from the bus stop to her apartment. *Love you, too.*

Her cat, Alan Turing, greeted her at the door. Lauren was too tired to avoid tripping on him if he wound between her legs, so she picked him up to keep him out of the way. He nestled close in her arms.

"You want a nap, buddy?" she asked him. "Let's take a nap."

She didn't bother turning on lights in her cramped apartment as she picked her way through the mess to the couch. The sun went down at five in mid-February, and the windows didn't let in much light anyway, so she'd gotten used to the dark. The dirty clothes on the floor and dirty dishes in the sink were familiar now, too. She tossed her button-up over the back of the couch, set an alarm on her phone, and went to sleep with Turing on her chest.

* * *

At six fifty-five that evening, she climbed the porch ramp of the yellow Healing House at a run, her breath visibly gusting in the cold. She was only five minutes early, as opposed to her usual ten, because she'd spent too much time picking her way up the slushy highway through the mountains north of Holderness, driving overcautiously on unfamiliar roads that led to unfamiliar destinations she didn't want to arrive at.

Still, Lauren was here now. This was all Tracy's idea, but Tracy was usually right. Taking a deep breath and squaring her shoulders, Lauren pulled open the Healing House door and stepped inside.

"Hello! Welcome!" an out-of-breath redhead called to her before rushing after a kid with boxing gloves on, saying, "David, we only wear those in the rec room, you know that."

Another kid shrieked, and Lauren watched a pair of twins wrestle over a piece of pizza they'd just dropped on the floor while an adult chose not to intervene. The noise, the chaos, was everywhere.

She took her coat off, but she wasn't sure she planned to stay. Maybe she was in the wrong place. Tracy hadn't warned her about kids being here.

"I like your shoes," a little voice said, quiet in the pandemonium.

Lauren looked at her soggy boots, then in the direction of the voice. There was a little girl with honey-blond hair crushed under a pair of over-the-ear headphones sitting on a beanbag chair in the corner. She had a phone in her hand, even though she had to be less than ten. Her shoes lit up as she drummed them hard against the beanbag.

"I like *your* shoes," Lauren said.

"Do you have a cat?" the girl asked. Her eyes were laser focused, but not on Lauren's face.

"Why do you think I have…" Lauren started to ask, then mentally slapped herself. She'd slept in a white shirt, with Turing on her chest, and hadn't changed it. She buttoned her flannel over the visible patch of black and gray cat hair the kid was staring at. "Yeah, I have a cat."

"Do you have a picture of your cat?"

"No."

The little girl didn't look disappointed. She just adjusted her headphones and started texting, still kicking the beanbag. A sudden bang in the house made both her and Lauren jump.

"The adult room is in the back," an Asian woman with a brace on her wrist said as she strode by.

Lauren latched on and followed her. Past the squabbling kids and through a kitchen that reeked of fast food, a door opened on a cistern of coffee and a cluster of adults chatting quietly. The closed door shut out the noise.

"Yikes," Lauren breathed.

"I know," the woman said. "I'm Annabel Liu, the adult programs coordinator. We only have two new folks tonight, and the other one's already here, so you must be Lauren, right?"

"Right. My sister mentioned your name when she ordered me here."

Lauren winced at her own phrasing, but if the comment offended Annabel, she didn't show it. She gestured with her coffee cup. "Feel free to introduce yourself around, Lauren, and we'll get started in a few minutes."

"Hey, young lady," a short man in a sweater vest called. He held up his arm, which had the same brace on it as Annabel's. "One of us is going to have to change!"

Annabel laughed and crossed the room to talk to her friend. Lauren was left alone to observe the scene and try not to feel abandoned. Every window was covered with cheap but heavy curtains, for privacy and to preserve the best efforts of the clanking radiator. The chairs set up in a circle in the middle of the room were a step above metal folding chairs, and the people seated in them seemed comfortable. They knew each other, at least a little bit. This bereavement group had only started last week, but that was enough to make these people not quite strangers to each other. Lauren felt distinctly on the edge of things, like the little girl in the corner who'd talked to her.

Just as the thought crossed her mind, Lauren felt the same intense gaze on her that the kid had given her dirty shirt. Against the opposite wall, obscured by the group of chatting people, another woman was sitting alone. She stared openly. Lauren guessed she was the little girl's mother, because they had the same honey-blond hair curling down in waves over their shoulders, but where the girl's look had been placid, this woman's face was blank with shock.

Lauren felt her cheeks and ears heat up. Sometimes it was comforting to know that someone else was having a worse day than her, but she hadn't intended to personally ruin an entire Tuesday for Georgia Solomon.

CHAPTER TWO

Georgia didn't stop herself from staring when Lauren Ashburn walked into the room. She watched the woman's eyes meet hers and her ears turn red under the shaggy ends of her short brown hair.

Should she say something? What was there to say? Hello, I don't know why you're here, but I wish you weren't, so please leave? Lauren might do it. If Georgia was reading her body language correctly, Lauren wished she weren't here, either. She looked right into Georgia's eyes, and the sweet natural smile on her lips was melting away.

Four seconds in, Georgia couldn't take the direct eye contact anymore, so she returned her attention to her phone. Hannah was texting her from the next room, trying to recover from the sensory overload a group of other children always caused. Georgia wanted to be sure she'd talked her through until she was well enough to participate in her meeting.

Everything would be fine already if Kyle were here, because he wouldn't be distracted and overloaded himself, like Georgia was, but that was the whole point of coming to the Healing House: Kyle wasn't here.

Lauren knew that. Lauren was about to know far more about Georgia than she should. Maybe this was a mistake, for Hannah and herself both. Maybe they should leave while they still could, before the meeting started. They could go home and—

"Okay, folks, gather around," Annabel said above the quiet murmur of conversation.

Too late to leave now. Georgia left her comfy, separate chair and joined the circle. The space was tight, especially for a large person like herself, and she struggled to squeeze herself between people to reach a chair. She fumbled with her purse and almost spilled it while she dug out her notepad and pen. Across from her, Lauren paused in the process of sitting down and raised an eyebrow.

Annabel said, "We have a couple new people today, so let's go around and introduce ourselves again before we start. Name, pronouns, something about yourself, and what brings you here today. Doug, would you start?"

Georgia rehearsed the list in her mind and started to practice, while also trying to keep track of people's names as they introduced themselves. What was something about herself? What did that mean, exactly?

"Lauren Ashburn, she/her. I'm a programmer for Green Mountain Software, and my dad is dead."

Half the circle flinched at the way Lauren said "dead." Other people had used phrases like "passed on," and Lauren's directness seemed to strike them between the eyes. The comfortable looseness of Lauren's body melted into slouching disengagement after she spoke, a lack of poise Georgia never would have dared in public. Georgia turned her attention to her own behavior. She kept her posture erect, her eye contact indirect but attentive, and scribbled quietly to release the tension of wondering how Hannah was faring, surrounded by strangers in the other room.

Then, suddenly, it was her turn.

"I'm Georgia Solomon, she/her," she said, then stumbled. She'd forgotten the script she'd planned, and everything there was to say about herself. "I'm…I'm really just here to find out what to do for my daughter, Hannah. Her father died, and it hasn't been easy."

Oh no, she'd said "died." Was that as bad as Lauren saying "dead?"

She looked at Annabel, who nodded. "A lot of people come here to help their children."

Georgia scribbled more on her notepad and let the tension go. What she'd said was good enough. The way the group had bristled like porcupine quills must have been more about tone than word choice. As long as she didn't slouch like Lauren was doing, she'd be fine, and they could ignore each other peacefully.

She got so good at ignoring Lauren, who didn't say another word, that she didn't see Lauren bolt for the door in the same moment she did once the meeting had ended. Lauren was shorter, and her hair was exactly under Georgia's nose when they ran into each other. Georgia caught a whiff of her shampoo, delicate and authentically floral, not chemical like most people.

"After you," Georgia said.

She waved Lauren through the door and followed behind, almost stepping on her heels.

Hannah had her ear defenders on. She ran to Georgia, and Georgia wrapped her up in the comforting tightness of a hug.

Annabel came out of the adult room and approached them.

"Do you mind if I check in with you both in my office?" she asked.

For a second, Georgia froze. Had she done something wrong after all? Had Annabel noticed the tension between herself and Lauren? But no, Annabel had said she might ask this, so Georgia didn't need to be nervous.

She and Hannah followed Annabel down the hall into a little room with a glass door. Hannah took her ear defenders off once the door was closed and the noise of the other children was reduced. Good. Maybe she hadn't spent the whole meeting so overwhelmed she needed to block things out.

"What did you think of your session, Hannah?" Annabel asked.

Hannah shrugged. "Fine."

"Was there anything about it you liked especially?"

Hannah swung her feet and kicked Annabel's desk by mistake. Annabel didn't flinch.

"I like Ms. Deb's hair," Hannah said, "and a lady with a cat."

"Who's Ms. Deb?" Georgia asked.

"Deb's the redhead. Not sure who has cats," Annabel said. She looked at Georgia for a second, then slid a basket on the desk in her direction. It was full of fidget toys: some soft, some clickable, some that spun, and one large chunk of hematite.

Georgia realized she had both hands running through her hair and fisted her sweater sleeves to stop herself. Annabel was a specialist, so she'd recognized that Georgia was trying and failing to soothe herself with the repetitive motion. It was called stimming, and she usually tried to be subtler about it. She never encouraged Hannah to hide her autism or adjust her behavior to blend in, but Georgia still kept herself in check when she could. Most people didn't know she was autistic as well.

Annabel turned her attention back to Hannah and said, "I like Ms. Deb's hair too. I think she has a granddaughter your age. Do you want to be friends with Ms. Deb, have her hang out with you during the session and make sure you're doing okay?"

Hannah nodded. Georgia made the effort to smile at Annabel. She'd made the right choice, bringing Hannah here for treatment.

When they left Annabel's office, Hannah said, "I'm hungry."

Georgia wanted to bounce around when she heard that, because Hannah had skipped dinner last night and shown little interest in food for days. "What do you want to eat?"

Hannah shrugged again. She was doing that a lot lately. Georgia led her outside to the car, considering her options.

"How about this? If you see a restaurant you want to go to on the way home, we'll eat there, and if not we'll have macaroni and cheese."

Hannah nodded, and she squinted out the windows to study the name of every place they passed. All the squinting Hannah did had convinced Kyle for months that she needed glasses, but really she just had a hard time focusing her attention on things that were moving, which Georgia understood. Trying to read road signs, especially the weatherworn ones on the country roads in rural Vermont, was hell. They were all the way back to Holderness, and Georgia was praying that Hannah wouldn't refuse macaroni, when Hannah finally spoke up.

"What's a catamount?"

"It's a mountain lion, a cougar."

"A puma?"

"Yep, they're called pumas, too."

Hannah pointed behind her and said, "I want to eat there. I want a waffle."

Georgia had seen the sign for the Catamount Café a few times while driving this way, so she knew what Hannah meant. That Hannah also knew what she wanted was an extra delight— she was perfectly healthy, but Georgia still worried about her fickle eating habits and her difficulty finding something she could stomach in the moment. Kyle had been much better at cajoling her than Georgia was. If Hannah felt ill and didn't want to eat for an entire day, what then? Georgia followed that worn-out worry in circles as she turned around and drove back to the Catamount Café.

While Hannah ate her waffle, Georgia picked at an omelet that wasn't exactly what she'd wanted and fiddled with a plastic jelly packet on the table. Her worry about Hannah was temporarily eased, so she turned to another: work.

Len Rogers, the owner of Green Mountain Software, was an old high school buddy of Gerald Prysliak, her boss. Georgia thought he was about as full of hot air as a flying balloon. Kyle had agreed. He and Georgia had warned Gerald that Len seemed to be promising an awful lot in a short time and a contract that provided assurances for all his guarantees might be in order. Gerald had assured them that Len always came through. He and Kyle had argued bitterly for hours about it, and they never quite made up before Kyle's heart attack.

Gerald regretted that fight more than anything. Today's meeting had proved Kyle and Georgia right, but Gerald was still holding on to some optimism. He had to, Georgia supposed. What else was he going to do, regret harder?

"I'll talk to Len," he'd assured Georgia before she left the office. "I'm sure they'll clean things up for next week. We'll be his top priority."

Much as Georgia wanted to believe him, seeing Lauren at the Healing House had banished any hope she had. If Lauren brought the same bitterness to her work that she had to the group, how good could her products possibly be?

And if the product was bad—which it was—the work they did on it would be bad, and they'd lose grant funding and fall behind on projects, and there was no plan B because Gerald had been so sure, and Gerald would be so sorry, but sorry wouldn't fix it, and—

"What are you thinking about, Mommy?" Hannah asked.

Georgia snapped out of her panic spiral and tried to make her face look reassuring. "Nothing, sweetie."

"Are you sad?"

"No."

"Am I eating too slow?"

"Of course not, you should always take your time."

Hannah stared at her for a moment, and Georgia stared back, thinking about how she could almost use that little face as a mirror, and she really needed to brush Hannah's hair tonight, if it wasn't too uncomfortable, and—

"You have to eat, too, Mommy."

Georgia looked guiltily at her half-full plate. She needed to stop thinking about work, regrets, and other worries that would come later. Right now, she needed to set an example, because her daughter was watching. Her daughter needed her.

"You're right! Thank you for reminding me."

Hannah slowly pushed a bite of waffle into her mouth, still staring. Georgia looked away and tried to eat.

CHAPTER THREE

"You're cutting those mushrooms wrong," Lauren told her sister.

"How can you cut mushrooms wrong?" Tracy said.

"I ask myself that every time I watch you do it."

Tracy rolled her eyes and handed Lauren the knife. Lauren finished dicing mushrooms in quick, even strokes while Tracy buttered a frying pan and gathered up cheese and eggs from the fridge.

Tracy liked having someone around in the mornings to keep her on track, so Lauren came over for breakfast when she was up early or, more commonly, up so late it became early. She was here today, instead of sleeping in like she'd wanted to, because she needed the comforting rhythm of making omelets in Tracy's clean, sunny kitchen. Not that she'd ever admit that.

"So the presentation was a disaster," Tracy said, bringing Lauren back around to her extended rant about yesterday. "We knew that was coming. What about the group?"

Lauren scraped the mushrooms into a dish and let Tracy whisk them with the cheese and eggs.

"A kid asked me if I had a picture of my cat," she said, because that was the only good news.

"Did you show her one?" Tracy asked.

"I don't have any."

Tracy almost spilled eggs into the stove burner when she jerked her head up to gawk at Lauren. "You don't? I have pictures of your cat! You're some kind of alien."

"We already knew that. You know what I don't know? Why people say they're 'celebrating the life' of people who die, like we're gonna throw a party or some shit."

The pan sizzled, and so did Tracy's glare.

"Please tell me you didn't say that."

"Didn't get a chance to. All I said was my name and that Dad's dead, and that was enough to put people off."

"You make first impressions like a cheese grater," Tracy grumbled. "*Why* did one instance of you opening your grumpy trap put the whole group off?"

Lauren could still picture the way Georgia's hands jerked across her notepad, scratching her pen on the page during the whole meeting. She'd driven the guy next to her nuts, but she hadn't seemed to notice.

"Well, one of them works at the architecture place, so she was already sour on me."

"And you got all negative and spiteful about that, and everyone heard it in your voice," Tracy guessed.

Lauren didn't waste breath admitting she was right.

Tracy shook a spatula at her before she folded the omelet. "You cannot let one person harsh your process! She doesn't know you, so who cares what she thinks? Focus on connecting with people who understand you."

Lauren let a little warmth seep into her voice when she said, "You understand me."

"I thought I did, but you willingly spoke to a human child and you don't take pictures of your cat! I don't know who you are anymore!"

Tracy launched into the dramatic monologue from the community play she was starring in, dropping to her knees on the kitchen floor. Lauren flicked pieces of eggshell at her, which made twice the mess she'd intended, and the cleanup made them both late for work. So much for keeping her sister on track.

On their way out the door, Tracy stopped her.

"I'm not gonna get another try out of you, am I?" she asked.

Lauren wanted to say no, but she hadn't really tried the first time. Of all the things she was failing at these days, sitting in a circle and trying to be pleasant shouldn't be one of them.

"Maybe one more try," she said.

Tracy's eyes lit up, and she hugged Lauren so hard they both slid a bit on the icy porch steps.

"I just want you to be happy," Tracy said.

Lauren hugged her sister back. She knew the feeling.

* * *

Felix insisted on using the squeakiest whiteboard marker while he wrote up the endless list of problems with the Green Mountain Architecture Suite. All employees were required to spend at least half their time in the office in order to build team cohesion, but Lauren felt she'd cohere with people much better if anyone bothered to replace the office supplies. Or at least the burnt-out fluorescents.

Lauren did her damnedest to slouch in her ergonomic office chair, even though she knew it made her look like she was being manhandled by a giant pleather lobster. Jamar, the third member of their team, hung his head back over the top of his chair. Even his tulip-yellow shirt, which in proper lighting would have brought out the warm earthen tones of his brown skin, looked dull in this environment. The only thing that stood out was Felix's blinding optimism.

"Prysliak and Associates still expect us to deliver a cutting-edge, professional program," he said, "and we have one week to do it. Can we do it?"

"No," Lauren said.

Felix scowled. "Can we do it?"

Jamar gave him a thumbs-up without lifting his head.

"If this is the kind of energy you've been bringing to this, no wonder it's a mess!" Felix whined. "Green Mountain Software makes dynamic programs, and we hire dynamic people to do it! Can we do it?"

"Do what, exactly? Where do we start?" Lauren asked.

This was a question Felix had never answered clearly. Priorities had shifted as Len's promises grew bolder, and Felix had discouraged them from examining other architecture programs because he wanted to "reinvent and reinvigorate the drafting experience." Lauren had ignored him on that, but it had only showed her just how far from the mark Green Mountain's project was veering. She still had no idea what architects actually wanted. Everything was half-done, and she needed to know what mattered before she decided what to do.

"Start with something you're passionate about," Felix said.

Jamar lolled his head over to roll his eyes at Lauren.

"Sure, man," he said. "We'll get right on that."

"I'm pretty passionate about not having memory leaks," Lauren said.

"Same."

Felix sighed and left them to it while he prodded his broken 3D feature.

By the end of the week, Lauren felt confident the program wouldn't shut down, and the Bezier curve function worked in 2D. It caused the entire 3D experience to curve, but that was fine in her opinion, because it was the closest to workable the 3D feature got anyway. Jamar was tantalizingly close to completing a clean interface; Lauren could see what he was going for, if Felix's pop-art predilection would get out of the way. Neither of them was sure what, exactly, Felix had accomplished. The night before the second presentation, he was still needling them about rewriting the whole program in LISP, which he claimed was "the most powerful programming language," even though he still couldn't articulate why.

On Tuesday morning, Lauren emerged from the pile of canned coffee and microwave meals she'd become buried in, almost fell asleep in the shower, and tripped on the third step onto the bus.

Her mother called just as Frank pulled away from the stop.

"Have you read the paper today?" she asked.

"No, Mom." Lauren never read the paper. These days she didn't need to, because Mom told her all about it.

"Ed Garritsen wrote another letter to the editor, and it is just exhausting. Listen to this!"

Lauren closed her eyes and let the gleeful sound of her mother scolding local fools soothe her. Her parents used to read the *Holderness Herald* together. She'd loved the sound of Dad's voice when he read a particularly silly headline aloud, like the one last year about someone stealing seventy whole pounds of organic broccoli in the night; laughter and affection had made his baritone growl smooth.

"Were people this ridiculous in Philadelphia?" Mom asked, and Lauren's chest tightened with anxiety again.

"Not that I noticed."

"I know you were planning to go back there, when we thought your father would bounce back from his first stroke, but it's not the only option in the world," Mom said. "If you got a job in Albany you'd still be close to Tracy. Not that you should be hunting for jobs based on how easy it is for your family to keep smothering you. It's just a suggestion. Have you looked there?"

Lauren hadn't been looking for jobs anywhere. She should have been—she'd said she had been—but it was yet another thing that slipped through her fingers when she tried to get a grip on her life.

"I'm heading into a meeting, Mom. Gotta go."

Mom hung up, and Lauren rubbed her eyes and tried to settle her heartbeat. This was not the state she needed to be in when she walked into Prysliak and Associates. She needed to stay calm and professional, no matter how bad it got. It would be over soon.

God, she really did need a new job.

The receptionist frowned when Lauren entered the building. Felix arrived a few minutes after Lauren did, and they set up at the front of the conference room and watched the architects gather, exactly on time.

Georgia cast a glance at the group photo on the wall as she passed it to sit at the very front. Her fingers twisted near her shoulder, where the ends of her hair would have been if it hadn't been pulled back in a bun. There was a bright green Band-Aid on her thumb, loose at the end from being picked at. The vibrant color choices made more sense now that Lauren knew Georgia had a kid, but the constant need to bandage herself up was a mystery.

Lauren tried to ignore the way she noticed and speculated on little details about Georgia. They'd met twice. After today, they'd never meet again.

"Ladies and gentlemen," Felix began, "may I present the new and improved Green Mountain Architecture Suite!"

Georgia raised her hand before the program had even finished opening. Lauren had planned to stand back and let Felix do all the flailing, but when he tried to ignore Georgia, she couldn't let it stand.

"A question already?"

"A few, actually," Georgia said. She tapped a notepad on her knee, and Lauren was close enough to see a long, numbered list written on the page.

"If you wouldn't mind holding questions until the end—" Felix said.

"I'd rather she didn't," Gerald Prysliak interrupted. "Go ahead, George."

Lauren nodded, though she didn't expect Georgia to need her approval.

Georgia cleared her throat and reversed the cross of her legs before she began. "The program Green Mountain Software described to us included a lot of enticing features, but at this time, we're concerned about the fundamentals. I'd like to see your program run the paces of a regular project. If you don't mind?"

Felix gulped. Lauren yanked an extra chair from the head of the conference table and sat heavily. She needed her tablet.

Georgia drilled down to the basic necessities of a program and pushed Felix to show her that his creation could provide any of them. She asked questions, explained best practices, and Lauren used a voice memo app to record every word she said.

Just when Lauren was ready to let go and give up, she felt herself getting a grip on this project at last. Felix clicked a button he shouldn't have—Jamar had told him that feature wasn't ready yet—and the program started to glitch and shudder to a halt again. Lauren barely noticed until Gerald spoke up.

"Does the lag I'm seeing mean the program is going to shut down your computer again?"

"There's no reason to expect that problem will arise again," Felix said. "We made repairing the memory leak our first priority, so—"

"So you want us to trust your abilities, despite not seeing any of them?"

Felix gaped like a fish. Lauren stepped forward and closed the program.

"I'm sure Len will be happy to hear your concerns," she said. "We'll continue working on the issues, as well as the separate interior design suite. You can expect to hear from us within the week about any updates."

It was a closing statement, poised and final. Felix turned his hanging jaw toward her, but she didn't care. They were done here. She had what she needed.

Gerald dismissed the meeting, and Lauren and Felix packed their equipment in chilly silence. Lauren turned back just before she left the building, in time to see Georgia turn on her heel and slam the door of the office at the top of the stairs.

"We need to have a team meeting," Felix snarled when they were alone in the parking lot outside.

"Sure," Lauren said, "but not this evening. I have another meeting to go to."

The Healing House wasn't where Lauren wanted to be tonight, but not going felt like running scared, and that wasn't her plan. Besides, she'd promised Tracy she'd keep trying.

Felix said, "I'll talk to Len first, then."

"You probably should. I'll put my notes in an email."

She sent the email to Len, with the audio file of Georgia's comments attached, on the bus ride home, and she set an alarm before she lay down to sleep. She drifted off to thoughts of

Georgia's steely eyes, her incisive comments, vast expertise, and professionally restrained disgust.

Right now, Georgia believed this mess was the best Lauren could do. Any other day, Lauren might have agreed, but Georgia herself had shown her the way. She could fix this.

Lauren lint rolled her shirt before she left the house and brushed her hair and teeth while she was at it. Just before she walked out the door, she yanked her phone out of her pocket and turned on the camera.

"Smile, Turing!" she called.

Turing lolled his head over the edge of the fridge, where he'd been sleeping, and preened. It was like he knew what a photo was.

"Perfect. Good boy!"

Lauren snapped a few pictures, then hurried off to meet her fate at the Healing House.

CHAPTER FOUR

Lauren Ashburn was not going to scare Georgia away from the Healing House. The thought of seeing her made Georgia's blood pound, but Hannah had mentioned the fish in the freshwater aquarium near the entrance a dozen times during the past week, and she'd asked more than once if Georgia thought the cat lady would describe her cat, since she didn't have any pictures to show. Hannah wanted to come back, which was more than Georgia had hoped for. She couldn't let anyone get in the way of that.

Besides, maybe Lauren wouldn't even be there. It didn't seem like she'd wanted to be last time.

Georgia kept her voice level when Hannah couldn't find her gloves, instead of letting the anxiety creep into her tone. She didn't tear the living room apart looking for her keys until Hannah had gone upstairs to check the bathroom for her gloves, either. They weren't even running late when they left the house, though they hit every red light on the way there.

"So you're going to spend the meeting with Ms. Deb tonight, right?" Georgia said as she hurried toward the yellow house.

Kyle had always reminded Hannah when there were plans in place, and it seemed to reassure her. He'd done the same for Georgia when she was upset.

Hannah nodded, hopping through the frozen snow in the yard instead of on the shoveled sidewalk. She had to stomp a lot, and Georgia scraped some snow off with her bare hands, to prevent tracking an entire flurry into the building. The already half-ruined Band-Aid on Georgia's thumb fluttered loose. She ripped it off and stuffed it in her coat pocket before twisting the freezing cold doorknob. They were now seconds away from being late.

The first person Georgia saw when she opened the door, of course, was Lauren. That would have been bad enough, but then she walked up to them, waving at Hannah. Hannah waved back.

"I took a picture of my cat," Lauren said.

Hannah bounced on the balls of her feet. "For me?"

Georgia froze. Lauren was the cat lady Hannah had liked? Hannah usually had good instincts about people.

Lauren looked at Georgia like she might bite and held up her phone. "Can I show her?"

Georgia glanced at the children's room, where the circle was waiting. Ms. Deb waved like Lauren had, but Hannah wasn't looking at her. She wouldn't be able to focus until she'd seen this cat picture. Did Lauren cause problems everywhere she went?

"Quickly," Georgia said.

Lauren knelt down and presented the phone.

"What's their name?" Hannah asked.

"His name is Alan Turing. Do you know who that is?"

"Yes! He studied secret codes, and he was autistic like me and Mommy!"

"Oh. I didn't know that about him."

Georgia was too frustrated to even try to guess what Lauren thought of Hannah's revelation about the two of them. She growled, "He's one of the most famous autistic people in history."

Lauren stood and put her phone away. "Clearly my professors left some things out. They didn't talk much about him being gay, either. It wasn't a history class, but still."

"Hannah, are you ready to start?" Ms. Deb called.

Hannah skipped over to her, explaining Alan Turing while Ms. Deb tried to settle her in. Georgia turned her back on Lauren and saw Annabel waiting for them in the doorway to the adult room. Did she look angry? They were definitely late. Georgia hurried into the room with Lauren close behind, and she didn't even have a second to appreciate that the chairs had more space between them this week. Annabel began the session immediately.

"Last week," she said, "I asked you to think about specific challenges you've had since your loved one passed, things about your life that changed or made it difficult to move forward. Would anyone like to share a challenge they identified?"

Julie, who had been reticent at the previous session, ran her fingers along the edge of the scarf covering her head and admitted softly, "This feels so trivial, but I didn't wash my hair for two months after Henry died. I didn't brush it, either. I dragged myself out of bed, dragged the kids to school, went to work. I did okay, getting things done that needed to be done. But I didn't take care of my hair, and now I'm afraid I'll have to cut it all off, it's such a mess."

"So why don't you?"

All eyes flashed suddenly to Lauren.

"You have a lot going on, right? And hair care isn't a priority right now, so just cut it off. It'll grow back."

Julie reached under her scarf, tangling protective fingers into the greasy hair at the back of her neck. "My husband loved my hair! I can't just get rid of it!"

Lauren leaned back in her chair and held up her hands. "I was just trying to be practical."

"*Practical* isn't always what people want," Georgia snapped. And who was Lauren to talk about practical after she'd made that useless disaster of a computer program? The fact that Hannah struggled with her own hair made Georgia even more defensive, coiled tight and ready to strike.

But Lauren said, "You're right," then turned to Julie and added, "Sorry." It was the last thing she said all night.

Georgia deflated, the passion she'd built up settling hotly in her cheeks. She scribbled violently on her notepad, scratching the paper audibly, heedless of Dylan's annoyance at the noise. When the meeting ended, she snatched her purse off the floor and stormed out of the room. She felt Lauren's eyes track her as she left.

What was this woman's deal?

She fumed into the children's room and found Hannah wrist deep in a sand table, chatting with Deb and clearly not ready to leave. Georgia waited in the hallway. Her fingers gripped and dug at the knitted patterns in her sweater until Annabel turned the corner and Georgia made herself stop.

"I'm so sorry we were late," she said. "It won't happen again. Lauren had something to show Hannah."

"That's fine. It didn't bother anyone. How was Hannah's second session?" Annabel said.

She seemed sincere, as far as Georgia could tell, so she relaxed. "Good, I think. She's talking to Deb right now, which is huge."

They both watched Hannah for a moment. She was crouched on the floor, holding a dustpan steady while Deb swept up loose sand.

"I thought those two might be a good fit," Annabel said.

Georgia made herself smile to indicate her pleasure. "It's definitely better than the Holderness Health Center. That guy was all over her, pushing and pushing for her to answer specific questions, and it seemed like she pulled into her shell more every time she saw him."

Annabel hummed, a noise Georgia assumed meant she understood. "I'll admit I was nervous about putting her in a group given her sensory issues—I know you were, too, but the direct approach just doesn't work with a lot of kids. Group sessions can take the pressure off. Your instincts are good."

Georgia puffed up with pride. Her instincts were just about all she had to go on these days. "Thanks. I'm just grateful to be working with someone who knows what they're doing."

"Hey, the health center workers know what they're doing, too. They're just doing it on hard mode. It's all forms and formulas down there because that's the only way to handle the massive caseload, and if they weren't handling it, no one would be."

"I guess I hadn't thought of that," Georgia said, and she didn't think of it now, either. "We're lucky you're out here."

Annabel smiled, but she seemed distracted. Georgia looked behind herself and spotted Lauren in the kitchen, draining a cup of coffee.

"Drive home safely," Annabel said, and she made a beeline for Lauren.

Georgia watched them for a moment. Did Annabel want to say something to Lauren about what happened in the session? Were they going to talk about her? Had Georgia been wrong to snap the way she had? Clearly she had been. What was she thinking? What were Lauren and Annabel going to do about it? Would they kick her out? Should Georgia apologize, like Lauren had? She couldn't right now, because Lauren and Annabel were talking. Should she wait?

Hannah tugged on her sleeve and asked, "Can we go to the Catamount again?"

Georgia stalled for a few seconds by thanking Deb, but Hannah was restless and Georgia was no good at apologies, so she left without saying anything. Lauren and Annabel were still talking.

* * *

Georgia was only a mile down the road when the back driver's side tire blew. The sound wasn't as dramatic as the way the car lurched under them, and Georgia swerved a little in her lane before pulling over.

"What was that?" Hannah said. She looked out all her windows frantically, trying to spot the sudden problem.

"Just a flat tire, nothing to worry about," Georgia said while she started to worry. They were just far enough away from the Healing House that it was dangerous to walk in the cold and dark, but it was also dangerous to flag down a random stranger for help. How did one go about calling a tow truck? There wasn't enough signal for the Internet to run efficiently, so she couldn't google it, and she didn't know who to call who would know. God, this was going to be expensive, a tow plus a replacement tire plus a change, and who knew how long it would take for a tow truck to even get here. Could she keep Hannah warm enough while they waited? They could both get frostbite and—

Someone had pulled over behind them. The driver's door opened, and a familiar figure walked toward Georgia's car, strangely shadowed in the streetlights but identifiable nonetheless. Georgia rolled down her window.

"Need help?" Lauren Ashburn asked.

"We have a flat tire!" Hannah said, still panicked.

"I saw that." Lauren nodded, calm and casual. Hannah started to mirror her, bobbing her head up and down while Lauren asked, "Do you have a spare?"

"I don't know how to change a tire," Georgia said.

"Lucky I do, then. Do you want me to do it for you, or show you how?"

"Show me!" Hannah said, already unbuckling her seat belt.

Georgia followed Hannah's lead and got out of the car. She was startled by the sudden change in Hannah's mood. One smile from Lauren, and she was ready to stand around in the wind and learn new things?

Lauren asked Georgia to pop the trunk, and Georgia remembered the mess piled back there. How embarrassed should she be? Lauren simply gathered it all up in her arms and tossed it into the backseat, so Georgia let it go. She was more concerned about the fact that Lauren insisted she could change a tire on her own despite not looking like much of a beefcake. The last thing Georgia needed right now was more of Lauren's incompetence.

"Are you sure you're strong enough to do this? It seems like something that requires some…torque."

Lauren pulled the spare out of its hidden compartment in the trunk and dragged it over the back bumper until it could slide to the ground under its own weight. Georgia winced. A scraped bumper would be the cherry on top of this mess of a day.

"There's more than one way to skin a cat," Lauren said. At Hannah's gasp, she changed metaphors. "To peel a potato. You just have to lean into your own strengths."

"That's my point. I don't have any strength."

Lauren looked up sharply from the metal tools in her hand. "Look," she snapped, "I'm saying you can do this. If you've decided you can't, then you're wrong, not me."

Georgia's look of shock fell on Lauren's back, because just as quickly as her mood had swerved, she turned away and knelt beside the punctured tire. Chastisement wasn't something Georgia usually handled with grace. Hannah was watching her, though, and Lauren kept reacting in ways Georgia didn't expect or understand, which meant she'd misread the woman somehow. Apologies didn't come easily to Georgia, but there was one way forward now that might be an olive branch.

"Teach me," she said.

Lauren tossed her head in an odd way, and a few seconds later, she said aloud, "Come here."

Georgia crouched on one side of her and winked at Hannah, who was already squatting at Lauren's other elbow and pointing a flashlight under the car.

"These ridges in front of the tire here? That's the jack point. It's a strong spot on the car's frame that can handle holding up the weight of the body. You put this—" she waved a diamond-shaped metal device in the light—"under here and line it up with the jack point."

She hooked a metal bar through a hole in the jack and began turning it. Slowly, the car rose up until some weight had been taken off the flat tire but the treads were still touching the ground. Then she held up another tool: a long, angled wrench.

"Now this is the part where all that torque you're worried about comes in. Upper body strength doesn't tend to be a specialty in people with our build, but we come with advantages too. Lower center of gravity, for one, and leg strength. So you put the wrench on the bolt..."

Lauren showed Hannah the hexagonal hole in the wrench, then lined it up with a bolt so the handle pointed diagonally up. She stood, grabbed hold of the bike rack on the roof of the car, pulled herself up, and put both feet on the handle of the wrench. Then she hopped on it.

Georgia instinctively tried to catch her, but Lauren slid off the now downward-pointing wrench and landed comfortably on her feet.

"See? You can use your entire body weight to loosen and tighten the bolts. You try."

She pulled the wrench off the tire and held it out to Georgia.

Well, Georgia thought as she took the wrench in her hands like a live snake, *I do have plenty of body weight.*

The shoulder of the road was damp and gritty, so she continued to crouch rather than kneel to plug the wrench onto a bolt. Lauren stood close when Georgia put one foot on the wrench.

"Get a handhold before you step up," she advised.

A sound suggestion, Georgia had to admit. The cut on her thumb was tightening in the cold, and the scrape on her knee, which she'd earned tripping up a client's porch steps, had only recently healed. It'd be just her luck to tip over backward now and crack a tooth or something.

Georgia gripped the bike rack and pulled herself up like Lauren had. Both her feet were on the wrench, and it didn't budge. She bounced a little, and her flats slid. Lauren caught her by bracing one arm against the car, not touching her directly.

Oh, but she was so close. The smell of her shampoo filled Georgia's nose again, and that sweet curve of her lips made Georgia's former anger simmer into something else. Lauren was aloof and incompetent, except when she was sincere and able, and the fact that she was so handsome didn't make that less confusing.

"Shift your weight forward," Lauren said, "and put your feet closer to the end of the wrench."

The tire. Right.

Georgia followed Lauren's instructions, and the bolt turned slightly. Emboldened by the hint of success, she hopped. The wrench dipped down under her weight, and she slid off it into Lauren's steady hands.

"Yay Mommy!" Hannah cheered.

Lauren moved Georgia aside and pulled the wrench off, then instructed Hannah on how to unscrew the bolt the rest of the way by hand. They leaned in close, their heads together and fingers bumping in the small space, but Hannah didn't seem to mind.

Another car slowed, but Georgia waved them on. She had all the help she needed.

CHAPTER FIVE

Lauren waited until Georgia and her daughter had successfully pulled onto the road and turned a corner before she drove away. It had taken almost an hour to replace the flat tire, but Georgia had agreed when Lauren said a tow truck would have taken just as long and been far more expensive. Georgia had been pretty agreeable overall, once Lauren proved she knew what she was doing and had the strength to do it. That was deeply satisfying. There was a time when Lauren wouldn't have been quite this winded, though. Where had all her muscle gone?

She was almost home and half asleep when she got a text from Tracy: *Check on mom plz?*

You check on her if you're so worried, Lauren wanted to say, but Tracy lived on the other side of the state line and didn't know Lauren hadn't made it home yet. She bypassed her driveway and continued toward downtown Holderness.

Ashburn's Art Supplies was the only store still open on Main Street, its lights burning clean and golden in the winter dark. The dusty windows of the empty storefronts on either side made it seem like Ashburn's was the only oasis of life in a ghost town. Lauren came in through the front out of habit, because her dad had always insisted that it made it seem like there were more customers coming and going. The sleigh bells tied to the door thumped and jangled. Lauren's mom was behind the checkout counter, but she didn't look up from her knitting.

"Aren't you supposed to greet customers, Mom?" Lauren asked.

"Oh, you're buying something, are you?"

"I'm here to help you close up. It's almost ten."

"So what?" Her mom leaned back in her chair and put her feet up on the counter. "You know classes are going at the college. A desperate art major could burst through that door any second. Why are you filthy?"

Lauren took the hand wipe her mom shoved at her and scrubbed as best she could. "Tracy said you were open past ten last night too. And that you sat down in front of the TV instead of going to bed when you went home."

Mom threw her knitting down in disgust. "That traitor."

"You know she tells me everything. Always has," Lauren reminded her. She didn't bring up other things Tracy had mentioned, like the way Mom had cried when she finally threw out the lilies that had been on the counter or the uneaten food Tracy cleaned out of the fridge at their parents' home. Partnership was what Tammy Ashburn was built for. Being alone was taking a toll.

"Do you want to stay at my place for a while?" Lauren offered, even though she hated the thought.

"I don't want to be within ten feet of a cat and you know it. I'm fine."

Mom picked up her knitting and scrunched further down in her chair, as if she could make Lauren go away by getting comfortable where she was. Lauren hated when her mom had the same body language as her. She put her elbows on the counter, leaning in close and forcing Mom to make eye contact.

"Tracy sent me because I'm not gonna be nice," she said. "I'll tie you to a hand truck and wheel you to bed if I have to."

"Doesn't Tracy want you to be nicer?"

"Not to you."

Mom shook her head as she wound up her yarn. "That girl is so sentimental. She doesn't understand that we need to sell off as much of this inventory as we can before our lease is up in May. Everything must go!"

It was useless to protest that maybe Tracy just wasn't ready for everything to change all at once, that maybe a little sentiment was in order. Whether or not the store closed didn't matter to Lauren. Let some other tenant take over the ghost of all those summer days wasted behind the counter, running the register while her friends ran around in the hot sunlight. Let new initiatives replace the same old displays that had stood in Ashburn's for decades, and maybe there'd be some joy here again, instead of wasted possibilities. Let her father and his goddamn store go. Good riddance.

"Store's barely been profitable for years now," Mom mumbled. Lauren took her elbow when they reached the front steps. Mom locked the door with a sharp clack. "It won't do any better with me running it by myself. It's just not practical to keep it."

Those words reminded Lauren of Georgia's glare and the angry way she gripped her pen. When Mom asked how the training had gone, Lauren lied. The confidence she'd felt this morning was being eaten away by the exhaustion seeping out of her bones. She'd worked over one hundred hours in the past week, and it had gotten her almost nothing. Was it really practical to try to tackle this program again? It probably wouldn't be enough to save the contract. She should spend her energy jumping ship, not trying to plug the hole that was making Green Mountain Software sink. This morning wasn't the first time a pretty face and a good pitch had gotten her hopes up.

Lauren waited until her mother had started up her car and driven away, just like she'd watched over Georgia and her daughter, then finally drove home.

Turing had choice words for her when she made her way into the kitchen. He'd been starving all day without her, he seemed to insist, not that she cared. Lauren filled his bowl before she even took her coat off.

"Someday I'm gonna get a bowl with a timer on it so you don't have to wait for me, buddy," Lauren said, just like she did every night she was out past nine. Turing blinked his eyes at her, loving now that he was able to eat dinner.

Cereal was the easiest thing available for Lauren to eat, so she poured herself a bowl of Raisin Bran and headed toward her computer room. When Tracy called, Lauren reluctantly answered.

"Did Mom go to bed?"

"I've had a long enough day without trying to parent Mom," Lauren told her sister while she tossed her glasses aside and rubbed her eyes. She shoved her dinner dishes from last night aside and put her cereal bowl on an empty square of desk. Turing took a sip before she could stop him.

Tracy hummed in knowing sympathy. "The presentation went badly."

"It wasn't gonna go well. Then I went to the Healing House for some stupid reason, even though I knew the architect and her kid would be there, and...What'd you say last week, about harshing people's process? I don't think I'm going back."

"I'm surprised you went today. She must be hot."

Lauren relived the buzz she'd felt standing close to Georgia, ostensibly to catch her if she fell off the tire wrench. Her wide hips had filled the circle of Lauren's arms, and the shimmer of her hair in the streetlight was almost irresistible. Even the redness of her face when she was frustrated was as enchanting as it was intimidating. So yeah, Georgia was hot, but that was irrelevant.

"Sure, I'm going to a bereavement group to cruise for sexy single moms. And did you miss the part where I made an ass of myself in her workplace and she's pissed at me?"

"Tina dated you for fifteen months after you ran her over with a shopping cart."

"Tina had bad taste."

"So what are you going to do about this?"

Lauren groaned. "Hell if I know. For a while today I thought if Jamar finished the layout and got all the bells and whistles out of the way, I could—"

"I meant about the hot architect mom," Tracy corrected, even though they both knew Lauren had understood her the first time. "You went to the group to see her, so you obviously care. What's your next move?"

Lauren considered denying it, but there was no point. She told Tracy everything eventually.

"I fixed her tire."

"Are you the reason it was broken?"

"No!"

"Good, then. The Ms. Fix-it look suits you, all greasy and sweaty and muscled."

Lauren scoffed. Her lips were cracked and flaking from the cold, she'd smeared road grime on her forehead when she'd pushed her bangs back, and she stunk from overheating in her coat while she worked. Super sexy.

"I got the job done," she said, "and next time she won't need help. I taught her and her kid how to fix it themselves."

"Did you eat a candy bar and supervise while they cried, like Dad did?"

Tracy laughed, but Lauren swallowed bile. He hadn't let her help her sister at all, even when Tracy caught her finger in the jack. Everything worth doing, he'd said, you should be able to do on your own.

"Was she impressed?" Tracy moved on when Lauren didn't respond to the joke. "Did you talk about the program? Did she swoon into your competent arms?"

"Not the point, Trace," Lauren said. She refused to think any more about Georgia in her arms.

On the floor by her feet, Turing was kneading on her workbag. She thought about Georgia's voice, loud and slightly shaking as she laid out exactly what her company needed from a program. Once again, code scrolled out in her mind's eye like the horizon in a dream about flying.

That damn architecture software couldn't stand. She could fix it on her own, like she'd planned this morning, couldn't she? The nightmare scenario had already played out, so she definitely couldn't make it worse.

"Are you finally going to bed now?" Tracy asked.

"Nah," Lauren said. "I have work to do."

CHAPTER SIX

It had been a long time since Georgia spent all night thinking about a woman, and the previous times had been more pleasant. Her current fixation on Lauren was irksome, and it brought her mind back to very urgent problems at work and at home. She was drawn to gentle, loyal people, the kind who took the time to understand and make space for her oddities instead of rushing ahead and plowing over. Lauren had thundered over people's feelings with her brusque attitude before, and she'd sat back and fiddled with a tablet all morning during the second presentation, leaving her coworker to the wolves. Last night though, working on the car tire, she had been so diligent, so patient and insistent on teaching, even when Hannah dropped the bolts. She'd also brought a picture of her cat to share, just for Hannah, who she didn't even know. Had those just been apology gestures? Because it didn't make up for the crisis that was the Green Mountain Architecture Suite.

Georgia knocked lightly on Gerald's office door. He hadn't asked her to stop by, but after nine years working for him, she knew she should. She only wished Kyle were with her.

Gerald let her into the office, then sank back into his place on the couch, gripping his head in his hands, while Georgia closed the door.

"So now we know what the 'old high school friends' discount buys," he said.

"What do you want to do about this?" Georgia asked.

She sat next to him, probably a bit too close, but he didn't move away.

"What can I do?" Gerald said. "We've canceled our contract with the other program, and it runs out next month. If we went back, we'd have to pay out the nose, and we'd have the same old problems we were trying to avoid with the new system. And still no interior design suite for Bev to work with! God, we did all that work to clean up our files and transfer them to another program."

"Did you know it can take a year or more to program something like this? I looked it up. Len gave his people nine months. It could have been better than this, but it wasn't going to be great."

"I could always trust him on the lacrosse field, I figured..." Gerald rubbed his face with both his hands. "I'll call Len, see what he has to say, but if he rushed this, he's probably rushing other things too. Doesn't leave a lot of time to backtrack and repair. God, how'd I let myself get into this mess?"

"It's not your fault that you trusted your friend."

"I should have trusted you and Kyle. You two never let me down."

Gerald swallowed hard, like he had at the funeral. Had he cried eventually, or had he kept it in all the time like he was now? He'd been so strong for her and Hannah. Georgia patted his knee, trying to be strong for him now.

"We'll work it out," she said.

When she left work that evening, though, she was troubled by it, and after she'd eaten dinner with Hannah she was still troubled. She had to force the whole issue from her mind in order to get to sleep. She kept imagining an office with no software, doing things by hand and trying to explain that to clients while Green Mountain Software promised a solid product and failed to deliver week after week. Money, time, and contracts hemorrhaged in every scenario she envisioned. Lauren loitered at the edge of every worry, looking up from her tablet to smile at the bedlam.

* * *

Georgia was on her way out of work the next week, still stewing, and worst of all worried about what it would be like to face Lauren at the upcoming bereavement group meeting, when she stopped short on the staircase.

Lauren was in the lobby. Her gaze was fixed on the middle distance, the natural smile on her lips at odds with the way she ran a hand through her short hair and tapped her foot. Of course she was a woman who hated to wait. But who was she waiting for? Was Gerald using her to talk sense into his high school buddy?

"Hi," Georgia said when she reached the bottom of the staircase.

"Do you have time right now?" Lauren said. She clearly expected a particular answer.

Georgia checked the clock on her phone before answering. "A few minutes."

Lauren nodded and started up the staircase, brushing past Georgia and heading directly for her desk. She yanked a laptop out of her messenger bag and snapped it open.

"Try this."

"What is it?" Georgia said as she settled in her chair. Lauren knelt beside her, balancing with her elbow on the armrest of Georgia's chair.

"It's the program. Try it."

The familiar Green Mountain Software logo stood open on the laptop screen. Just the sight of it raised Georgia's blood pressure, but she clicked the icon. What unfurled before her, smooth as butter, was a cleaned-up version of the previous software layout with neat rows of toolbars and features. The laptop hummed steadily as Georgia opened menus, and the pen tool didn't lag when she sketched a cartoon house on the drafting page with the track pad.

"Jamar got it to hook up with a tablet. I know that's better for drawing," Lauren said.

Georgia hummed distractedly, focused on how easy it was to create Bezier curves. Then she found the file download menu. Ready for disappointment, she stuck a random flash drive into the laptop's port and uploaded the biggest file she could find. It loaded. It opened. It wasn't distorted by translation errors because of the file type. The program didn't crash.

"You fixed the button to nowhere."

Lauren nodded, grinning when Georgia looked down at her.

She had fixed everything. In just a few days, from top to bottom, Lauren had fixed it.

"Did you do this on your own time? Len said you were all too busy to get changes made before the end of next month."

"It's easy once you identify the problem," Lauren said. "And you said you needed a functioning program right away. I took that seriously."

Lauren's voice was firm, but her grin hadn't faded, and her eyes were sparkling with pride. Her eyes were dark brown. They were beautiful, and now was not the time to be noticing that.

Georgia turned away from Lauren's steady gaze and futzed with the program. This woman had taken *her* seriously, had been listening to her the whole time. And the program she'd made...

"It's wonderful. Why is this so wonderful when the original was so bad?"

Lauren shrugged, sinking down to sit cross-legged on the floor by Georgia's chair. "Not enough time was one issue, and our priorities were really mixed up. A lot of daring new ideas, not a lot of follow-through. We'll get to the fancier features eventually, but this should have everything you need to get by for now."

Lauren came into sharp focus for Georgia in that moment. Her circumstances were tragic—she'd lost her father, which Georgia hadn't given her much sympathy for—but she made no excuses and cut herself no slack. And she cared, and she was so pretty.

Georgia cleared her throat to help clear her mind. "So what do you do now?" she asked.

Lauren's grin faded. "Felix is the project manager. Jamar and I'll take it to him so he can—"

"Screw it up or take all the credit? No. Kyle can…" Georgia mentally staggered at the slip-up, the instinctive turn toward Kyle's expertise and steady presence. "We should take it to Gerald. You can count on him."

"How did you make that work, being coworkers with your ex?"

Georgia paused. Lauren really, really listened to her, it seemed.

"He wasn't my ex, he was my co-parent. I mean, we were together a few times, but not…together. We worked together the whole time we knew each other. It's how we met."

"That's asking for trouble."

Georgia remembered trying to explain the situation to Gerald when it had first arisen and frowned fondly.

"I guess," she said. "We always agreed it wasn't serious between us, and maybe we should have just not been together, but it was fun. Then we found out we were going to have Hannah. Neither of us expected to ever have the usual kind of family, so we decided we wanted to have her. We weren't a couple, but we were a team. It honestly might have been harder to work together if we hadn't had the excuse to stay close."

Georgia noticed she was rocking her chair back and forth and stopped. Kyle's office was right below Georgia's desk. He used to tease her about being able to hear her rolling around and fidgeting in her chair. One day, he said, he was going to bang on the ceiling like she was a rowdy neighbor, but he never did. He never would. Georgia shook her head so hard her neck popped, dislodging her helpless thoughts like buzzing flies.

"I need to pick up Hannah," she said, "but we should set up a time to present your program. I'll talk to Gerald."

Lauren looked up at her for a long moment before she hauled herself up from the floor and started searching her pockets. Eventually she produced a business card. "My schedule's flexible," she said. "Just call and tell me when to show up."

She gathered her computer and headed for the stairs, rubbing her eyes as she went. Georgia followed her all the way out to the parking lot. Lauren walked down the block toward a bus stop, and Georgia stood beside her own car and watched her go.

"How about that?" she muttered. Georgia felt like she'd been shoveling mud for weeks now and suddenly struck gold. Kyle would have teased her for hours.

CHAPTER SEVEN

Lauren went to bed the moment she got home from Prysliak and Associates, and she slept until the early hours of the next morning. Georgia Solomon had already texted her when she got up, proposing a meeting time with her and her boss. Lauren texted back that she'd be there. Then she started sorting garbage from recycling and piled all her laundry in one corner. At seven, just when she'd soaped up a sponge to do dishes, Tracy called.

"Do you know where Mom is?" she asked. "I called the house and the store and her cell, but she hasn't answered."

There was panic in her voice, and Lauren caught it quickly. "Are you at home?"

"Yeah. I'm sorry, I know it's early, but you're closer. Could you—"

Lauren rinsed the dish soap off her hands and said, "I'm on my way."

* * *

She found her mother pacing in circles around the fountain in the town square. She was drinking coffee out of the mug Tracy had made her at camp fifteen years ago, pausing when she took a sip so she didn't spill anything on the clothes she'd been wearing since yesterday. Lauren took a deep breath. She smelled her mother's coffee and the chill of fresh snow.

"What are you doing out here, Mom?"

Mom stopped her pacing and smiled at Lauren, waving her over to join her. "I'm having my first cup of coffee and enjoying this beautiful morning!" she said.

"You didn't want to sit down?" Lauren asked, pointing to one of the wrought-iron benches a little farther back from the fountain.

"Can't sit still," Tammy grumbled. "Too cold to enjoy my pastoral scene."

It was cold, but the sprawl of New England houses draped in white was a sweet enough view that it didn't seem so bad. The snowy ground reflected up into a pale, colorless sky that was still dropping flakes. Black branches, sagging with the weight of white, barely etched a border between above and below.

Lauren followed her mom around the fountain in silence, watching her as she scuffed snow off the bricks under her feet. The town had constructed a timeline of Holderness along the path, then sold commemorative bricks that locals could get inscribed, which Lauren hated. Mom stopped and ran her sneaker around one brick fondly.

"Here's the one your father put in for you girls!"

Etched in black on the red stone was the message FOR LAUREN AND TRACY ASHBURN, FROM LUCAS ASHBURN, ASHBURN'S ART SUPPLIES.

Lauren scowled. "He didn't put it in, you made him put it in. And he made it weird by putting the store name on it."

"It's wonderful advertising. You wouldn't believe the number of customers who mention this brick when they come in. And besides, it's not nearly as tacky as this one." Tammy scuffed her heel on a brick that said FOR OUR BELOVED KITTY. "Why would you pay fifty dollars to put in a brick for a cat?"

"It's not for a cat, Mom. It's for a person named Kitty."

"Oh. Not Kitty Bakerson?"

At Lauren's parents' wedding, Kitty Bakerson had elbowed the maid of honor in the face to catch the bouquet, which had resulted in a hospital trip and an unreturned deposit on the maid of honor's rented dress because the blood wouldn't come out. Mom had asked Kitty to pay for the deposit, but Kitty had loudly and publicly refused. The enmity between her and the Ashburns had been burning steadily ever since. Lauren didn't know for certain that she was the Kitty this brick was for, but she told her mother it was probably was.

"Ugh." Tammy took a drink of coffee and continued her walk. "See, there's another reason why you'll be happier when you get out of here again. No more living in the same town as Kitty Bakerson."

"Can you finish your coffee and come inside, please?" Lauren said. She loved listening to her mother rant about her mortal enemies, but she did not want to be reminded of her failure to launch at seven thirty in the morning.

Tammy swigged her coffee and crossed the street without looking. Lauren followed, calling Tracy as she went.

"Found her at the fountain."

"The one that has the brick with our names on it?"

Lauren rolled her eyes. "I hate that thing."

"Why? It's great advertising," Tracy said. There was a sizzle on her end of the phone, and Lauren started planning to come over and steal Tracy's breakfast. "Did you show off that program you worked on all week?"

"Yeah, I—" Lauren covered the phone to tell her mom, "no, I'm not staying, I just wanted to know where you were," then continued despite Mom's continued questions. "I took the program out there yesterday. Georgia said it was good."

"Georgia did, huh?"

"Shut up, Tracy. And make extra bacon for me."

"I already am," Tracy said, and when Lauren arrived at her house twenty minutes later, there was plenty to go around.

"I told Mom to keep her cell phone on her from now on. She went on that jag about 'why don't we just put her in a home already.'"

"I figured you'd get an earful of that. Sorry," Tracy said while she packed her briefcase. She wiggled her eyebrows when she returned to the table and said, "Now, tell me about Gina."

"Georgia," Lauren corrected. She chewed bacon and waited a minute while Tracy repeated the name to herself, memorizing it. "She got the meeting set up immediately. It's first thing Monday morning."

"That makes sense, given that they expected the program to be ready, what, two or three weeks ago? But why didn't you take it straight to the boss?"

"Georgia would have told me if there was anything wrong with it. I respect her opinion. Plus, I'm technically not supposed to go over Felix's head and interface with customers on my own."

She didn't mention that she'd gone along with Georgia's plan to bring the program straight to Gerald herself instead of following up with Felix right away. Neither of them had any reason to trust him with Lauren and Jamar's hard work.

"So she's brilliant and efficient," Tracy said, "she has a kid, she lives in town. What else?"

Again, Lauren stuffed her mouth and paused before she spoke. Tracy had had a friend in middle school who was autistic, if Lauren was remembering correctly. Maybe she could answer some of the questions Lauren hadn't had time to ask the Internet about.

"Do you know what the odds are of a kid and a parent both being autistic? I thought it just popped up sometimes, like your dyslexia thing."

"Autism and dyslexia are both genetic, so sometimes it pops up and sometimes it passes down. Why? Do you think Georgia's autistic?"

"No, but her kid said they both are. Maybe it's like Asperger's or something?"

Tracy stole the last slice of bacon right out from Lauren's hand. "Asperger's is mostly just autism that doesn't look how people expect it to. For some people the separate label is important, but if Georgia calls it autism, you should stick with that."

"I don't know what she calls it, Hannah just blurted out that they're autistic when I showed her a pic of Turing."

"The kid has a name!" Tracy gasped. "And you remember it! You're almost as bad at that as me."

Lauren stuck out her tongue. At least Tracy hadn't latched on to the fact that she'd gone out of her way to take the picture.

Instead, Tracy sighed wistfully. "Your first crush since you left Philly. I never thought I'd see the day."

"I've had dates in the past two years, Trace."

"None that I've heard of!"

"Well, you don't hear about everything, what do you think of that?" Lauren lied.

Tracy swatted her shoulder. "I think you need to get out of my house so I can go to work."

"Ah yes, the thrilling world of accounting awaits," Lauren said. "I'll leave when the dishwasher's loaded."

Tracy rounded up her belongings, hugged Lauren, and headed for the door. Before she closed it, she called back, "From now on, I expect to hear *everything*, got it?"

"Yeah right," Lauren said. A few minutes later, she left the house behind with the dishwasher humming. It was eight thirty, which left her just enough time to get to work.

* * *

Sunday night found her working late again, playing catch-up on another work assignment she'd been neglecting in favor of the Architecture Suite. At ten, when she was half dozing, the phone rang. She jumped and spilled coffee on her lap, which contained a sleeping Turing. The poor cat yowled and ran away, clawing a loose thread into Lauren's jeans as he went. Lauren swore while she hunted around for her phone and doubled her gripes when she saw it was Georgia calling. What the hell could she possibly want?

"Yeah?"

"Have you checked the weather?" Georgia demanded on the other end of the line.

"No." Lauren fumbled for her glasses so she could look out her window. It was a perfectly normal early March night.

"There's going to be a lot of snow overnight, and I don't think you should trust the bus system to get you all the way to Hadley in those conditions. I know you have a car, too, but the driving route is different than the bus route, and people get lost on the back roads. Why do the back roads here not have signs? Anyway, I'm going to pick you up and drive you. My snow tires should be able to handle the slush, but I'll leave early just in case, and then we can make sure to not be late."

"What are you talking about?" Lauren said.

"The meeting. Tomorrow. Which you can't take a bus to."

Lauren took her glasses off again and pinched the bridge of her nose. "The buses are fine, they can drive in snow," she said.

"But they will be running late. You really need to check the weather and plan your transportation accordingly, especially in winter."

"Where are you from again?" Lauren asked, trying not to sound like she was laughing. Snow brought out the weirdest hang-ups in people.

Georgia's voice, previously high from anxiety, dropped into a deeper rumble of annoyance. "I've seen snow before, if that's what you're asking. Text me your address, I will pick you up by eight, and we will go to the meeting, on time, together. Please."

The demanding tone baffled Lauren. Did Georgia not think she could handle a damn bus schedule or road map by herself?

"Why are you so wound up about this?" she growled.

A sigh crackled through the phone line. "I assumed it would be important to you. You did good work. I want to make sure people see it."

Oh. That was actually kind of…

"There's a fine line between helping and micromanaging, you know," Lauren said, because Georgia's kindness made her skin crawl. She didn't need more people telling her what to do or what she was doing wrong.

For a long moment, Lauren sat in her chair drying Turing off with a paper takeout napkin, waiting for Georgia's biting reply. It didn't come.

Instead, Georgia groaned. "I swear I'm not a control freak. I've just been getting bent out of shape since...I've been more anxious lately, is all."

"Yeah, okay," Lauren said, because she suspected now what was going on. She hadn't heard anyone mention how Kyle had died, but he'd been young. Even with some prior warning, it would have turned Georgia's entire world upside down, and maybe it had been sudden. Cautiously, Lauren offered, "Sometimes you want to control what you can, right?"

"Right."

Lauren didn't know what else to say, and Georgia was so quiet that she might have hung up, but then she cleared her throat loudly. Lauren startled again.

"So," Georgia said, drawing the sound out to make it seem casual, "looks like it's going to snow a lot tonight. Would you like a ride in the morning, or are you all set?"

"I'll text you the address," Lauren said.

CHAPTER EIGHT

Georgia had learned through years of experience that the clothes you needed were always at the bottom of the laundry hamper. She wanted to dress more nicely than usual for Lauren's presentation, but her newest pair of slacks hadn't been hemmed yet and her second pair had a stain, so the wrinkled pair she'd worn last week would have to do. Febreeze took care of the dirty laundry smell, and she ironed the slacks with care. She kept a nervous eye on the smoke detector as she worked. Hannah was eating breakfast with her ear defenders on because half the time when Georgia ironed, it went off. Kyle said most people didn't have this problem, but he'd never been able to tell her what she was doing wrong. At least she managed not to burn herself this time.

Hannah made it to school a little early, and Georgia drove slowly to Lauren's apartment. The roads had been plowed and salted, but there were still flurries falling. The fresh coat of snow had made the old, muddy drifts beautiful again and also very bright. She had to put her sunglasses on to see.

At exactly eight o'clock, Georgia pulled into a parking spot in front of the address she'd been given. Lauren was already waiting. Judging by the amount of snow buildup on her hat and shoulders, she'd been waiting for a while.

"For someone who was worried about being late, you're cutting it pretty close," Lauren said. She kicked the snow off her boots before she got into the passenger seat.

"It's eight o one."

Lauren held her hands up to the heating vents. "My dad always said that early is on time and on time is late."

"On time is on time," Georgia said, "and I'll make better time than the buses anyway."

They drove in silence for nearly twenty minutes, until Georgia turned a corner and spotted a bus.

"Look!" she said, pointing down the block to their left. "That's the eight fifteen bus, and it's eight eighteen now! It was late."

"That's the red line. It's always late."

Georgia pouted. "You have to be right, don't you?"

"I don't have to be. I just am."

It sounded pretentious, but when Georgia looked at her, Lauren shrugged in a way that was almost helpless. What can you do? she seemed to say.

She was small in the seat, with so much legroom that Georgia could see her shoes. The seat was still adjusted for Kyle. "Forget days," she used to tell him, "you've got legs for weeks. Possibly months." He'd protested that the phrase wasn't usually applied to men, but it was one of Georgia's best jokes, so she'd kept telling it.

"Kyle always said that what really counted was whether or not something sounded right when you said it out loud. Which sounds like a lawyer thing, but he actually learned it in a writing class, about dialogue. I think he thought of law that way, though. You can read a law in different ways, right? So you just kinda..." Georgia wove her hand back and forth in front of her, "wiggle your story in between the lines and hope it sounds better than the other guy's."

Lauren frowned. "I think I'd rather just be right."

"But right in what way? By the letter of the law, or the spirit of it? And what if the law is wrong? You have to make a judgment call eventually, which means what's right is up to you."

Georgia expected a debate or at least a response, but Lauren stared out the window, her face as blank as the untouched snow. They didn't talk for the rest of the drive.

Lauren's unsettling silence was amplified by another when they arrived at Prysliak and Associates and walked past Kyle's dark and empty office. Georgia paused to glance through the window in the door, as if he might be there. Lauren went on down the hallway without her, entering Gerald's office after a sharp rap on his open door. Georgia grimaced at the sound and hurried to catch up.

Gerald sat at a table, not behind his paperwork-smothered desk like usual. There were new pictures of his husband and their nephew on the wall, but Lauren was too busy getting down to business for Georgia to have a chance to comment on them. The battered laptop Lauren worked on booted up while Gerald quizzed her. Even sitting while she stood, he seemed so much bigger than Lauren, watching and judging from above. The scale was tilted in Lauren's favor of course—they'd already paid Green Mountain Software a deposit and turned down generous offers from other companies, and Gerald wanted his friend's company to come through for him—but what if Lauren said something to turn him off? What if something went wrong at the last minute, or what if—

"I like that," Gerald said about something, and Lauren glanced up and gave Georgia a thumbs-up behind Gerald's back. There was confidence glittering in her eyes. She was doing just fine.

"We'll continue to update gradually until you have everything we promised, and you can call us anytime if something goes wrong."

Gerald tapped his thumbnail against his lips. "And you like this version, George?"

Georgia straightened her spine and tried to look confident. "I do."

"Well, my first mistake in all this was not hearing anyone else's opinion, so if it has your stamp, it can have mine. And I'll make sure Len hears about all the work you and your team did for us, Ms. Ashburn. Thank you."

He shook Lauren's hand in both of his massive ones, and finally, he smiled. Georgia offered to see Lauren out, and once they were in the hall again, she struggled to get her flapping hands in her pockets and out of sight.

"God, that was like getting interviewed all over again!"

"How were you getting interviewed?" Lauren said.

"Because I vouched for you! I wanted it to go well so badly." Georgia started to climb the stairs to her office, but Lauren headed toward the door. Where was she going?

"Well, thank you for vouching for me. I'll see you later?" Lauren said.

Georgia tilted her head in confusion. "I drove you here. How are you leaving?"

"There's a bus in ten minutes."

Ask her to lunch, Georgia urged herself, even though it was only midmorning. Ask her something, make her stay. But if Lauren wanted to go, why bother?

"See you later," Georgia said.

Lauren stood for a moment longer than Georgia had expected, just smiling at her. Did she want to stay? The moment ended before Georgia could decide whether or not to change her mind, and Lauren nodded goodbye and walked away.

From his office doorway, Gerald said, "You're lucky I saw you going all googly-eyed *after* the demonstration. Though I guess you do tend to like the competent ones."

He glanced at Kyle's doorway, which Georgia had just walked past without pain for the first time while escorting Lauren out. The viper of grief struck at her then, but it missed. She needed to reassure Gerald about Lauren.

"I do like her, but it's all professional between us. Sorry I was being obvious just now."

Gerald huffed. "You weren't the only one being obvious. I'm pointing it out so you don't miss it."

"I like your new family pictures," Georgia said, because she remembered it while she retraced every interaction, looking for what Gerald had seen. He smiled and told her to get started on the day's work.

Georgia had expected her mind to settle after this meeting, but her anxious morning bled into an absentminded afternoon. Lauren was taking up more of her mental space, not less. Was it possible Lauren was thinking of her, too?

CHAPTER NINE

To her own surprise, as well as Tracy's, Lauren went to the Healing House that week. She passed a pleasant hour sitting next to Georgia in the circle, admiring her doodles and the crisp lines of her handwritten notes. A week after that, when Lauren arrived ten minutes early for her fourth session, Annabel caught her by the elbow and asked for a moment in private. She led her to a small office with a glass-paneled door and sat behind the desk. Lauren sat in a boxy fabric chair in front of her. Was this what it was like to get sent to the principal's office in school?

"You don't talk much in the group," Annabel said. "I'm concerned you're not getting much out of it."

"Oh."

Lauren intended to stay quiet and read all the plaques on the wall and the names of all the people who'd signed all the thank-you cards that were displayed just as proudly as the awards. She expected Annabel to say more, but it seemed like she was willing to wait Lauren out.

"I guess I don't have much to say," Lauren said.

"Do you talk to anyone else?"

"My sister."

"Ah." Annabel smiled like they were talking about a mutual friend. "She's the one who told you about the program, right? Does she want you to come here?"

"She wants to help," Lauren said, leaving off the part about Tracy being a pain in the ass while helping.

"And are the sessions helpful?"

Lauren shrugged.

"Do you want to be here at all, or are you just coming because of your sister?"

"I wouldn't drive thirty minutes out of my way every week just to please my sister."

Annabel steepled her fingers, pressed them to her lips, and stared at Lauren. There were not enough plaques and cards on the wall to keep Lauren's eyes away from hers. Was she going to have to come up with something to say again? She was running out of energy to be polite.

Finally, Annabel sighed and asked, like she was contemplating a riddle, "If you're not sure it's helping, and it's not for your sister, and it's so far out of your way, why do you come?"

Lauren looked away again, through the glass panels of the door, and saw Georgia and her daughter coming down the hallway. Georgia noticed her looking and waved. Hannah stared at Lauren until they were past the door and out of sight. Annabel coughed, or maybe laughed, and Lauren had the sinking feeling that at least two people had found out more about her than she had meant to share.

"Look," Annabel said, "I want you to be here, and I want to be helpful to you. Would it be okay if I pushed a little? Asked you some more direct questions?"

"Yeah," Lauren said. "Sure."

It was what Annabel wanted to hear, and while she still looked at Lauren with something like suspicion, she led them out of the office and back to the group. Lauren slid into the chair next to Georgia, and the session began.

Annabel said, "I asked you all to think about coping

mechanisms this week, to observe your own behavior and consider where it might be coming from. Who would like to start us off?"

A man, one-half of the couple whose son had died, raised his hand like he was still in high school. "I've been busy," he said. "Busier than I've ever been, and I barely have time to think. I'm not sure I'd like what I thought about if I slowed down, so I just keep hopping from one thing to the next."

"It's easy to let activity take over our time. Who else has had a time in their life when they felt like they were too busy to think?" Annabel asked.

Several people raised their hands, so Lauren joined them.

"Lauren, what was that like for you?"

"What?"

Annabel said, "What time in your life were you busiest? What were you doing?"

Lauren rubbed the palms of her hands together slowly. She'd agreed to this, like a fool, and now she had to play ball. "I did a lot of sports and after-school stuff in high school, pretty much took over my life. Résumé building for college."

"Were there things you avoided or neglected while you were so busy?"

The memory of fainting during volleyball practice because she'd skipped both breakfast that morning and dinner the day before rose up so quickly she felt the heat of it again. The team had been losing badly that season, and Dad had insisted on reading the scores from the paper every morning.

"Why are we talking about this?" she demanded. She was getting defensive, she knew, but she didn't retreat or restrain her tone. Who here needed to know about her miserable high school days?

Annabel explained, "We were talking about coping mechanisms, such as staying busy. You said you did this when you were in school."

Lauren recognized the look on Annabel's face from earlier in the evening—searching, intelligent, intent. She'd probably push with that silent look for the whole hour if she had to.

It was quiet now. Lauren felt everyone's eyes on her and

refused to meet them. She couldn't even remember the names of everyone here. Who was the sweater vest guy? Dale?

"Did you enjoy having all those after-school activities?" Annabel asked.

"I guess."

"Which was your favorite?"

Lauren looked at Georgia. She was frowning in concentration, her pen still, totally alert.

"I dunno."

"Do you have a particularly happy memory about one of them?"

"Not really. I wasn't very good."

"Okay, so what got you so involved in—"

Lauren's patience snapped, and she almost shouted, "I didn't want to go home, okay? My dad put me under a lot of pressure, so I avoided him by doing stuff. Then when I sucked at that stuff, I had to avoid him even more. Is that a good enough answer? Is that therapeutic for the group?"

Annabel leaned back in her chair like Lauren's outburst was exactly what she'd expected. The sweater vest guy cleared his throat, and Lauren turned her sharp gaze onto him. He didn't flinch.

"I did the same thing with my mother," he said. "There were a hundred things I did to stay out of her way when I was young, because it felt like every time we crossed paths, she had something harsh to say. I rarely thought about that part of her once I left home, because we had so many good years together, but now that she's gone...I wish it had been different. I wish she'd been different."

"What's the point of that?" Lauren grumbled. Her father had never changed, and he never would. That was part of why Lauren had left Holderness after high school, with no intention of returning. Looking back or staying still was how you got stuck.

Annabel refocused Lauren with another question. "So you did all those sports to avoid other feelings, like the pressure from your dad?"

Lauren shrugged.

"What's your activity level like now?"

"My job takes a lot of time," Lauren admitted. It wasn't the same thing, right?

"Have you done anything lately, besides work, that you felt strongly about, or are you just keeping busy, like in high school?" Annabel asked, because of course she'd zeroed in on that.

Again, Lauren looked at Georgia. She was sitting sideways in the chair beside her, chin in hand, drumming her fingers against her jaw. A shift of Lauren's knee brought her into contact with Georgia's crossed leg, and Georgia subtly pressed back. Georgia had protected and supported Lauren's work. She'd inspired Lauren and forgiven her. Gratitude was a pretty strong feeling.

"I uh…" Lauren said, clearing her throat around a slight lump. "I guess I made a friend?"

Annabel said something about avoidance and how letting yourself rediscover feelings, even unpleasant ones, would help return normalcy after loss or whatever. Lauren wasn't listening as much as she should. The contact between her knee and Georgia's was too distracting, and much more worthy of attention. When someone else started speaking, Georgia turned her head, but she didn't shift away from Lauren in her chair.

Lauren felt happy about that.

When the meeting ended, Hannah entered the adult room and said, "Mommy, can Ms. Lauren come to dinner with us?"

The question shocked Lauren like static electricity. Georgia's reaction was unclear. She stared her daughter down, and some invisible exchange happened between them. Finally, Georgia said, "I think that's a great idea. Lauren?"

Lauren froze and struggled to respond. "Uh, where do you go?"

"We go to the Catamount Café," Hannah said. "It's not the most nutritious place to eat, but Mommy's just happy when I eat anything. She thinks I'm going to starve, but she's just being dramatic."

Georgia gasped. "Me, dramatic! How could you, my own child, accuse me of being dramatic?"

Hannah looked at Lauren. Lauren got her coat.

* * *

Lauren had lived in Holderness for most of her life, but the inside of the Catamount Café was alien to her. At eight thirty on a Tuesday night, the slightly off-kilter tables were all vacant. The gray-haired server hid a paperback novel under the counter before she approached them.

"What can I get for you?"

Georgia said, "We'll be getting the usual, but I think our guest needs a minute with the menu. Coffee to drink?"

She turned to Lauren, who ordered decaf on autopilot while thinking that Georgia looked like an old-fashioned movie star. Her fluffy jacket was wrapped around her like a mink stole, and her posture pulled everyone into the scene. One arm was draped across the back of Hannah's chair, her body was turned toward the server, and her bright eyes looked sideways at Lauren. The server left, and Lauren threw her full attention toward the menu to avoid Georgia's gaze. Everyone was quiet.

Once the food was ordered and brought to the table, Hannah broke the silence by saying, "Did you know axolotls don't chew?"

Lauren looked up from her eggs and toast, startled. "Axo… What?"

"Axolotls are endangered salamanders from Mexico, and they don't chew," Hannah said. "They suck food up like a vacuum. They still have teeth, though. They're just really small. It's called 'vestigial,' like people's wisdom teeth, but all their teeth are wisdom teeth. When they want to eat they seal up their gills and suck food into their mouths. Some people think axolotls eat little rocks, too, to grind up the food in their stomachs, like chickens do, but we're not sure yet, scientifically."

Hannah looked down then and started carefully pouring syrup into each little pocket of her waffle.

"I didn't know that," Lauren said. She glanced at Georgia, who winked at her around a mouthful of sandwich. "Are they the ones that regrow their legs?"

"Not just legs," Hannah said, not looking up from her food this time while she spoke. "Tails and livers and brains sometimes, too. And you can take an eye from one axolotl and put it in another one. Hopefully scientists switch axolotl eyes instead of just taking one away and not giving any back. That'd be mean. Or maybe they take the eyes after the axolotls die, like organ donation. Either way, it works, and that's pretty cool."

"That…is cool."

"Sometimes when an axolotl has a broken leg, it heals the leg and grows a new one at the same time, and then—"

"Eat, honey," Georgia said.

Hannah put a bite of waffle in her mouth, chewed deliberately, and swallowed. "I'll show you the axolotl habitat I made when I'm done," she said.

The kid ate fast, then pulled a forest green notebook, the size of Lauren's spread hand but large in Hannah's grip, out of a canvas pouch on her belt. Lauren had wondered what that was about, and now she knew. This well-used, overstuffed notebook was the kind people paid top dollar for at the art store, leather-bound, acid free, water resistant, and god knows what else, so attaching it to herself was a good way to make sure she didn't lose it.

Hannah wiped the table before she put the notebook between their plates.

"This is the overall design," she said, and she unfolded a long page four times wider than the book itself. The aquarium drawn on it was childish in some ways, like the dopey smiles on the axolotls' faces, but Georgia had clearly shown her daughter a thing or two about perspective and steady lines. There was a mosaic-ed floor, and the little animals had multiple hiding boxes, climbing ramps, and lush plants to enjoy. If Lauren could breathe underwater, she wouldn't mind living in a place like this.

"Gorgeous."

On the next page, which Hannah turned when Lauren voiced her approval, there was another well-drawn aquarium with measurements along the sides. There were notes in looping kid letters about brand, materials, and other details that quickly boggled Lauren's mind. Next were various filters, pasted in from magazines rather than drawn, and Hannah started lecturing on the pros and cons of each model. Thankfully, Georgia intervened.

"It's time for you to go to bed," she said, "and Lauren has to go home."

"She can come to our house," Hannah said, then turned to Lauren and added, "Daddy liked to have people at our house when I went to bed. Mommy should do that, too."

Lauren wasn't sure if that meant what it sounded like, but Georgia didn't blush or correct her daughter. She just put enough cash on the table to cover all three meals and a generous tip, then led Hannah, who clung to her side like a limpet, to the parking lot. Lauren followed, and paused when Georgia didn't immediately get into the car like Hannah did.

"I don't know if the invitation is appropriate," Georgia said, "but you are welcome to come."

There were several reasons to say no, not least of which that she wasn't sure what Georgia was angling for here, but Lauren found herself following the Solomons' car through the outskirts of Holderness to a pleasant little duplex in the woods. The lights were all off, but it still looked warm inside somehow.

Georgia unlocked the back door on the right-hand side of the duplex with one hand, fumbling a ring of too many keys in one hand because Hannah had her other pinned in a clingy hug. Lauren turned her attention to the window beside the door, not wanting to stare. The kid had gone from mile-a-minute chatting to seemingly nonverbal in an instant, so anything too forward might melt her down like a nuclear reactor. At least, that's what Tracy and the Internet said. Lauren wasn't here to cause problems.

Her reflection in the warped window glass frowned back at her. What was she doing here?

"There we go!" Georgia said when the door finally creaked open. She waved Lauren through the darkened doorway, then flipped a light switch with her elbow while kicking the door shut with her heel. The sudden brightness in the mudroom made them both blink. Hannah squeezed her eyes shut entirely. Georgia adjusted her arm under Hannah's grip, then led the way into the house proper.

"Make yourself at home, I guess, and I'll be back."

Lauren kicked her boots off before entering the living room, and Georgia whispered to Hannah to say goodnight as they made their way toward the stairs. Hannah gave Lauren a thumbs-up, but she seemed like she was pretty much asleep already. That was a good sign, right? Georgia would probably be back soon, and Lauren wouldn't spend too much time sitting on a stranger's couch, drumming her palms on her knees. The creak of mother and daughter moving across the floor above her didn't give her any guarantees.

Might as well take a look around, then. Lauren wandered past the stairs and further into the living room, turning on a floor lamp when she passed it. There was a plush area rug rolled out on the hardwood floor, and several plastic dinosaurs were lined up on it in rows. A stuffed rabbit sat by the fireplace, and a racetrack for little toy cars was put away in the corner. The neatness of Hannah's toys softened the chaos of Georgia's bookshelves along the walls. Volumes were crammed tightly against one another, piled on top of each other, and sitting in towers on the floor with no place to call their own. Bookmarks poked out and dangled from some of them, others had badly broken spines, and many looked like they hadn't been touched in years. A recent issue of *Architectural Digest* was draped over the back of the couch, presumably to save the place. There was a blanket falling half onto the floor, as if someone had kicked it off in a hurry, and a mix of older magazines and children's picture books lay in a short pile on the side table. The dregs of a cup of tea rested at the bottom of a mug on the floor. Lauren didn't live here, but the room felt like home.

A familiar name caught her eye as she scanned the books: Ann Bannon. Lauren was reading *Journey to a Woman*, starting from where the bookmark was placed, when the stairway creaked behind her.

"Find something you like?" Georgia asked, her voice quiet and deep in the low light.

Lauren looked up from the book to the tops of the shelves,

not turning around just yet. The intimacy of being at home with Georgia had just struck her, and she didn't want to look at her until her equilibrium recovered.

"Pulps are great, but your whole collection is pretty impressive," she said. "You've got some really old atlases here, first edition *Wizard of Oz* stuff, too. My dad would love your Golden Age sci-fi."

"Do you want tea?" Georgia said.

The abrupt question confused Lauren. She turned to see if she could get a hint of what Georgia was thinking. It didn't help, but the effect of Georgia's earnest eyes gleaming and her hair falling in her face, casting delicate shadows, made Lauren tremble. She couldn't remember the question she'd been asked.

"Yeah," she said to avoid being contrary.

Georgia tucked the loose hair behind her ear and winked at Lauren, which was an adorable thing to do, before wandering toward the kitchen. She flicked on a single dim light, which Lauren was grateful for. The white cabinets and dented appliances didn't cast a glare into her eyes, and it didn't wash out the deep shadows on Georgia's face that made it irresistibly inviting.

"I tend to like jasmine," Georgia said as she opened a cabinet stuffed to bursting with various boxes and brands of tea, "but I have a lot of different herbals, English Breakfast, and ooh, this raspberry stuff is good!"

Lauren shook herself and said the raspberry sounded good. She wasn't sure it actually did, but she'd try it. Georgia took two mugs out of a cabinet and filled an electric kettle with water.

"Can I ask you something?" she said while the kettle boiled. When Lauren nodded, she continued. "You and your dad. It was complicated, wasn't it?"

"What makes you say that?"

"Everything you've said about him. Which isn't a lot, but that's kind of meaningful, too."

This was a topic Lauren rarely broached, even to herself, even when the memories loomed large in comparison to the ones that would never be made. You weren't supposed to speak ill of the dead. But the lamp in the kitchen cast such a friendly light, and Georgia was leaning against the counter beside her steaming kettle, and there wasn't a single sound in the entire house, as if the two of them were cocooned in here and would never have to emerge.

"He wanted me to be a painter," Lauren said. "Which is weird, right? Most parents worry about their artistic kids and how they're ever gonna make money. My dad threatened to saddle me with all my student loans when I said I was switching from art to a computer science major, but I convinced him that programming was an art too. I think the money I make creeped him out, though, and I don't make nearly as much as I could."

"Was he a painter?" Georgia asked.

"Yeah. Well, no. He had great ideas and plenty of technical skill, but he never finished anything. Nothing he made looked like it did in his head. One time he loaded up all his old work in a truck and drove it to the dump. My mom had to hide the ones she liked so he wouldn't get rid of them, too. She has them framed now. He'd hate it."

The kettle clicked off, and Georgia poured two mugs of tea. She didn't have honey, and Lauren didn't want sugar, so they both drank their tea unsweetened. The raspberry was good, though.

"My parents definitely hated that I did art," Georgia said. "Not even good art, nothing that would go up in a museum. I never did anything to their standards, and when I finally found out I'm autistic, they took that as just another excuse. I have my own standards, though, and I'm usually good enough for me."

She frowned when she said it, which Lauren was starting to recognize as her version of a sincere smile.

"Were you diagnosed after Hannah was?" Tracy had said that was common.

Georgia nodded. "I didn't really talk until I was two, so someone probably should have known there was something going on. Of course, my parents didn't talk either in any way that mattered, so they got divorced when I was in middle school and got married to other people right away. My dad's divorced again. They only see Hannah once a year, during the summer. My stepbrother lives in England, so he's never even met her. He and I used to be best friends, but…Am I talking too much?"

"Maybe, but I like it. I want to know more about you." The sudden pause in Georgia's singsong speech disappointed Lauren more than having to listen to someone ever had, and she wanted her to continue.

"What do you want to know?" Georgia said.

All thought drained out of Lauren's mind in the face of this golden opportunity. What did she want to know? She could have answered that question ten minutes ago.

"Are you really going to build that axolotl habitat?" she managed to ask.

"She put in all that work," Georgia said, "so I guess I have to. No idea where to go to buy an axolotl, though. I've never seen one in a pet store."

"Me neither," Lauren said. She ran her thumbs over the raised design on her tea mug, a classic house with rose bushes in front. When she turned it around, she found the address and date of an architecture conference in New Hampshire. The mug's handle had been broken and glued back together.

"Have you always lived in Holderness?" Georgia asked.

"Yeah, except when I went to school. I came back when my dad got sick, because my sister was still in undergrad and my mom needed help. I didn't mean to stay so long, but it's two years later and I'm still here. My dad always asked me when I was going to leave again. I told him I'd get back on track when he got better."

Which, of course, he hadn't. Lauren braced herself for the questions people asked about the "getting back on track" part: When was she leaving? What jobs had she applied to? Could she not get a job? What was she waiting for?

Georgia didn't ask those questions. She asked, "Back on track to where? Where would you want to go?"

Lauren's head spun, because that was the heart of it, wasn't it? There wasn't any place she wanted to go. Honestly, she didn't even want to leave this kitchen, this moment. She wanted to stay exactly where she was.

Her eyes swept toward Georgia's, and that was when she noticed the clock on the oven. It was well past ten.

"I should let you get to bed," she said, and she downed the last of her tea. "Thanks for inviting me."

"Of course," Georgia said. She looked confused. Maybe she'd been under the spell of the moment, too. Lauren had thrown cold water on it just in time, because no one needed to know that she was, at heart, an unambitious slob. She was working too hard to overcome it to let anyone see her that way, especially someone she liked.

Georgia put the empty mugs in the sink and led Lauren through the mudroom to the back door. Outside, it was dark and bitterly cold. Lauren braced herself for a second before she plunged into it, hoping to make the journey to her car as quickly as possible.

She was ten feet from the door when Georgia said, "Wait!"

Lauren turned back to her, hunched deep in her coat in the driveway. Georgia was huddled down in her sweater exactly the same way.

"What's your Thursday afternoon like?" she asked.

"I'm around," Lauren said, though she wasn't sure she was. She could make time, right?

Georgia winked again, radiant as she shivered in the wind. "I'll text you."

She shut the door, and Lauren stood in the driveway a minute more. The blush on her cheeks kept her warm.

CHAPTER TEN

It was early evening, and the day had been good to Georgia. Everyone was getting used to Lauren's program, she'd solved a difficult issue with a client, and Hannah was enthusiastic about karate for the first time in months. Then there was Lauren. Georgia hadn't imagined she would be so open last night, and she did shut down suddenly, but Georgia had taken a chance, asking about her Thursday plans, and the intimacy between them had stabilized again. They were officially friends.

As Georgia pulled into her driveway, she noticed a car with Connecticut license plates on the other side of the duplex. It sent a quiver of dread down her spine. What was Kelly doing here?

There were lights on in Kyle's apartment, and the front door opened when Georgia turned the knob. Kelly Gray, Kyle's sister, was sitting on the living room floor just inside, surrounded by stacks of old files.

"Hello?"

"Hi, Georgia." Kelly finished leafing through the document in her hand before she looked up. "Do you know where Kyle's copy of your custody agreement is?"

Sirens went off in Georgia's mind, and she hunched her shoulders like an angry cat. "We're Hannah's parents. That's the agreement."

Kelly sighed, looking over the sea of paperwork around her. "You really never signed anything."

"We didn't need to. Kyle always told you, 'Law is a hammer—'"

"'And your relationship was not a nail,' right." Kelly looked away from Georgia, mumbling, "All well and good until someone gets screwed."

"Well, see, we did that first."

Kelly glared.

Nice to know that Kyle being gone hasn't changed anything between us, Georgia thought. She waded through the files on the floor and sat on her old familiar spot on the couch. Kelly would probably change the subject now, regroup, and return to this issue when she'd built up a new argument for her case. Such a lawyer, like everyone in her family. Georgia stared at the bookshelf across the living room, waiting.

"You haven't started going through his stuff," Kelly said. "He's been gone for months now."

"Hannah's not ready to let go of the apartment yet, let alone have strangers move into it. The lease doesn't end until November, anyway. We're taking our time, adjusting gradually."

The apartment was changing gradually, too. The smell of the place was already different—Georgia had noticed that weeks ago. Kelly stirring up dust and moving things around didn't help, and she'd wafted in the smell of her cigarettes, which she kept trying and failing to quit.

"That's expensive, paying rent all those months," Kelly said.

"It's important. Were you looking for anything else?"

"Where's Hannah?"

"Karate practice," Georgia said. "I'd have made arrangements if I knew you were coming."

No one ever knew when Kelly was coming. She just "dropped in" on her way back from one meeting or another and expected to be accommodated. Georgia never understood why Kyle tolerated—even enjoyed—that kind of guerrilla socialization, but then again, Georgia never really enjoyed Kelly at all.

"I'd like to know when you do start going through Kyle's things," Kelly said. She brushed off her slacks and left the paperwork where it was on the floor. "There are mementos the family wants, so I'll help you sort that out. It might also be a good time to come up with an agreement about Hannah's time with everyone. We all expect to see her."

"Does that mean you plan to schedule your visits from now on?" Georgia asked. For once, the idea soured in her mouth. It implied far too much about the Gray family's rights and entitlements regarding *her* daughter.

"No, it means I plan to be around. Tell Hannah I'm sorry I missed her."

Kelly breezed out of the apartment, her exit made slightly less haughty when she tripped over the corner of the rug. Eddies of dust spun in the air when the door closed. Another puff went up when Georgia flung herself down sideways on the couch, her knees pulled tight against her chest.

It was the twenty-first century, in Vermont, which meant the law was on Georgia's side regarding custody, despite her sexuality and her autism. That fear was vestigial, like axolotl teeth, left over from a darker time that had passed. But without Kyle to shield her, the Grays might hammer at Georgia in other ways: their whimsical comings and goings; their loud, crowded Christmases; the proud chefs in the family who took offense when food was refused, even after they'd been told a hundred times that texture was difficult for Hannah; their quiet insistence that what Georgia and Kyle had had wasn't family, wasn't love. It didn't matter to the Grays that Kyle had been her best friend. It didn't matter that Kyle had never wanted a romance, let alone a marriage. In their eyes, Georgia had scorned their darling son, and for that, she would never be forgiven. Now they wanted to take apart Georgia and Kyle's life together.

Georgia had moved often as a kid and split her time between two households when her parents divorced. Removing Kyle's things from his apartment filled her with the same kind of upheaval and dread those years had. Precious memories would be taped into boxes and hauled away, treasured keepsakes might be lost or broken, and the life that had been lived in this house would be over. Hannah wasn't ready for that. The very thought made Georgia squeeze her eyes shut and ball up more tightly on the couch.

It was too late in the evening to wallow for long, though. Georgia uncurled herself and put Kyle's papers away, then set out to pick up Hannah from karate.

* * *

Despite the best efforts of the staff, who scrubbed everything down with tea tree oil-scented cleaning wipes between classes, the Green Mountain Karate Dojo still smelled faintly of sweat and feet. For her part, Georgia thought feet was a better smell than tea tree oil anyway. She sat in one of the wobbly metal chairs at the back of the class while the kids did their last drills. A wall of mirrors let her see Hannah's face, even though she had her back to her. It was twisted in concentration, and she mouthed the count along with the instructor as she carefully moved her limbs in the proper direction. Kyle had said karate would help with Hannah's poor coordination. Georgia was still trying to decide if he was right.

A man entered the dojo and sat next to Georgia. "Which one's yours?" he whispered.

"The blonde with the scrunched-up nose," Georgia said. "Yours?"

The man smiled as he pointed out the little girl whose gi was grass stained, the one right next to Hannah.

"She just started, but she loves it. Thank god, because she needs something to do with all her energy, and I can only play tag and softball with her for so long before I have to lie down. I'm Ben."

Georgia introduced herself, shaking hands with Ben while the kids bowed to their instructor and scattered to chat with their friends or put on their shoes. Normally Hannah came straight to her, but today, Georgia saw her standing by the mirrors, talking to Ben's daughter. They put on their shoes together, and Hannah stomped around to show off her light-up shoes before leading the other girl over to the chairs.

"Mommy," she said, "this is Abby Lennox. Abby, this is my mom, Georgia Solomon."

"Not Solomon-Gray, like you?" Abby asked.

"No, just Solomon, but you can call me Georgia. It's nice to meet you, Abby. Hannah, this is Abby's father, Ben."

Hannah shook Ben's hand firmly, introducing herself with her full name, and Ben laughed. Georgia frowned. What was funny about being formal? At least Hannah was polite. Abby was picking her nose and asking Hannah why she and her mom didn't have the same last name. Before Georgia could think of a way to stop her, Hannah had answered the question in full, including the facts that her mother was bisexual and her father had died. Ben turned to Georgia with obvious interest. Abby looked at her dad with wide eyes. She had probably never considered the fact that dads could die.

"We should get going!" Georgia intervened, too loudly. Several of the parents who were trickling in to pick up their kids stared at her while she shepherded Hannah toward the door.

Had Hannah been this open with other kids? The thought made Georgia's head hurt. There were already enough things about Hannah that stuck out. She didn't need to add conversations about her weird mom and dead dad to the mix. She also didn't need to be going around making other seven-year-olds confront their parents' mortality. God strike her if she knew what to do about it though.

Maybe the group at the Healing House would know. Annabel always asked if people had other questions before the session started, and she was there to help Hannah, wasn't she? She hated the idea of looking clueless in front of the other parents, but she didn't have anyone else to turn to. Not anymore.

When she and Hannah had buckled themselves into the car, Georgia said, "So, is Abby your new friend?"

Hannah shrugged. "She talks to me, and she said I could come to her house to practice karate more if I wanted."

"Sounds like a friend to me."

"Are you friends with her dad now?"

Georgia opened her mouth to say no, then closed it again. She would probably have to be, if their kids were going to be spending time together.

"We'll find out!" she said. Her voice was too loud again, and Hannah watched her for a moment before she started answering Georgia's questions about what else had happened in karate practice that night.

In the back of Georgia's mind, one thought still needled her, long after she'd fed her daughter and put her to bed: maybe the Grays were right to look down on her. She had no idea how to do this.

Kyle's voice answered her from seven—almost eight—years ago, when he'd held Hannah for the first time: "No one knows how to do this. The fun part is that we get to find out."

And it had been fun. Hopefully it would be fun again, once she found out how to do it alone.

CHAPTER ELEVEN

It was a busy day at Ashburn's Art Supply Store. Lauren consolidated the glues and pastes onto one rack and carefully slid the price tags over. Mom had relented to Lauren and Tracy's demand that she close the store on time, and for some reason, even though she'd never gotten around to all the big sales she'd said she was going to advertise, enough of the store's regular stock was gone that some of the shelves could be cleared and dismantled. That task had to happen right away, because Tracy had had the bright idea to host a goodbye party for the store, in the store, on Dad's birthday, which was in two weeks. She kept calling it a birthday party, as if that was a normal thing to do for dead people. The vibe about it was weirdly chipper. Opening up the floor was something Tracy had always wanted to do, and her happy humming was audible two aisles away in the pastels section.

It wasn't entirely clear to Lauren why they were having a birthday party at all. The guest of honor wouldn't be in attendance, and everyone else had just seen each other a few months ago at the funeral. What was there to celebrate? That it was Tracy's idea was even stranger, because Tracy had never let their father have a single peaceful birthday in her life. She'd been ten months old and feverish the first year she was around, she'd spent Dad's fiftieth yelling at and breaking up with her then-boyfriend over the phone, and when she was nine she'd tripped while she and Lauren were carrying the birthday cake, with candles lit, to the table.

Lauren paused, thumbing the price tag for one-pound pats of modeling clay. The year after Tracy had tripped, Lauren was fourteen. She'd started studying art in school, and she spent a month secretly painting a portrait of the house her father had grown up in. He had talked about that house, which had been built on a hill in East Holderness in 1883, as if it were the only place in the world he'd ever been happy, so Lauren had put all her new knowledge into her watercolor reproduction, as if maybe this would make him happy too. Her mom had bought a frame to put it in, solid wood and real glass that Lauren had cleaned until it squeaked and shone. The wrapping paper she'd used was crisp and new, not the reused stuff they always had, and it had folded in perfect angles when she creased it between her fingers. It had been the centerpiece of the gift pile. Lauren didn't remember what her father's complaints had been about the cake that year, though she did remember the smell of chocolate mingled with the smoking candles. She remembered the tearing of the paper. She remembered the way her dad had propped the picture up on his knees and studied it.

"Boy," he'd said. "You sure let these colors run all over, didn't you?"

And before Lauren's heart could fully break, Tracy had thrown the cake at him.

The current moment invaded her thoughts when an unsharpened pencil clanged against the shelf next to her. Lauren spun around and glared at her sister.

"Pencil for your thoughts?" Tracy said.

"If we have a cake at this party, what are the odds it ends up on the floor?"

Tracy joined Lauren in the task of moving clay, calculating before she answered. "We've dropped a cake three times in twenty-seven years, so that's a one in nine chance that we lose another one. Maybe we should put down some, uh…doormats."

"Drop cloths?"

"Yes! Why were you thinking about cake?"

Lauren leaned back against the shelves. Tracy kept consolidating clay, but she was watching her sister out of the corner of her eye.

"What do you do when you remember bad stuff about Dad? I mean, we're supposed to honor the dead, right? And love our parents, but…" Lauren grimaced.

"Honestly," Tracy said, "I stopped thinking about Dad a long time ago. It was easier for me because he never really thought about me, either. He was a miserable old man who was too stubborn to see how great things were because they weren't the way he wanted them. For a while I resented him, felt sorry for him, but now I just…I take things the way they are."

"Things could be better," Lauren said, thinking about Sweater Vest Guy at the Healing House, wishing his mother had been different too.

"So make things better," Tracy said, "but don't spoil what's good by expecting it to be perfect, and don't miss out on perfect because it's not what you thought it would be. And if it wasn't good, let it be. Happiness is a choice Dad never made. I don't live that way."

Lauren studied the empty, dusty shelf she'd cleared. She ran a finger along one rusty scratch in the metal and wondered how old it was, because she knew the shelves themselves were older than her. This had been their grandfather's store before Dad ran it, and it hadn't changed once until now. Every empty space was full of their family history, and soon it would be gone. The idea of standing in the middle of an empty floor made Lauren smile. Tracy, she noticed, was smiling, too.

"Are you making happiness choices?" Lauren asked.

"Yeah."

"Tell me about them."

Tracy's smile faltered. It was like she'd been reading and hit a word she couldn't make sit still on the page, and Lauren sensed it was her fault somehow. There was something Tracy wasn't telling her.

The phone rang, and Tracy went to answer it without giving Lauren any clues. Lauren shrugged it off, finished the clay section, and moved on to pastels and pens. Her mom was silent when she came up from behind and grabbed Lauren's elbow, which made Lauren jump and throw expensive pens everywhere.

"Tracy's pregnant!" Mom whispered as loudly as she could.

Lauren pulled away from her mother and knelt down to gather the pens. "Why would you think that?"

"Because she's all nervous about this party, and she asked me to have lunch with her this weekend! I just know she has something big to say, and what else could it be?"

"About a hundred things. Tracy hasn't said anything about trying to get pregnant. She doesn't even have a boyfriend."

That Lauren knew of. Maybe that was Tracy's secret.

Mom helped Lauren off the floor, smirking. "These things aren't always planned, you know."

"Tracy's on birth control, Mom. She's not pregnant."

The smirk faded, and the dour look that replaced it brought out harsh lines on her mother's face.

"Well, *something* is going on, and we're going to be surprised big time."

Lauren watched her mother swan away as worry knotted her stomach. The only time Tracy didn't tell Lauren about something the second she thought of it was when she knew Lauren wouldn't like it. And whatever it was, her mother was going to find out before her and gloat, which would make her unbearable, because there was nothing Tammy Ashburn loved more than being in someone's secret circle. God, this whole birthday party was going to be unbearable, whether or not the cake ended up on the floor. How was she supposed to make happiness choices in the face of that?

She pulled out her cell phone and called Georgia. She was the only pleasant thing Lauren could imagine at the moment.

"Don't tell me your afternoon got filled up," Georgia said when she answered.

"No, tomorrow's good. I was just wondering: what are you doing a week from Friday? Because I'm recruiting allies."

* * *

They met at Northway Coffee on Main Street the next day. Georgia had only ever been to one coffee shop in town, apparently, but Lauren knew for a fact that Northway had the best hot chocolate, so she convinced Georgia to branch out. By the way she licked whipped cream off her spoon, it seemed like she agreed with Lauren's assessment.

"So," she said, "your sister is throwing a birthday party for your dad in his store, something's up with her, and you hate this because you don't know what it is?"

"Yeah, basically," Lauren said.

"Why would I be a helpful addition to that situation?"

Lauren looked into her coffee for a second before she admitted, "If people are talking to you, they won't be asking me questions I don't have an answer for. Like what I'm doing with my life or what's up with Tracy. Plus, you'll be the most pleasant person there."

"Ah," Georgia said. "One of those parties. Does everyone else want to know when you'll drop all this money-making computer nonsense and do some art?"

"I wasn't supposed to come back to town after I left for college. Now that Dad is dead, they're expecting me to leave and do something better than hang around here. I expected better, too, but…" Lauren took a long drink of her coffee.

"Well, now you know the most pleasant person in Holderness, so it can't be all bad. I'll prove it at the party."

Lauren beamed. The anxiety that had rumbled in her stomach settled into contented butterflies. Georgia started asking the crucial party questions, like what the dress code would be and what she should bring, and Lauren did her best to answer in reassuring detail.

* * *

Time passed comfortably for a little while. Len wasn't insisting it was "crunch time" like he usually did, which left her plenty of time to spend with Georgia. They drank tea and read after Hannah had gone to bed, and they went for walks in town during Georgia's lunch hour several times that week. It was almost possible, in those times, to not worry about whatever it was that Tracy wasn't telling her.

On Saturday morning, while she was working at her desk at home, Lauren got a text from her mother: a selfie of her and Tracy at their favorite weekend brunch spot. Because of course she had to rub it in that she knew something Lauren still didn't.

Also on her phone was a picture from Georgia, of Hannah lying on her back in last night's fresh snow. It was probably the last snowfall of the season.

Happiness choices, Lauren thought, and suddenly she was on her feet.

She sent up a flurry of dust when she opened her blinds and peered out the window of her living room. Down the road, between the houses and apartment blocks, the mountains were just barely visible. They looked like a delicate pen and ink drawing, gentle black lines denoting the negative space of white curves against cloudy sky. It was a little above freezing now, cold enough to preserve the snow, but it would warm up in a few hours. "Last chance to come out and play," the winter beckoned.

At the back of Lauren's closet was a set of cross-country skis, which had gathered even more dust than the blinds she rarely opened. She'd hardly ever had the time to go skiing these past two years, and when she had time, she didn't have the energy. She often wanted to go, but she didn't. Eventually the wanting had faded.

Lauren rushed to her room now, grabbed her skis, her coat, and the mittens and hat her mother had made her. She scampered out into the cold before the urge deserted her again.

The next morning, Lauren heaved her sore, out-of-shape body upright and dragged herself to the Unitarian Universalist meeting. She was greeted at the door by someone who'd joined more recently than ten years ago and who thought she was a visitor.

"I'm an Ashburn," Lauren explained. "I grew up here, just haven't been back in a while."

Tracy and Mom were in the same seats they'd always been in, close to the piano and as far away from Kitty Bakerson as they could get. It took Lauren until the bell rang for the start of services to make it over there. A lot of people remembered her and wanted to know what she'd been up to.

"Working," she told them.

It was mostly true, which had never struck her as sad before. Her father had rarely been to meetings, either, because he opened the store at eleven and refused to push that time back by even half an hour on Sunday to accommodate services. Ashburn's was open every day of the week, always had been.

"Did you get pod peopled?" Tracy whispered when Lauren settled in beside her. "Is your new lady friend religious?"

"Not everything is about Georgia," Lauren snarled, although admittedly a lot of things lately had been.

Tracy made a suspicious noise while they stood up for the opening words. Lauren leaned against her, half to share her hymnal and half to whisper at her under the muttering of the congregation.

"I went skiing yesterday."

"Is that why you're limping?"

Lauren elbowed her. "I'm thinking I might establish this thing called boundaries, right? It's where you don't work all the time and you have a life and stuff. I hear that's trendy these days."

"It's really not, but good for you," Tracy said. "Of course you'd decide to chill the hell out at the same time I take up your work ethic."

The congregation sat down. Lauren almost missed the cue because she was too busy staring her sister down, hunting for clues about this mysterious whatever-it-was she had going on.

"What do you need my work ethic for?"

Their mother popped both of their knees with her own hymnal, hissing, "It is the moment of *silence!*"

Lauren intended to take up the issue later, but her terse, monosyllabic antisocialism didn't deter UU people who wanted to chat, and Tracy kept up her silence.

"Can you help me set up for the party at four?" was the only thing she said about it all week. Lauren resentfully agreed.

* * *

On Friday, Lauren showed up at Ashburn's Art Supply Store at three fifty to set up tables, hang decorations, and shove aside the last of the empty shelving units. Tracy was following their mother around with a large poster board, asking how to spell several different words.

"Use a dictionary, Tracy!" their mom said, as if she didn't know Tracy struggled with using dictionaries too. Then she turned to Lauren. "You have cat hair on that nice shirt. Go find a lint roller before you do anything else. I'm going to pick up the cake."

She went out the door, leaving her daughters staring at each other in silence.

"There's a lint roller in my purse. I figured she'd say you needed one," Tracy said, trying to hide the fact that one side of her poster board said Happy Brithday on it.

Lauren smiled as she dug through Tracy's purse on the counter. "I'll go through the letters with you if you want, after we get the heavy lifting done. You have to write them, though, because my handwriting sucks."

"You do have trouble with straightness," Tracy agreed. She took the lint roller out of Lauren's hand to clean up all the spots she'd missed. "There's probably a reason for that."

The two of them worked well together for fifteen minutes, until Lauren made the mistake of saying, "Go to your right" while they were carrying a table. Tracy moved in the wrong direction quickly and yanked the table out of Lauren's hands. The table dropped on Lauren's foot.

"God damn it!" Lauren yelled, too loudly to hear the sleigh bells on the door jangle.

"Mommy," Hannah said from the entrance, "Ms. Lauren said a bad word!"

Uh-oh. What was the kid doing here?

Lauren turned around, ready to be shamed, but Georgia was coming toward her with a look of concern on her face. "Are you okay?" she asked.

"Yeah, I just dropped a table on my foot. My right foot!" Lauren said, shaking her injured limb in Tracy's direction. Tracy ignored her and introduced herself to Georgia and Hannah.

"Are you a good speller?" she asked Hannah. When Hannah nodded, she said, "Do you want to help me with a project? I need someone to tell me all the letters in words, one at a time, so I don't get them mixed up."

"Okay," Hannah said, and Tracy led her to the checkout desk at the back of the store, away from Lauren and Georgia.

"Why does she need Hannah's help?" Georgia asked.

"She's dyslexic. Which is why I should have known better than to say 'right' instead of just pointing while we were moving tables. You're really early."

Georgia frowned. "You said early is on time and on time is late."

"I didn't mean an hour early."

It was obvious Georgia was embarrassed from the way she retreated slightly into her sweater. Lauren backpedaled. "You're on time to help with decorating, though! Clearly Tracy and I need it."

The tables got settled and covered with cloths, and the Happy Birthday sign was hung up. Mom had driven off with all the party food when she went to get the cake, so that part would have to wait. Georgia agreed to spot Lauren while she climbed on the precarious shelving against the wall to hang streamers.

After a few minutes of quiet work, Georgia said, "I couldn't come up with anything better to do than hang out with you, and Hannah was bored, too. That's why we're so early."

Lauren almost fell off the shelving. The wording made it sound like Lauren was simply better than nothing, but she knew that wasn't what Georgia meant.

"I invited you because you're better company than anyone else who's coming, so I'm happy you're here," she said. She smiled down at Georgia before she shuffled down the groaning metal shelf, unrolling a length of paper streamer behind her.

Lauren and Georgia wrapped the streamers around to the back of the room near the checkout register, where Hannah had started talking about axolotls. Tracy struggled to pronounce the word. Hannah coached her with gentle but dogged persistence.

"Ask-o-little," repeated Tracy.

"Ax-o-lot-el."

"Ask-o-*lot*-el."

"*Ax*-o-lot-el. Stress the first syllable, and take out the s."

"Ax? Like a…" Tracy made a chopping motion.

Hannah frowned, and Tracy apparently assumed she was wrong again, because she shifted to "ass."

"Ass-o-lot-el. Like a lot of asses?"

"I don't think you're supposed to say that."

Lauren would have broken a rib laughing if her mother hadn't entered right then and scowled at Hannah.

"Excuse me, little girl. Should you be here?"

Lauren hopped down from a shelf. "She's Georgia's daughter, Mom. And this is Georgia, my friend."

Georgia waved. Mom looked skeptical. "You do know this is an adult party? There won't be very many children here."

"I like adult parties," Hannah said. "They're quieter than kid parties, and usually there's cheese cubes."

"Did we get cheese cubes for this?" Lauren whispered, surprised to be so concerned about Hannah's enjoyment of the party. Tracy gave her a thumbs-up.

Lauren's mom looked from Hannah to Tracy and said, "Would you girls unload the car while I meet your new friends? I bought more wine, since your uncle Ned is coming."

Lauren hesitated, but Georgia pushed her gently toward the door. Tracy told Lauren to prop it open on their way out to the car.

"I like that kid," Tracy said as she piled trays of fruit, crackers, and yes, cheese cubes, into Lauren's arms. "She's weird. Is that why you tolerate her so well?"

"She's not weird, she's just…serious, like Georgia. What do you think Mom is saying to her?"

Tracy hauled a box full of wine bottles out of the backseat and knocked the door shut with her knee. "By now? Probably that I'm the better daughter and she should run away from you screaming."

"Ha ha. I'll come back for the cake. Don't you even touch it."

Having food platters stacked up to her chin made it hard for Lauren to see what was happening, but she heard her mom's laugh immediately when she came into the shop. It almost made her drop the cheese cubes.

Georgia took the top two platters out of Lauren's hands, and they made their way to the main table.

"I can't believe you got my mom to laugh. How did you do that?"

"I'm the most pleasant person at the party." Georgia winked at her.

It was like that for the entire evening. Georgia talked about knitting and rheumatism with several family friends, let Uncle Ned saw on about cricket for half an hour, and introduced Hannah to anyone who needed an extra infusion of adorable. Hannah seemed genuinely happy, too. She listened closely to discussions of the stock market.

There was only one moment when Georgia faltered. She had just said Hannah was taking karate lessons.

"Is that so?" Dad's college roommate's wife said.

"Yes."

Everyone paused, and Lauren realized Georgia hadn't picked up the cue.

"Tell us more about that," she said, and Georgia slid back into the stream of conversation.

During the one instant when they weren't surrounded by partiers, Georgia whispered, "You weren't kidding about people asking a lot of questions about you. Isn't it kind of rude to pry so much?"

"They've known me my whole life, which makes them feel entitled to the gritty details," Lauren said. "Do your parents' friends not do this to you?"

"My parents didn't have many friends."

It occurred to Lauren that maybe that was sad, but right now it sounded wonderful. Placing Georgia at the center of people's attention spared her most of the intrusive pressure she'd endured at her father's wake. It didn't stop people from telling stories about Dad, though. If anything, meeting someone who hadn't heard it all a hundred times drew out new material along with the old familiars. Lauren hadn't anticipated that.

"Uncle Luke had so much talent," Cousin Dave said. "I still have a sketch of his from when I was five. He was brilliant. It's such a shame."

A friend from the UU said, "He came out in the middle of the night to jump my car when I was stuck up in Arlington once. He looked like the Abominable Snowman when he was done, but he didn't care one bit."

Uncle Ned recalled, "He met Tammy at an ice cream parlor, and he looked at her so much he stuck the ice cream on his nose instead of in his mouth! Took him down a peg or two. But Tammy brought him a napkin, and he said right then he was gonna marry her. They were crazy in love, like doves. Or rabbits."

"One time back in high school," another friend said, "Luke came up with the best prank the school had ever seen. The English teacher was…"

Lauren turned away from that story, leaving Georgia behind. She knew more than enough about her dad's hilarious pranks: tripping her in mud, hiding plastic snakes in her bed, revving the lawn mower at her and running behind her laughing because she was afraid. It was always funniest when someone was afraid. Makes you tough, he'd said. God help her when she'd tried the bucket-over-the-door trick on him, though. She could see his red, dripping face so clearly.

She was standing alone, her typical party move, when Tracy climbed up onto the checkout counter and tried to get everyone's attention by tapping a plastic knife against a plastic wineglass.

"Nice try, dweeb," Lauren teased.

Tracy stuck her tongue out at her, then shouted at the top of her lungs.

"Okay, folks! Before we cut the cake—"everyone hushed at the mention of cake—"I'd like to say a few words."

Mom caught Lauren's eye and danced in gloating excitement. Hannah was standing with her, eyes locked on the cake. Where was Georgia?

Tracy started in on her speech. "It's been a joy spending time with you all, remembering how much my father meant to you. And we all know this store meant a lot to him. It was his crowning achievement, if you don't count me and my sister. He poured hours into this place, made sacrifices and took risks, and so did our family. I remember doing my homework here. I never did it very well, but…"

The crowd laughed lightly.

"My grandfather had a vision when he built the store, of supporting this community and bringing their imaginations to life, giving them the tools to create their own visions. My dad carried on that vision. And I have a vision, too: of what Ashburn's can be now, with my father's and grandfather's memory and our family's love and care. You may have been told this was a farewell party, but it's not. It's the official announcement party for the grand reopening!"

A surge of murmurs, then cheering, rose up from the party guests. Lauren stood in the midst of it, stock-still, watching her mother make her way to the checkout counter with a manila folder and a bottle of champagne.

"Here's the papers that transfer all assets, rights, and responsibilities of Ashburn's Art Supply Store, LLC!" she said, holding the envelope high. Then she turned around so Tracy could crouch and use her mom's back as a firm surface to sign her name.

"It's signed!" Tracy said when she stood up, waving the pen in the air. To riotous applause, she popped the cork on the champagne. Hannah jumped at the sudden sound. Wine boiled up from the neck of the bottle and splattered on the counter. "Let's cut the cake!"

Tracy stepped down to the floor, her hand dripping with champagne. Lauren elbowed her way through the crowd and pulled her between two of the remaining shelves in the store.

"Surprise! Isn't it great!" Tracy crowed.

"Great? No, it's not great, Tracy. What the hell are you thinking?" she demanded.

The glee on her sister's face ran down like the champagne now dripping from her elbow. Lauren didn't care. "You can't buy the store! You'll go under in months."

Tracy ripped her arm out of Lauren's grasp. "Who says? I'm an accountant. I can run a business."

"Everything on this street goes under, Tracy. You know that."

Everything in Holderness turned bitter and burned, like their father. Tracy lived out of state now. Why would she tie herself to the store when she was already free?

Tracy widened her stance like she was ready for a physical fight. "Everything goes under except Ashburn's."

Lauren was silent. That was a mistake.

"You don't think I can do it! I knew you wouldn't," Tracy said. "You think I'm too stupid to do anything, just like Dad did, don't you? You hate the idea that I might succeed at something while you sit behind your computer being miserable and getting told what to do."

The last insult was intended to pierce deeply, but the idea that Lauren was anything like her father struck much harder. She pulled a napkin out of her pocket and gave it to Tracy to dry her arm with.

"I don't think you're stupid, Tracy. I never did. I just…This place? Dad's place, the one he resented every day of his life? Why would you want to keep that?"

"Because I love it!"

"You do? Since when?"

Tracy handed the soggy napkin back to her. "I don't tell you everything. And this is why. You think you know it all already."

Lauren knew what it had been like growing up with her parents pouring everything into the store and wringing nothing out of it. She'd had to compete with local boys for yard work and beg grandmothers for birthday money to buy track shoes, skis, computer repairs, and other precious things her family couldn't provide. Her father had wondered why she blew her hard-earned cash on shoes when she never even placed in a race or scored a winning point during her whole sports career. He also hated that summer practice pulled her away from the store. Everything was a balance of future success versus immediate reward, because running a store meant nothing could ever be wasted. Sacrifice and risk, like Tracy had said. She wanted kids one day. Did she want them to live like that?

"Don't you want something better than this?"

"No, I want this. There's nothing better for me. And better how? What does that even mean?"

"Don't you remember—"

Tracy looked to the rafters and put her hands on her hips. She looked just like their mother. "Yes, I remember how miserable you were. I remember how much Dad wished he wasn't here and how often he told us we should want more for ourselves. But I don't hate Holderness like Dad did. You don't either, and I think you'd notice that if you let go of your self-flagellating superiority complex. If you thought about what you liked instead of what makes life hard, maybe you'd finally figure out what the hell you want. Meanwhile, I have what I want, and you don't get to shit on that."

Uncle Ned, too drunk to sense the tension behind the shelves, stuck his head around the corner and called out to Tracy. She flicked good cheer on like a light switch and went to accept his congratulations. Lauren fled to the balcony of the store to hide, alone.

CHAPTER TWELVE

Georgia had noticed when Lauren peeled away from her during a conversation, but she didn't think much of it. She needed a break from parties sometimes, too. In fact, she took one shortly thereafter. Hannah had attached herself to Tammy Ashburn, who was giving her a detailed account of multiple family cake disasters, so Georgia had told them both she'd be back in a moment and climbed up the stairs to the art store's darkened balcony. The babble of people and noise was dimmed from up here, and the light was less aggressive to her eyes. She sat on the floor with her back against a wall and relaxed. Just a few minutes. A few minutes of what her parents had insisted was weird, antisocial behavior, then she could go back into the fray.

A wave of increased noise washed up from below. Georgia didn't hear why, but she decided to wait in her comfortable shadow until she was sure it wouldn't happen again. One minute, two minutes of quiet. She was on her knees, starting to stand, when Lauren appeared, slouching up the stairs and carrying her glasses in her hand.

"You okay?" Georgia said.

Lauren jumped. Georgia winced.

"Yeah," Lauren said. She rubbed her eyes and put her glasses back on. "Yeah, I'm okay. Why are you up here?"

"I just needed a break."

Lauren stopped walking toward her. "Should I leave? I can— Oh, man, I didn't think about the noise and the—I'm sorry, I shouldn't have—You don't have to stay for the whole party."

"I like parties. I'm just taking a break," Georgia said. She sat back down on the floor, and Lauren slid down the wall and landed next to her with a thump and a huff.

"You could have told me what a huge favor I was asking," Lauren said. "All these strangers, and they've been all over you. It doesn't freak you out?"

Georgia said, "My parents took me to parties all the time, especially when we'd moved to a new place and needed to meet people. I know how to regulate myself. I was nervous about meeting your family, but they're nice. I like Tracy a lot."

"Tracy's the best," Lauren agreed. "I mean, she's my sister, so she's the worst, but she's still the best. I don't deserve her."

Georgia didn't know what to say to that. She watched Lauren's profile for any sign she wanted Georgia to go away, but she didn't find any. After a moment of quiet, she pointed toward the store beyond and asked, "What's going on down there?"

"They're celebrating," Lauren said.

"Is that normal at a birthday party for a dead person?"

It looked like it hurt when Lauren laughed. "Tracy made her big announcement: she's keeping the store."

"Oh." Georgia grasped the emotional tone of this conversation about as well as she would a live fish, so that was all she said.

Lauren rolled her head to the side to look at Georgia, not lifting it from the wall. Apparently Georgia had configured her face into the correct expression, because Lauren continued, just as Georgia hoped she would.

"I hate this store. This fight I'm suddenly having with my sister? I've never not had a fight in this store. Or heard someone else having a fight. Tracy used to bicker with my dad constantly about how he ran things, trying to get him to remodel or upgrade or whatever other change we couldn't afford. Mom and Dad would go over the books and yell about money. Customers bitched, I bitched, Tracy's friends bitched about her working during the summer. God, it gets hot here in the summer." Lauren rubbed her face and wiped her forehead like she was sweating, even in the cool darkness. "Tracy can do anything, so why do this?"

Georgia mulled this over for a moment, then began to put forth her hypothesis. "You really like your sister, right?"

"In general? Yeah."

"So do you think she might make a store that you like? One that makes people happy?"

Lauren cocked her head to the side, face constricted in thought, then sighed. She put her hand over Georgia's on the floor.

"I'm glad you're here," she said.

Georgia turned her hand over so she could hold Lauren's properly. She realized that even while she'd been searching for a break from other people, seeing Lauren had made her happy. Touching Lauren was soothing, not overstimulating. She wanted to be the person Lauren wanted to see, even when Lauren didn't want to see anyone else.

"I'm glad I'm here, too," she said. "Sorry I didn't save you from fighting with your sister."

"You don't have to save me, it's fine. Tracy'll text me in a few days. A week, maybe, because I really screwed up, but then we'll talk."

"Really?"

"Yeah. It's not like I haven't done worse than this before." Lauren grinned at her, but it faded. "Does your family not work like that? You said you're not close to your parents."

Georgia shook her head. "We don't have little, fixable fights in the Solomon family, just nuclear blowups. No one's really big on saying sorry."

It had rubbed Georgia wrong at first, Lauren's willingness to screw up and then own up afterward, as if mistakes should be apologized for instead of avoided. But she and her family could recover from mistakes and move past them, and they listened to each other. There was no going back for Georgia. No one was all that sorry, either. Lauren squeezed her hand, probably trying to be comforting, and Georgia felt like she'd said too much.

She asked, "Do you think you're forgiven enough that we can go back to the party and have cake?"

"God, I want cake right now," Lauren said, and Georgia pulled her to her feet. It was a terrible shame to let go of her hand, though.

* * *

Hannah was silent and pressed tightly against Georgia's side when they left the party, very shortly after they had their cake. Georgia could have lasted an hour more, but Hannah clearly couldn't. When they got home, Hannah went straight to the shower, and from there she planned to go to bed.

At a few minutes past nine, Kelly Gray called.

"I'd like to talk to Hannah," she said.

Georgia clenched her teeth. God forbid Kelly consider anyone else's schedule when she wanted something. "She's too tired to talk right now, but I'll tell her you—"

"Oh, come on, it's not hard to talk on the phone for two minutes."

Snapping at Kelly would not improve things, but being interrupted ground Georgia's gears. "It's also not hard to call back later!" she snarled.

Kelly paused. Georgia could hear her thinking and rethinking. Then she said, "Kyle could always pep her up enough to say hi, at least."

"Well, Kyle was better at this than me," Georgia said. "Call back tomorrow. Good night."

She gave Kelly time to say good night back, but when she continued arguing instead, Georgia told her she was going to hang up and then did so.

Upstairs, Hannah's footsteps were audible as she walked down the hallway to her bedroom, and then the house was silent.

It rarely ever used to be totally silent. Georgia huddled under a blanket on the couch, listening to her ears ring and trying not to remember all her childhood fears of the whole world vanishing overnight. Kyle was usually still up at this hour, and the sound of him rattling around in his own apartment had been audible through the thin walls between them.

But Kyle was gone. There were no more noises in the night, no more pep talks, no one taking the time to understand or stand firm between Georgia and the rest of the Grays or between Georgia and the rest of the world. The world was still out there, but it was hostile and strange, full of noxious smells and spicy food and people insisting that you can't know you don't like something until you try it. There was no more calm presence with her at the edge of it all. That was worse than her childhood nightmares had been.

Just as the wave of lonesome nausea was sweeping her stomach away, her cell phone chimed. Georgia took a shaky breath before she got up and dug through her purse.

There was a text from Lauren. *Did you make it home safe?*

No one had asked Georgia that before. It seemed like a silly question, really, because how much could go wrong during a short drive on a pleasant night? Her mind started filling with visions of all that could go wrong, and she gripped her phone tightly to ease the nonsensical worry.

Perfectly safe, Georgia answered. *Did you?*

Yeah. Then, *What did you think of the party?*

Eager to reassure, Georgia told her it was lovely. It was always lovely, being with her.

Lauren, usually quiet, turned out to be quite the avid texter. She was also precise and clear in her wording, which kept Georgia safe from the fear that perhaps she was misreading tone or intent. The conversation flowed with no uneasy pauses, and Georgia tucked herself in on the couch and let the mundane chatting comfort her—soft noises from elsewhere, reminding her that she was not alone.

CHAPTER THIRTEEN

Lauren's new sneakers weren't going to be broken in without a fight. They still gripped around the ball of her foot wrong after three weeks, and the left one was chafing as she ran toward Northway Coffee.

Focus on birds, Lauren reminded herself. *Don't get pissed off, think about the birds.*

Identifying local species of plants and animals by common and scientific name was the one skill Dad had taught her for fun, because his dad had taught him, instead of coaching her to perfect it. All three of them, grandfather, father, and she, repeated the memorized names to steady themselves and focus.

A red-breasted robin (*Turdus migratorius*), always the first to return in spring, gave up pecking the meager grass that had been uncovered when the snow melted and flew into a tree that was starting to bud. It was nice. Robins always looked a little disgruntled, which made them some of Lauren's favorites. Soon there would be blue jays (*Cyanocitta cristata*) around again, then red-winged blackbirds (*Agelaius phoeniceus*).

Georgia was outside Northway, her blue knit sweater as bright as the sky. Lauren put on a burst of speed when she saw her.

"So athletic!" Georgia said.

"I'm an athlete," Lauren confirmed before she tripped over the curb. It landed her right in Georgia's arms, which wasn't the worst outcome possible.

"That looked like one of my signature moves. Is klutziness contagious?" Georgia asked.

"Not that I know of," Lauren said, getting her feet under her. "But let's go in before I pull any more stunts."

Georgia linked their arms and led Lauren, who was breathless now for more than one reason, indoors.

It was still cold enough today for Georgia's habitual hot chocolate order not to seem out of place. Lauren was prepared to give the stink eye to anyone who thought it was odd when she inevitably ordered it all summer, too, but the cashiers liked Georgia so much already that maybe they'd accept it. Like how Lauren had casually accepted thinking about hanging out with Georgia several months into the future.

"Is it okay if we drink this outside?" Georgia asked when their drinks were in hand. "Maybe we could walk. It's so pretty today."

Lauren agreed, and they strolled down Main Street side by side. The way Georgia tilted her face toward the sun and breathed in the spring breeze that ruffled her hair gave Lauren an idea.

"How do you feel about hiking?" she asked.

Georgia stopped on the sidewalk. "You want to go hiking?"

"All New England lesbians hike," Lauren said. "It's in the bylaws."

"Oh. Do bisexuals have to do it, too?"

"Only half the time."

That got a laugh out of Georgia, and they continued walking.

"Where would we go?" Georgia asked.

"There's all kinds of options, but my dad and I went to the Appalachian Trail a lot. For the prestige of it, I think. He loved saying that he'd hiked on the Appalachian Trail, even though it's just this little spit right outside of town."

"It sounds impressive to me. Is it difficult?"

"It's a little hilly in places, but it's not an expedition. There's a lookout spot a couple miles in that's great for snacking and taking pictures. Sometimes we'd even take naps up there."

Georgia bumped into Lauren's shoulder and smiled. "It sounds gorgeous. I'm in. Hannah might get tired before a mile or two, though. Would that be okay, if we had to turn back early?"

Lauren had to adjust her vision of the hike on the fly, like she had when Hannah appeared at the party. She wasn't used to spending time with parents and kids, who apparently always did things together.

"Totally okay to turn back," she said.

"Thank you."

"How's Hannah doing?" Lauren asked. She wasn't sure she could carry a conversation about it, but Georgia talked about her kid all the time, and Lauren had found herself oddly interested lately.

"Normal, I think." Georgia squeezed her coffee cup lightly and twisted her free hand in her sleeve. "I keep expecting her to have a crisis like I did, but…I mean she cried the day we found out, and she had a lot of questions, but I lost it. Is she not going to lose it? And if she doesn't, how do I know how to help her?"

That wasn't a conversational direction Lauren had expected. Georgia's soft brown eyes met hers briefly before they flickered away again, and Lauren found herself groping along anyway, eager to comfort.

"I didn't cry," she said.

"You're an adult."

Lauren shook her head. "My grandmother died when I was a kid, and I didn't cry then, either. I don't remember my grandfather dying because I was so young, but Mom says I didn't cry. I've never cried. It's not my thing."

"What did you do?" Georgia asked.

A smile cracked Lauren's face as she turned it toward the sun. "I went hiking."

* * *

They planned their outing for Saturday morning. It rained overnight on Friday, but by morning it had stopped, and Georgia and Hannah got into Lauren's car dressed for walking in the damp forest.

"All the backpackers I see in town, and I've never known where they come from," Georgia said. "How did I not know there was an entrance to the Appalachian Trail right here in Holderness?"

Lauren said, "It's not really well marked. The sign is on the opposite side of the road from the actual trailhead, and it just lists the local nickname, not the Appalachian Trail aspect."

She parked carefully, avoiding the large potholes filled with muddy rainwater. Hannah got out the car and waded straight through a puddle on her way to a boulder on the edge of the woods. Lauren prayed the damp wouldn't melt her down or give her blisters.

"Are there any salamanders here?" Hannah asked. "I saw salamanders when I went hiking with my school."

"Wrong time of year, but soon there'll be fat little red newts around."

"With spots on their backs?"

Lauren nodded.

"Eastern newts," Hannah intoned. "Juvenile stage."

She marched toward the trailhead and waited for the adults to join her.

The gravel parking lot faded quickly into wet soil, leaves, and stones. The path curved gently at times, but many steep slopes were not undercut by switchbacks—they climbed upward, straight as the birches that stood out, stark white, among the darker trees. With mud season setting it, these patches were slippery. Lauren could have chosen a better time of year for this.

"Do you know why different trees have different colored leaves in the fall?" Lauren asked Hannah. The kid liked science, clearly. When she looked over her shoulder, Hannah was staring off into the forest.

"I don't know," Georgia said. "Tell me?"

Lauren smiled. "Chlorophyll is a pigment, so it absorbs sunlight, but it also makes things green. When the chlorophyll breaks down, tree leaves get their color from other chemicals that are still in the leaves. The red pigment in leaves is the same one that makes blueberries that purple color on the inside. Different trees turn different colors because they have different kinds of pigment, at different levels. Even the same kind of tree can look different in different places, though, because different soil gives the trees different nutrients to make pigments with."

She looked over her shoulder at Hannah, who was now watching her own feet.

"You said 'different' eight times," Hannah said.

Closer to the river, the trees were starting to bud, and the current carried muddy water and winter debris over the rocky riverbed. Hannah stopped at the edge of the wooden bridge, then bolted across like a squirrel crossing a highway.

"She doesn't like bridges," Georgia explained.

She leaned against the railing of the bridge and watched the water bubble below them. Lauren waved to Hannah, who was waiting for them on the other side.

"Does she like any of this?" Lauren asked. "I can't tell if she's having fun or not."

Georgia rubbed Lauren's back. "She's having fun," she said.

Lauren wasn't convinced, but she relaxed anyway because Georgia's hand was still resting against her shoulder blade.

It was late enough in the morning that the mist was thinning, so the first several feet of woods around them were completely clear, but farther away the sugar maples and other trees started to lose their hard edges and color until they dissolved completely in a bruised gray fog. Georgia's panting became audible as she crested a particularly demanding hill, and Hannah was falling farther behind. Going as far as the overlook would be too difficult for them, and there wouldn't be much to see on a day like this anyway. Lauren instructed Georgia and Hannah on the best way to descend the muddy slopes they'd climbed, and they shuffled back to the mouth of the trail. When they reached the parking lot again, Georgia tapped Lauren's arm and passed her a smooth rock from the ground. Lauren slipped it into the largest pocket of her jacket to fawn over later.

She was unlocking the car when she heard Hannah sing to herself, "Orange leaves and yellow leaves and leaves like blueberry guts!"

Over the roof of the car, Georgia caught her eye and winked. While Lauren drove them home, Georgia nearly fell asleep, but she perked up when Hannah asked for hot chocolate. By the time the three of them had settled in the living room with warm mugs, she seemed to have recovered her energy. She shuffled close to Lauren on the couch so she could whisper while Hannah lined up her dinosaurs on the other side of the room.

"She listened to you."

"Yeah," Lauren said. "Does she always listen on a half-hour delay?"

"I panicked for months a couple years ago, because I thought she was ignoring me. Kyle pointed out how she brings things back around after a while. It just takes her some time to process, you know? She listens, and she communicates. It's just not always the way adults expect."

Lauren drank her hot chocolate cautiously before she responded. "My dad used to always say I didn't listen to him, but he just wasn't listening to me. It's nice that you do. With Hannah, I mean."

"There's a big difference between listening and obeying."

"Yeah," Lauren sighed. "That, too."

She thought about her boots, laced exactly the way her father taught her. All day she'd placed her feet exactly the way he had, while the names of every plant around her, common and scientific, rattled through her head like a familiar army drill. Even the trail she'd chosen was their habitual choice, leading up to the spot where they always stopped and drank at least eight ounces of water, and then when they got home there was the mandatory—

"Shit! Sorry, crap," Lauren corrected. "We forgot to do a tick check."

"Tick check? It's forty degrees out, aren't they dead or hibernating or something?" Georgia said.

"It's never too early to start tick checks," Lauren said, muffled by the sweater she was pulling off over her head. She looked it over and found no sign of the nasty little bugs, but that was just the top layer of her clothes.

Georgia hustled Hannah upstairs to the bathroom, almost tripping on the hot chocolate mug she'd left on the floor. "You can come up next," she said.

Lauren, already examining her socks, nodded. She finished her clothes check, and after a few minutes of nervous waiting, she checked the couch, just to be safe. A few minutes after that, she finished her hot chocolate and washed her mug in the sink. She washed the pot Georgia had heated the milk in, too. Then she went to the mudroom to check her boots, even though they had tick-proof spray on them. Nothing made her more anxious than ticks.

It took a full twenty minutes for Georgia and Hannah to come back downstairs, and Lauren went straight up when they returned. Georgia followed her.

"Do you want me to check your back or your hair?" she offered.

"Sure," Lauren said. "Thanks."

Georgia closed the bathroom door behind her, and Lauren realized what she had agreed to. She was going to have to take off her shirt. In front of Georgia.

It didn't seem to affect Georgia at all. That was... disappointing, which in itself was surprising, and the effort of untangling that was enough to distract her from the actual act of taking her shirt off.

She could see Georgia in the mirror, holding a hand up but not touching, checking the full terrain of her back. Then Georgia's hand moved forward and combed through Lauren's hair. Whether or not Georgia looked at her when she did it, Lauren couldn't say, because her eyes closed. She luxuriated in Georgia's careful fingers questing all the way to her scalp, all over her head, much more thoroughly than necessary,

before brushing it all back into place and patting Lauren's bare shoulder, so briefly it might have been accidental.

"Okay up top," she said. "Good luck with the rest."

"Sure," Lauren said again. "Thanks."

Alone in the bathroom now, Lauren stripped off her clothes and gave herself a once-over. There were goose bumps down her arms. Ridiculous. Sexy thoughts were not what tick checks were for.

Still, sexy thoughts were happening. Georgia's clothes were flowing and layered, which left plenty of space for the imagination to conjure visions of several different, equally tantalizing bodies that might be found under them. Was her stomach as warm as the palms of her hands? Were her breasts as small under her shirt as they seemed, or did they have the same wonderful heft as her thighs and hips? If Lauren could gaze at the skin of her back, like Georgia had just looked at hers, would it be clear and uniform or spotted with freckles? What did her stretch marks look like?

Too bad Lauren would probably never find out. She'd been ignoring her attraction for two months now, and she wouldn't let a momentary slip lead her fully astray.

Tick free and dressed, Lauren left the bathroom, and she recited the scientific names of native species in her head as she descended the stairs to help gather her thoughts.

Betula papyrifera, paper birch (She just lost her partner.)

Acer saccharum, sugar maple (Not a romantic partner, but still.)

Notophthalamus viridescens, eastern newt (She has a kid.)

Inonotus obliquus, chaga mushroom (And I'm not in the best place, either.)

Trifolium pratense, red clover (No point building something I'm going to leave behind.)

"Do you want to play a card game with us?" Georgia asked when Lauren reached the bottom of the stairs.

"Sure," Lauren agreed, because Georgia was still beautiful and she couldn't help herself. "Do you know how to play Hearts?"

CHAPTER FOURTEEN

Hearts proved difficult for Hannah to follow, so Georgia proposed rummy, a game all three of them knew. Lauren's shuffling ability fascinated Hannah. Georgia, meanwhile, found it hard to concentrate with Lauren sitting right next to her, knee against knee, hiding her cards close to her chest.

"Am I supposed to let her win?" Lauren whispered.

Georgia shook her head and made her point by playing three aces. She discarded the queen of spades, and Hannah wiggled.

"What's that about?" Lauren asked.

Hannah wiggled again. "I'm wagging my tail."

"Got it." Lauren's mild acceptance of Hannah's quirks charmed Georgia even further.

On Hannah's turn, she scooped up the queen and lay down a run of four.

"I handed you two all the good cards, clearly," Lauren said.

The next time Hannah wagged her tail, Lauren snatched the card first. Hannah pouted quietly, but the second time it happened she whined.

"You have a tell," Lauren said. "You gotta stop doing your dance when you see a card you want."

Hannah turned to Georgia, wide-eyed. "I can't stop. I can't help it."

This could unravel quickly. Georgia grabbed at the first solution she came up with. "We'll all have to wag our tails. Does that sound fair?"

It did to Hannah. Georgia looked at Lauren, worried that the proposal wouldn't land. Adults could get so competitive, even with kids.

Cautious as a cat, watching for approval as much as Georgia was, Lauren wagged her tail.

* * *

It was raining again when Georgia went to bed that night, a comfortable springtime patter on the roof and windows that banished any echoing silence from the house. The mismatched layers of blankets pressed comfortably on Georgia's body. Everything was sleepy except for Georgia's mind, which whirled through the day's events and those of the last two months since she met Lauren. Her laughter, her sweet floppy hair, and the way she always tried to drink hot coffee too soon enchanted Georgia in a way no one had since Hannah was born. There had been no time, no interest since then. She'd been thoroughly occupied.

Desire had stirred, however, when she gazed at Lauren's naked back and found herself wondering what the rest of Lauren looked like. Georgia's usual minimal facial expressions had done her a great service while she carded Lauren's hair with her fingers. She believed, she hoped, she had given nothing away.

Dating was a dangerous proposal. With Hannah's happiness on the line as well—change, good or bad, was difficult for her— any partner Georgia considered would have to be in for the long haul. No casual pleasures like she used to enjoy. Georgia pictured Lauren's natural smile and swallowed. Maybe she could pass the tests, if Georgia figured out what they should be. If it did work out...

It was an idle fantasy, Georgia knew, but her hands weren't interested in being idle. Such lovely thoughts deserved acknowledgment.

* * *

"I have a story," Mark said at the Healing House meeting, "that'll make Georgia feel better about Hannah telling people about her sexuality at school."

Georgia forced a smile. Mark was choking back laughter and looking at Julie, who kept rubbing her cheeks like they hurt. Was Georgia about to be made fun of?

"Quin and David just, they sa—oh god!" Mark dissolved into giggles, his dark skin turning darker, and waved his hand at Julie.

"Mark's son and mine just approached us with a proposal," Julie continued. She glanced at Mark, caught his giggles, and blushed. "I'm a mother, you see, and Mark's a father, so clearly we should get married. It's simple logic, right?"

Mark snorted. Julie lost her composure and laughed with him. Georgia looked from them to Lauren, delighted to see her laughing, too.

"Relationships are that simple when you're a kid," Annabel said when Mark and Julie had calmed down. "Has anyone had to broach the topic of dating with their children?"

Overall, it seemed, dating didn't have to be complicated. The advice of the group, particularly Annabel, was to answer questions, be honest, and proceed as normal. Georgia wasn't sure anything she did could be classified as "normal," but honesty was a specialty of hers.

"I like Lauren," she said in the car on the way home. "Do you?"

"Yeah," Hannah said.

"Would you like it if she came to dinner sometime this week?"

"Yeah, but not during karate."

Simple enough.

* * *

The next evening brought Georgia back to the Green Mountain Dojo, where she waited with Ben Lennox in the folding chairs at the back of the studio. Ben talked like he'd just finished a vow of silence and had three days' worth of stories to tell. Then suddenly he said, "Hannah doesn't go to the Moosewood School. Why is that?"

It was a question Georgia heard often. The people in East Holderness were evangelical about their tiny village school, and few of them considered the risks involved for a student like Hannah.

"Private schools aren't required to provide special education services," Georgia explained.

"Maybe Hannah wouldn't need that at Moosewood. They have smaller classes, extra staff, and they're super hands-on. I'm sure they'd be willing to help, even if they're not required to."

"Why doesn't Abby go to the public school? If she did, the school would get more state funding due to higher student numbers, and that funding could support students like Hannah. Besides, I have more legal recourse if something isn't being handled appropriately at the public school."

Ben stammered, then turned eagerly to their approaching children.

"How'd it go, Abby-cakes?"

"Good," Abby told him. "Can Hannah spend the night this weekend?"

"If it's all right with Ms. Solomon, sure!"

All eyes turned to Georgia, but the only gaze she cared about was Hannah's. "Do you want to go?" she asked.

She saw no doubt in her daughter's face when she nodded.

It wasn't what Georgia had expected, and it yanked the rug out from under her. Hannah had never been away from her overnight before. Her coworkers' children had started spending the night with their friends when they were younger than Hannah, but Hannah had never shown an interest, and Georgia hadn't felt the need to push. She liked having Hannah at home. When had her little girl taken a step away from her?

She turned to one of Kyle's strategies: negotiate and delay.

"Let's think about it, and we'll let you know on Friday if Hannah can stay on Saturday. Does that work?"

Abby looked disappointed, but she and her father agreed, which allowed Georgia to flee from the situation. Hannah didn't seem surprised by her behavior, which was a sweet, intimate understanding Georgia was grateful for.

Once home, she texted Lauren.

I don't know how to do my due diligence with something like this. Should I run a background check on Ben? Do I need to stay up until she calls? How much medical information should I disclose for an overnight visit?

Asking the wrong person, Lauren's first response read. It was followed by, *Do you want to do some research and talk through what you find?*

Georgia's anxiety about Hannah spending the night away collided head-on with her uncertainty about how to ask Lauren on a date, and like many things with Lauren at the center, the impact left Georgia with a startling sense of clarity.

Do you want to have that conversation after dinner tomorrow? she asked. *If you're going to help me, I want to feed you for your trouble.*

You're not obligated, but I don't turn down free food. What can I bring?

It wasn't the most romantic answer, but Georgia hadn't said this was a date. Maybe it wasn't. Should she specify? Was she ready to specify? It was probably easier to retreat if she didn't state an intention. Did that make it not a date, if she didn't name it? Would Lauren still come, if she knew Georgia wanted it to be a date?

When the details were settled, Lauren said, *I can't wait.*

That, Georgia decided, was all she needed to know. Lauren was coming and was excited about it. They'd eat and talk, and everything would work out like it always did when Lauren was around. Georgia went to bed feeling as eager as she did anxious, and she slept far better than she'd expected to.

CHAPTER FIFTEEN

Lauren wasn't clear if this dinner at Georgia's house was a date. At first she'd thought it was an April Fool's joke, but Georgia didn't joke that way. It probably wasn't a date, since the kid was going to be there. Although who knew what parents thought of as dating. The Healing House discussion had made Lauren feel like you had to date the kid as much as the adult, which was so not her kind of arrangement.

Tracy usually helped her pick her clothes out before a date, but Lauren was only in the "texts about Mom and work" stage of being forgiven for her little scene at the party, so that wasn't an option. She sure as hell wasn't going to call her mother. It was probably sad that she couldn't think of anyone else to ask. The few friends she'd made in high school were gone now, casualties of distance and neglect during Lauren's college years. Her college friends were distant now, too. A couple had reached out with kind words after Dad had died, but she hadn't known how to reply.

Sometime soon, Lauren resolved, she'd try to make new friends. It had gone well with Georgia, after all. To address her immediate problem, she turned to the Internet, which told her nice jeans and a button-up would do.

She picked up a bottle of sparkling apple juice at the grocery store (Hannah didn't like grape) and spent several minutes standing in the floral section, staring at daisies and carnations like they were aliens on sticks. In the end, she left without them and insisted to herself that the drink was enough. This wasn't a date.

Hannah answered the door and said dinner would be served shortly, then took the bottle of sparkling juice to her mother in the kitchen. Georgia was pulling pans off the stove. The setting sun passed through several stained glass birds hanging in the window and soaked colors into her golden hair.

I should have brought flowers, Lauren thought.

"It's good to see you!" Georgia said. "Do you want to pour your juice into the glasses on the table? I love that stuff, thank you. I'm gonna plate this food and I'll be right with you."

Hannah pulled out a chair for Lauren and herself and gathered the three glasses near the seat she'd chosen for Lauren.

"Thanks," Lauren said, and she poured the bubbly drinks while Hannah watched.

"Okay, ready now," Georgia said.

She passed Lauren a plate with steak, green beans, and mashed potatoes. The red fluid seeping from the steak flowed across the plate as it tilted, dyeing the nearest portion of potatoes a bloody pink. She tried not to cringe. With the plate in front of her now, Lauren debated her best approach. The already wet potatoes might work as a barrier wall, as long as the vegetables hadn't been contaminated. She moved some aside—and found red pooled under them, too.

Georgia stopped halfway through the process of seating herself at the table.

"What's wrong?" she asked. Because of course she had noticed Lauren's hesitation.

Lauren winced. "Nothing, it's good."

But Georgia was watching her with real concern, and Hannah was eating from a sectioned plate. This wasn't home.

Her parents weren't going to jump out from behind the fridge and tell her not to be a baby. There was no reason to lie, even if she felt stupid telling the truth.

"The meat blood is touching the potatoes."

"I hate that," Hannah said.

"It's not blood," Georgia said, "it's hemoglobin."

Lauren frowned. "Isn't hemoglobin blood?"

"No, it's a component of blood. The blood gets taken out of meat before it's sold, and the hemoglobin gets released when the meat is cooked. I'll get you another plate. Do you want me to rinse the vegetables off?"

Lauren shook her head. Georgia pulled a plate out of the cabinet and passed it to her, but Lauren didn't start her potato rescue right away. She was mesmerized again, this time by the beauty of Georgia's brain as much as her body.

"What?" Georgia asked.

The way she squirmed made Lauren shake off her haze. "Nothing. I just like that you know stuff."

Georgia whispered a thank-you in the direction of her meal. The table was quiet for a while, until Hannah announced that she was tired of chewing. Lauren and Georgia split the rest of her steak, and Hannah piled more mashed potatoes in the potato section of her plate. She was learning a lot about potatoes in school, apparently, including the fact that they're very nutritious. When she started talking about the Irish Potato Famine, Lauren wondered if that was age appropriate—why teach seven-year-olds about mass tragedy?—but then, she didn't know jack about child development, and Hannah wasn't distressed. Not that Hannah was your average seven-year-old… Lauren sighed. Best to leave these decisions to the professionals.

After dinner, when the moon was high and the birds were quiet, Lauren and Georgia settled on the couch to watch a movie. Hannah went upstairs to read. Lauren watched Georgia watch her go.

"You're good with her," Georgia said, turning back to Lauren.

Lauren started. "Really?"

"You don't treat her like a baby or make her feel weird. She likes you. That's why she talks so much when you're around."

"Oh." Lauren wasn't sure if she should explain that she had no idea how she'd accomplished that.

"You don't spend a lot of time with kids, do you?" Georgia asked.

Lauren felt her gaze, soft and a little drowsy. She was so comfortable right now that it made Lauren fidget, because she knew where this conversation was going. Best to get it over with.

"No," Lauren said. "I don't really like kids."

"Oh."

"Hannah's okay, though!" Lauren added, eager to sugarcoat the subject in the wake of Georgia's disappointment. "She likes cool stuff, and she doesn't do that thing some kids do where everything she touches gets sticky somehow."

Georgia's face was blank.

"You know, like when you give a kid a glass at dinner and when they're done it's, like, opaque with grease and stuff? Tracy did that, it was gross. But Hannah's not gross."

"I'm glad Hannah's not gross," Georgia said.

Lauren could hear the clock on the wall tick. She cleared her throat, and it made her ears ring. Georgia's arm was held at an odd angle, as if she were so deep in thought that she'd forgotten to complete whatever motion she'd been making with it.

"Um…do you still want to watch a movie?" Lauren whispered.

The suspended arm revived itself and reached for the remote before the rest of Georgia came back to reality.

"Are there any good movies about cows?" she asked.

When they found one, they watched it without looking at or speaking to each other. They were supposed to talk about Hannah's sleepover, but Georgia didn't mention it, so Lauren slunk out to her car when the movie was finished without bringing it up.

She wanted to call Tracy. Instead, when she got home she parked herself in front of her laptop and worked, with only

Turing for company. She hoped Georgia didn't feel as adrift as she did.

* * *

Sunday morning started off with a video call from Felix, who was monkeying with Lauren's perfectly good code. Work was getting busy again, and while Lauren was keeping up with it, the random schedules and constant demands from Felix were cramping her new "boundaries" style. She'd rather be at the UU meeting, but he had to be stopped now.

"You're going to take up too much RAM again, I told you…" Lauren was revving up for a full tirade when her cell phone rang. She didn't recognize the number.

"Hello?" she answered, holding a finger up to silence Felix.

"Hi, is this Lauren? It's Ben Lennox. Abby's dad? Abby is—"

"Hannah's friend, yeah. She's mentioned you guys. Why are you calling me?" How did Ben even have her number?

"I've called Georgia five times, texted her…oh gee, I don't know how much, but she won't answer."

Lauren scrolled through her mental calendar of what Georgia's plans were, because that was something she kept track of now, apparently. "She's in Shaftsbury, I think, out in the mountains. She probably doesn't have reception."

"Can you help me, then?" Ben sounded helpless. Lauren wondered how many skills exactly he'd had to learn from scratch when his wife left him.

"With what?"

"Hannah fell. She won't talk, but when I say anything about the hospital she screams! I don't know what to do, and if I can't call Georgia…"

Then Lauren was the only other person he could call.

Her mother always said Lauren was a lion with a small pride, protective and territorial when provoked. She had protected her father for years, before she understood how much pain his pain had caused her. She had protected Tracy against him when he said community theater was only for retired gay men with nothing better to do, and then every day after that. She was even protective of her code.

Now, Lauren felt that flood of stinging warmth in her gut. Her muscles wound tight for springing into action. Her mind rushed through a bare-bones plan of approach.

"Text me your address," she said, "and tell Hannah I'm on my way."

CHAPTER SIXTEEN

Corina Lewis, the site superintendent at the Mueller house, fussed the entire time Georgia climbed the stepladder to the roof.

"I've watched you trip over nothing at all. Why do you wanna take chances?"

"I want to get a picture from this angle for the project records," Georgia called down. "It's great work!"

She hadn't been up on a roof for a while now, which was a shame. Adjusting to single parenthood had drastically reduced her time on job sites this year, and she'd hardly picked up her camera at all since Kyle had died. Other people's photos lacked the particularity and detail that Georgia usually insisted on when taking pictures for her project records. She was eager to get back to doing things her way.

She reached the top of the ladder and pulled herself over the gutter and onto the gray slate roof. The mason, brick in hand, nodded to her. He was finishing the new chimneystack, which both Corina's and Georgia's levels and measurements confirmed was straight as a rail.

"Say cheese!" Georgia said, and the mason grinned. The picture was perfect, and Georgia always loved having the people involved on record in project files too. "Roger, right? Would you mind escorting me around so I can take pictures of the sides of the chimney?"

Roger took her hand and helped her balance as she minced across the slate. He hovered close while she took her pictures, then guided her back toward the ladder.

"Why are you even on site now?" Roger asked before Georgia began her descent. "It's Sunday, Ms. Solomon."

"Well, I heard you'd be finished by Tuesday evening, and I'm booked tomorrow. Last photos before the finishing touches are done! Thanks, Roger."

Georgia climbed down, and Corina eased her off the last few steps.

"You want to see the floor realignments now, or do you want to hop around like a goat some more?"

"Is the fresh air intake all set?"

Corina confirmed, and Georgia continued eagerly through her onsite checklist. The Mueller house was old and, like many houses in the area, uneven. The crumbling chimney had been the worst issue, but flattening out the second floor had progressed slowly through several setbacks. It was wonderful listening to the way Corina unfolded Georgia's plans and the Muellers' vision. This late in the project, she knew the whole house better than anyone else.

Georgia was also in high spirits because she hadn't gotten any phone calls overnight. Hannah, it seemed, had been fine without her, and though Georgia slept poorly, she felt confident enough in Hannah's security to come to this site instead of waiting at home just in case.

It wasn't until an hour later, when she was halfway back to town, that her phone started chiming. Over and over again, it chimed, relentless now that there was a sliver of reception to deliver messages with. Georgia pulled over, her spine already frozen with dread. She checked the phone, just a cursory glance, and then sped forward. Damn any cop who tried to pull her over. She wasn't stopping until she reached Ben Lennox's house.

The driveway was full. She pulled to the curb. She scraped her hubcaps, but she didn't care. She jumped out of the driver's seat. Ben had heard her pull up. He already had the front door open. Georgia raced through it. Through the front hall, past the kitchen, into the darkened den. She stopped at the threshold so suddenly that Ben slammed into the back of her. She stumbled forward with a heavy thump, made louder by her sturdy work shoes.

Lauren looked up from her conversation with Hannah.

"All good here," she said.

Hannah gave Georgia a thumbs-up from the safety of Lauren's side.

The curtains in the den were closed, and all the lights were off, so Georgia saw the fuzzy idea of them on the couch together rather than a stark, well-defined picture. It would have been harder to believe if the lights had been on. Georgia tracked gravel from the Mueller site across the hardwood as she approached them. Lauren started to stand, but Georgia put a hand on her knee to still her as she herself knelt in front of Hannah.

"How are you feeling, baby?"

Hannah showed her the bag of frozen peas on her right wrist. When Georgia asked to see it, Hannah moved the peas to reveal a red, slightly swollen joint, plus gravel scrapes, clean and dry, on the heel of her hand.

Abby piped up from the other end of the couch. "We were just riding bikes, it was an accident. We were wearing helmets!"

Georgia squinted at her daughter in the dimness. "Riding bikes? With training wheels?"

Hannah had never let Kyle or Georgia take the training wheels off her bike. It was fun the way it was, she said, so why make it harder again? But Hannah shook her head now. No training wheels. Damn it, she'd give up after an accident like this, just like she had with downhill skiing two years ago. Even Kyle hadn't been able to convince her to try again.

"Everybody falls on their first try," Lauren said. "I was telling Hannah about how Tracy rode into our dad's car and scraped the fender. She got grounded, no dessert or TV for a week. Nobody's first fall is worse than that, right, Hannah?"

Hannah nodded.

"She didn't break anything," Abby said.

"Nope," Lauren said. "The bike's okay, you're okay, and you'll be ready to try again as soon as your arm feels better."

Abby nodded so hard her teeth clicked. Hannah didn't look at anyone, but she presented another thumbs-up. Georgia slumped back on her heels, tingling from the rubber band snap of released tension. Lauren tapped her with one foot. Georgia took hold of it, which was probably weird, but Lauren didn't seem to mind. It comforted Georgia almost as much as hugging herself did.

"Right," she said. "Everybody falls."

The way Lauren had said it, it hadn't sounded like a bad thing.

Soon enough, Hannah was ready to stand up and go to the car, so all of them went outside into the humid afternoon. Abby held Hannah's uninjured hand. Ben apologized all the way to the door.

"How did you find Lauren?" Georgia asked him when they were on the porch.

"You talk about her a lot. You said something about an art store, so I called and somebody there gave me her number. I didn't know what else to do."

Lauren punched him lightly on the shoulder. "No problem, man. You got me out of a really frustrating video conference, too, so…bonus."

Georgia felt the conversation freeze—she had learned the signs from experience—so she said goodbye to Ben and Abby and led Lauren down the sidewalk toward their cars. She helped Hannah buckle her seat belt, turned on the radio for her to adjust, then walked back to Lauren.

"I don't know how to thank you."

"I'm good in a crisis," Lauren said.

"You're good with Hannah." It was something special, and Georgia needed her to understand that.

Lauren scratched the back of her neck and scuffed her shoe against the sidewalk. Georgia waited. Silence didn't bother her.

"Did you learn that kind of quiet from Annabel?" Lauren asked when she looked up. "You both wait me out like you've got all day."

"I do have to leave soon."

"Right, yeah. Look. I'm sorry about what I said the other night, about kids being gross? I didn't think about how that sounded."

"Is it how you feel?"

Lauren shoved her hands deep into her pockets. "I'm not a people person, but sometimes you just click with someone. I like that I click with you and Hannah."

Georgia clutched at her sleeves to keep from reaching out to Lauren. "I like it too," she said.

She dragged herself away, too eager for time with her daughter to linger in the renewed peace with Lauren, but she knew they'd be together again soon. She felt the pull of Lauren's reckless, decisive personality and her soft stance, soft lips, soft eyes, like magnets. There was no reason Georgia could see to resist that pull much longer.

Mentally, she took a picture of this moment: the dust of doubt swept out of the corners, the finishing touches applied to her new home on Smitten Street.

CHAPTER SEVENTEEN

Lauren had a few things to be happy about as she drove away from the Lennox house. One was visible in her rearview mirror, headed in the opposite direction in a little Subaru. Another was that Tracy had just texted her:

Are you still busy, or do you have time to swing by the store?

Ben had called Ashburn's Art Supply Store to try to reach Lauren, and Tracy had connected them. She'd followed up to ask if Hannah was okay, of course, but Lauren hadn't expected more than that. Two people forgiving her in one day would be a record, if she pulled it off.

The storefront of Ashburn's had a sign in it, handwritten by Mom, that read UNDER NEW MANAGEMENT, CHECK BACK WITH US IN SEPTEMBER. The massive string of sleigh bells was still on the door. Everything else was gone.

"Weird, right?" Tracy called down from the balcony.

Lauren mounted the stairs with a spring in her step. "Yeah. Coffee?"

Tracy took the offered takeout cup gratefully, just like Lauren knew she would.

"How's Hannah?" she asked.

Lauren leaned against the balcony railing and groaned. "She fell and got freaked out. She's okay now."

"I bet Georgia loved seeing the knight in shining armor side of you."

"Luckily, yeah, since I put my foot in it the last time I saw her."

Tracy's laugh echoed through the empty store. "Of course you did. Good thing you made up for it, because I want her hanging around. I like her."

"I knew you would."

"You like her," Tracy said. She was sweating and sagging over the railing next to Lauren, but her jaw was set like stone. There was no way to lie about it.

"Don't start," Lauren pleaded, but that was useless, too. It was time for sage advice from little sister, whether big sister wanted it or not.

"You know how I told you at the party to stop being a grump and go after what you really want?" Tracy said.

Lauren frowned. "In my career, yeah."

"I didn't mean just your career. You've turned your life around, and I know that's not because of Georgia exactly, but she opened a door you kept shut for a long time. Don't you want to be open to more of that?"

The objections were immediate: Georgia had just lost her best friend, Georgia had a kid, Lauren wasn't going to be in town forever, there were plenty of dating options better than Lauren, and... "No," she said.

"No? Why not?" Tracy whined, then held up her hands to fend off Lauren's protests. "Actually, don't tell me why not. I'm sure there's a list. But here's the thing: there will always be a list. Yes, it might not work out, and yes, that would suck, but would never being with her at all suck less?"

The thought made Lauren flinch. She turned it away by asking, "Is that what you're doing by trying to keep the store? Taking a spontaneous risk?"

Tracy shrugged. "Yes and no. I've always wanted the store, but I thought I'd have a little more time to get my shit together first. It's now or never, though, and I can't live with never, so I guess it's gotta be now."

Lauren listened this time, and Tracy's vision for the store unfurled. They could both see it laid out on the floor below them, modern, dynamic, an adventure of an art supply shop. It was more than their father's store had ever been. Just like Tracy.

Before Lauren left, Tracy poked her in the chest and ordered, "Get what you want. 'Shouldn't' and 'can't' won't make you happy."

"Yeah yeah," Lauren said. "Okay."

* * *

The next week was normal, which meant Lauren continued to walk a tightrope of emotion when she had coffee or dinner with Georgia. She even came into the Prysliak office to deal with a programming problem and slipped on the stairs when Georgia waved to her. Thankfully that encounter didn't involve any coffee. Then one Saturday night, while Lauren was muttering curses and typing code, Georgia called in a panic. Her sitter had just called out, and there was some fancy work party Georgia had to go to, with grant funding on the line.

"I would normally never ask, but Abby's with her mom tonight and I don't really have anyone else to—"

"Georgia, it's fine. I can sit with Hannah for an hour and then chill in your house when she goes to bed. That's not a big ask."

It was, actually. The idea made Lauren twist in knots, but the relief she heard through the phone when Georgia thanked her made her own shoulders relax. She packed up her computer and drove to the duplex. Georgia already had a jacket on and was out the door almost before Lauren was in, tossing thanks over her shoulder as she charged toward her own car.

Lauren looked at Hannah, who was sitting on the living room floor in a neat ring of dinosaurs.

"What's on your agenda for the evening?" she asked.

"Hot chocolate and aquarium blueprints," Hannah said.

That was totally doable.

Hannah went to bed an hour later, and Lauren scrubbed the overboiled remains of failed hot chocolate off the stove before crashing on the couch. Georgia had said it was okay to sleep, and with Len crying "crunch time" again, a nap would do her good, so she got comfortable. Sleep took her eagerly.

When a key turned in the back door's lock at half past midnight, Lauren woke up and smiled. She rubbed her face while Georgia's high heels clattered to the floor in the entryway, and she sat up enough to watch her come in. The sight bowled her over.

The light caught Georgia's blue satin dress, shining gently and highlighting the curves it clung to and the loose folds of the skirt. A gold bracelet slid down her bare wrist when she lifted her hand to pull pins out of her hair, which fell, bit by bit, in messy yellow ringlets. When Georgia tried to run her fingers through it, she snagged her pretty opal ring. She huffed around a mouthful of hairpins.

"Need help?" Lauren said.

Georgia winked at her and shook her head, and the lipstick was almost all faded from her lips. She worked the ring free, then took the hairpins out of her mouth and dumped them carelessly onto a little table by the door.

"How was your night?" she said.

"Fine," Lauren said. She was ready to explain that the scorched milk in the saucepan would definitely clean up with a little baking soda, but Georgia had leaned her hip against the doorframe, and her hands were sliding under the hem of her dress, searching for the end of her nylons. "It was fine."

The nylons were rolled gently down Georgia's thighs, over her knees, down her calves, and abandoned on the floor. She started taking off her jewelry, her hands running over her fingers, her wrists, the back of her neck. Lauren wanted her own hands on that skin, gently baring the woman before her piece by piece. Next, she'd take hold of the zipper at the back of her dress and...

Georgia chuckled. "Nice hair," she said.

Lauren snapped out of it and patted her wild hair desperately, muttering, "Yeah, like yours is any better."

"I'm gonna go upstairs and clean up. Back in a minute?"

"Yeah."

Georgia's bare feet were almost silent on the stairs, but Lauren listened closely for the tiniest sounds of movement until the water running in the bathroom drowned out everything else. She got up then to make tea. It was ready when Georgia came back, in sweats and a baggy flannel, and they sat on the couch together to drink it. Lauren expected the erotic spell she'd fallen under to have faded by now. It hadn't. The underlying tension of desire had broken the surface and forced itself into full view, and now the sight of Georgia, barefaced and plain as always, only made Lauren want her more.

"How was the party?"

"It was all about the grant money. Nobody knew anything about architecture. And the cheese was all fancy and weird."

Georgia took a sip of her tea. Lauren licked her lips.

"Thank god I won't be here while Kelly is tomorrow," Georgia continued. "She's Kyle's sister, and I don't have the patience for that."

"Hannah mentioned her aunt was coming over, said she was looking forward to it."

The whole couch vibrated with the force of Georgia bouncing her leg. Lauren wanted to soothe her, but she didn't know what she'd start if she touched Georgia, so she put her feet up on the coffee table and kept her distance. They sipped their tea in silence. Eventually, Georgia settled down.

"Thanks for this," she said, and Lauren stared at her pretty fingers peeking out from the too-long sleeves of her shirt, wrapped around her warm mug. "It's nice to come home to hot tea. And a hot woman zonked out on my couch."

Both of them froze. Lauren was spinning from affectionate to salivating like a broken compass.

"Is that an okay thing to say?" Georgia asked.

"Yeah." *Say it again*, Lauren thought.

Georgia brushed an awkward piece of Lauren's hair down, then said, "I'm not kidding, you know. There are so many boring

people at these parties, it's a relief to see someone I actually like."
Her fingers ran through Lauren's hair to her jaw, and Lauren
felt the faintest touch of Georgia's skin on her own.

Please like me, Lauren thought.

"I really like you," Georgia said.

Lauren pressed Georgia's hand fully against her face,
nuzzling slightly into the flannel sleeve.

"You're so beautiful," she confessed. "Can I…"

Georgia nodded, leaning forward before the question was
out. The question was probably obvious, with the way Lauren
had been staring at her mouth. Lauren met her where she'd
stopped halfway, kissing her. When she pulled away slightly,
Georgia followed, so Lauren put her hands on Georgia's hips
to bring her closer. The kisses were deep, slow, and constant,
with neither of them pulling farther than a breath away before
coming back together. Lauren's hands flexed against the warmth
of Georgia's sides, feeling the gentle give and softness of her
body beneath her clothes. When Georgia's lips opened slightly
to release a panting breath, Lauren moaned.

Then, to her horror, the moan turned into a yawn.

"You're tired," Georgia said. "You should stay here tonight.
I don't want you to drive."

Lauren nodded. She kissed Georgia's jaw, but Georgia
wasn't finished talking.

"The couch is great for sleeping, as you discovered. Or you
could have the bed? I'm not, I haven't…We should sleep, not…"

"The couch is comfortable," Lauren said. She made a show
of leaning back on it, settling in and closing her eyes.

"You're not gonna brush your teeth or anything?"

Right. Lauren hauled herself up and followed Georgia
upstairs, where she received an extra toothbrush and soft cotton
pants to replace her jeans. They kissed one last time before
Georgia retreated to her room and shut the door. Lauren
dumped herself on the couch again and stared into the dark in
wonder.

Tracy's advice, it seemed, was easier to follow than she'd
thought. Kissing Georgia was exactly what she'd wanted to do
tonight, and she wasn't thinking at all about why she shouldn't.

CHAPTER EIGHTEEN

Georgia shambled down the stairs at eight the next morning, hoping she had enough pancake mix for her guest. Lauren was already in the kitchen, fully dressed in the previous night's clothes, and she smiled like a person who was far too awake.

When Georgia mentioned breakfast, she said, "I'm going to Tracy's place before church."

"Church?"

Lauren shrugged. "Not church-church. It's more like a social event than anything. Unitarian Universalist."

Right, this had been mentioned before. Georgia tried to look like she remembered what it was.

"What have you got going on today?" Lauren asked. "Besides Kyle's sister coming."

"She'll be here at three she said, which means she might arrive any time after noon. Ben invited me to dinner so I won't be underfoot while Kelly and Hannah bond. I think he still feels bad about letting Hannah fall off a bike. We're going to the Green Pepper in Massachusetts."

"With Ben?"

Now that the sunlight streaming through the window wasn't hateful, Georgia could admire the way it lit Lauren from behind, an enchanting silhouette. She stepped closer and swung Lauren's hands in her own.

"Don't worry," Georgia teased. "He's a nice enough guy, but he doesn't even know the difference between a gambrel roof and a mansard."

Lauren's hands stopped in their playful swinging arc. "I don't know that either."

"You have other redeeming qualities," Georgia said, and she kissed her.

The way Lauren's lips moved against hers was a long-lost pleasure, and Georgia wondered how she hadn't started kissing her first thing when she saw her, because one night's sleep seemed as long ago as the eight years that had gone by without a single kiss like this. When Lauren kissed her forehead and stepped back, Georgia knew that from this kiss to the next would be a long wait too.

"I'm still gonna look those words up," Lauren said.

"I know. It's one of those qualities I like."

Lauren kissed her again, and by the time they broke apart, she was running late. Georgia listened to her try and fail to shut the door quietly, and her heart shone like the sunbeams dappling the countertops.

* * *

That afternoon, Georgia clung to her lovely morning with white knuckles while Hannah stomped back and forth across the living room floor. Kelly was late.

"Do you want to play with your cars while you wait?"

Hannah didn't answer. Her stomping made the little cars roll out of the lines she'd arranged them in earlier, and that made her stomp harder. Georgia tugged at a lock of her own hair. She was trying to think like Kyle, but it was hard when she felt the same way Hannah did. They both needed to calm down before Kelly got here, though, because Kelly wouldn't be any help.

"Stomp for five more minutes," she said, "then we need to do something else, okay?"

"Stomp for five more minutes," Hannah said.

Kelly arrived an hour later, at the same time as Ben. Both of them waited by the door while Georgia and Hannah finished a hand of rummy.

"I'm sorry I was late," Kelly told Hannah.

"Stomp for five more minutes," Hannah said, but she gave Kelly a thumbs-up. They'd be fine.

Georgia put her cardigan on and announced that she'd be home by nine, not any later. It had the twin benefits of assuring Hannah that her nightly schedule was still on track and guaranteeing that no one could keep Georgia out later than she wanted to be.

"What's the stomping thing about?" Ben asked when they were in his truck.

"I think she means she's still mad that Kelly was late, but she'll be better soon."

"How long are you gonna be mad?"

Georgia smiled, because Ben was smiling at her. "Longer than five minutes," she said.

* * *

The Green Pepper had a vibe that passed for funky in Western Massachusetts, with mismatched chairs at recycled wood tables, a totally vegan menu, and obscure herbal teas served in mason jars. Really good obscure herbal teas, to be fair. Georgia was taking her second large swallow when a voice exploded from behind her.

"Hey look, it's Ben!"

Ben didn't respond. Georgia looked behind her and saw a white couple arm in arm, breezing past the hostess on their way to Ben and Georgia's table.

"It's been forever since we've seen you, Ben!" the man scolded. "What's up with that?"

"I've been busy. Good busy, though." Ben smiled at Georgia, but it didn't look right.

"Is this Georgia?" the woman said. "Oh, we've heard so much about you! I'm Ava Hayden, and this is my husband Evan. Can we join you?"

They did, despite the fact that Ben looked so nervous now. He perked up despite himself when the Haydens asked about Abby.

Children remained the topic of conversation, and it lasted until their meals arrived. Into the comfortable silence of eating, Ava Hayden dropped a question that almost made Georgia choke on her summer squash.

"How long have you two been together? I know you told me, Ben, but I forgot."

"We met three months ago," Ben said, not correcting the assumption behind the question.

Georgia was baffled. She knew she wasn't misunderstanding the connotations of that question. She knew exactly what it meant. Had the Haydens misunderstood whatever Ben had told them? Had she misunderstood Ben's intentions when he asked her to go to dinner with him? Had he misunderstood her friendliness as interest? She needed to say something, but Ava was asking her what she did for a living, and Georgia was helpless to do anything but follow the track of the new topic.

Unless…

"We just got new software in our office," Georgia said after she'd explained what her firm did. "The woman I'm dating designed it."

It didn't drop into conversation as smoothly as Georgia had hoped it would. Evan raised his eyebrows and looked at Ben, who was looking at his black bean burger like it was going to bail him out of jail. Ava let out one loud bark of laughter and slapped the table, which made Georgia and all the silverware jump.

"Please tell me everything about your girlfriend," she said.

Georgia was more than happy to. It turned out Ava worked with computers, too, so she was enchanted with Lauren's devotion and effectiveness in the face of an uphill battle for success. It made Georgia proud to see another professional so impressed with Lauren and her work.

When the meal was finished and they all set out toward their cars, Ava held Georgia a few steps back.

"He's been telling us about you for weeks. I'd think if you're gonna pull off a fake dating scam, you'd let the person you're fake dating in on it," she said.

Ava was smiling, like it was a joke, but Georgia didn't find it funny. It hadn't occurred to her that Ben might have done this on purpose, that it hadn't been her mistake. "He lied to you about us? Directly?"

The wattage of Ava's smile dimmed. "It's not like him, but divorce does funny things to people."

"Funny things like pretending you're dating someone?"

Ava grimaced. "Rachel, his ex-wife, is doing really well, and we're still close to her. He wanted his life to sound as good as hers, and he probably never expected us to meet you. We shouldn't have barged in on your dinner tonight."

Georgia still didn't understand and said as much.

"Some people get so focused on what they think they should have, they don't appreciate what they've got. You're a good friend. We'll make sure to remind Ben of that, in case he ever thinks of taking advantage of that again."

He wasn't going to have another chance to take advantage, but Georgia didn't say that out loud.

Ava and Evan shook Georgia's hand before climbing into their car. Ben stood stiffly at the passenger door of his truck, waiting to help Georgia up.

When he said nothing for ten minutes, Georgia asked, "Is this why your ex won't let Abby stay at my house during her weeks and doesn't want Hannah at her house? Because she thinks we're dating?"

"I don't know what Rachel thinks."

"I'd appreciate it if you found out."

Ben didn't answer.

Georgia continued, "My step-brother told me we'd go to the same college, then move to Vermont and buy some land together, build a cabin. It felt like he was my real brother. Real family. I was serious, but he was just playing pretend." Georgia turned to Ben and stared at him, knowing he wouldn't take his eyes off the road to stare back. "I'm not interested in friendships with people who are playing with me."

He said he was sorry, so quietly Georgia barely heard. She turned her back and stared out the window. She felt as far away as the stars looked.

When they pulled into her driveway, Hannah ran out to greet her. Kelly waited at the door.

"So he's a friend of yours?" she asked, nodding toward Ben's retreating truck.

"Not really," Georgia said.

Hannah became thoroughly absorbed in her racetrack and cars once they were all inside. She wouldn't have been able to hear when Kelly said, "I'm going to stay in Kyle's apartment tonight and head back in the morning."

The notion of Kelly, of anyone, sleeping in that apartment set Georgia reeling. She couldn't imagine anyone wanting to sleep in the bed Kyle had died in, and Hannah's little bed was untouched since that last time she and her father had made it up together. Kelly would disrupt the sheets and use the dishes and mingle her own steps and smells with Kyle's and set the whole place to fading away. She would make unfamiliar noises on the other side of Georgia's familiar wall.

"Why?" she asked.

"It's free, unlike a hotel room. You're keeping it, might as well use it, right?"

No! No, not might as well. It wasn't there to be used, it was there to be preserved, just for a little while longer. She couldn't explain that to Kelly, though.

"You can stay here," she said. "The couch is great, or I can change the sheets on my bed. Either way."

Kelly huffed. "Whichever way you want it, Georgia. It's always your way."

Georgia clenched and unclenched her hands as she considered. Surely Kelly had a preference, but it was impossible for Georgia to know if Kelly didn't tell her, so how was she supposed to make that decision?

Her phone chimed. She pulled it out of her pocket so quickly she almost threw it.

How was dinner? Lauren had texted.

Lauren. She'd slept so soundly on the couch last night; Georgia didn't want to share that with Kelly Gray. She gave up her bed and curled up downstairs, steadied by the memory of Lauren's presence despite the upheavals of the day. Tomorrow would be a new one, and maybe she would see Lauren again and be even more renewed.

CHAPTER NINETEEN

Lauren wasn't able to see Georgia at all during the following week, but the reason was worth it: Felix had taken a job with another company and left immediately, which sent everyone else scrambling to pick up his slack. One question dominated the minimal break conversation: Who was going to take Felix's place as project manager? A few people had high hopes for themselves, and Lauren was among them.

Moving up the ranks at Green Mountain had never been a consideration before. Lauren had always thought of her position as temporary, and the problems, as they revealed themselves, were short-term annoyances, not outlets for growth. Could she clean this place up if she were the manager? Would she want to? How would the position fit with the rest of her suddenly rich life? Those weren't questions she'd asked herself before. They sunk in more deeply when she made her first attempt to befriend Jamar.

The two of them had been ranting to a rubber duck about the latest bug they'd discovered, which was the tried-and-true method for solving a programming problem, but after forty minutes, they had gotten nowhere.

"Six o clock," Jamar said, setting the duck back on the tiny slot of desk space he called his own. "Time to pack it up."

Lauren glanced at their busy coworkers. "You're gonna leave right now?"

"I have dinner with my son every Thursday, so...yeah."

"I've literally never been in this office for a second when you weren't also here, including on Thursdays."

Jamar crossed his arms, and Lauren realized she'd sounded accusatory when he replied, "You leave when you want to. Why can't I?"

"You can and should. It's new, that's all." Jamar's posture relaxed, so Lauren decided to ask, "What changed?"

At first, Jamar didn't answer. Lauren could see the wheels of his mind turning. She'd known it was a sort of personal question, but she might be in over her head already in her attempt to be friendly.

Finally, he said, "Can I tell you something?"

"Sure, why not?" Lauren said, because there was no sense in turning back when she'd come this far.

"I decided to spend more time with my son, at least partly, because of something you did. Don't take this the wrong way, but when you joined that video call from the hospital..." Jamar shook his head, as if just remembering it rattled him. "That wasn't right. You should have been with your dad then. And I should be with my son right now, not working. I'm glad you're stepping back, too, taking time for yourself."

Lauren squirmed under Jamar's earnest regard. She remembered that call. Dad had been hospitalized for a week before he was released to at-home hospice care, and she'd spent every day in his room, balled up in a plastic chair, feeling useless. Then Felix had called.

"My dad told me to join that meeting. He said you guys needed me right then, and there'd be more time for us to talk after I did my work."

Jamar scoffed. "The man's dying and says he's got more time."

Lauren picked at the stitching of her chair for a moment, looking for the right thing to say before she said it.

"I'm glad you're spending your time how you want."

"Trying to," Jamar said. He tucked his chair in, ignoring the resentful glances he got.

Lauren packed her bag in a flash, saying, "Hold up a sec, I'll walk out with you."

Jamar waited, and he kept his stride slow so Lauren could keep pace with him as they left together.

"You wanna see a picture of my little man?" he asked.

Maybe it was the way his face lit up when he said it, but Lauren found she actually did want to see a picture of a kid. She even asked what his name was, and she remembered afterward that it was Alvin.

* * *

The next afternoon, while she was drafting a formal account of her accomplishments over the past two years, she got an odd text from Georgia.

Do you know anyone who owns a picnic basket?

Sure—Yogi Bear, Lauren said. *My parents had one. It's probably still in the attic. Why?*

Because Hannah and Abby want to have a picnic tomorrow. Can you come?

Lauren looked from her phone to the people around her, hunched over and dug in for the long haul. They'd get it done by tonight.

I'll be there, she said.

She wasn't able to get away from work until midmorning the next day, and when she swung her bag over her shoulder and headed for the door, several coworkers glared at her, just like they had at Jamar.

"Where are you going?" one of them asked.

"Got a date."

"And that's more important than the deadline? We're killing ourselves here."

Lauren gave them all finger guns as she retreated. "Can't code if you die. Work-life balance, bitches!"

Jamar would have laughed if he'd been there, but he was camping with Alvin, so no one was amused except Lauren herself. Too bad for them.

Half an hour later, stifling in her mother's hot, humid attic, she realized she was killing herself for this date as surely as the others were for their deadline.

"If you find my old bird feeder, bring it down, would you?" her mom called up the stairs.

"Sure, Mom," Lauren said. She'd broken that bird feeder and thrown it away years ago, but apparently she'd really sold the idea that maybe it was hidden in the attic.

A bead of sweat ran down her nose and hung there. Lauren considered giving up on the picnic basket, and for anyone else, she would have. But the thought of making Georgia happy was too much to pass up. This picnic scheme seemed like the kind of thing that she would want to be perfect, and having a basket would make her smile so widely that—

Lauren hit her head on a rafter and knocked over a box of Christmas ornaments. Thinking about Georgia's lips while navigating tight spaces needed to stop. She found the picnic basket, which for some reason was full of random candles, under the three-legged table Dad had always said he was going to fix. She picked a candle to bring to her mother and left the others wilting on the attic floor. A good look at the basket in the daylight showed that it needed a bath as much as Lauren did. She blew dust off the top of it just as Mom turned the corner. Both of them sneezed.

"Did you find the bird feeder?"

Lauren presented the candle she'd chosen, a little blue bird still in its plastic wrapper, and held it at arm's length toward her mother. "I found this!"

It was meant to be a small distraction, proof that she had truly dug around in the attic and looked as hard as she could, but her mother let out a small "oh" at the sight of it and took it from Lauren with both hands.

"Your father gave this to me," she said. "He just brought it home on a whim one day. I could never stand to light it, it's so pretty, but I never figured out what else to do with it. Thank you, sweetheart."

She put an arm around Lauren's neck, and Lauren tried to accept the rare hug without hitting her mother with the picnic basket. When Mom pulled away, she cupped Lauren's face in her hands and smiled with watery eyes. It took effort not to avert her gaze. Tracy had been distant with Dad, and Lauren's relationship with him was a turmoil of disappointment and longing for both of them, but Mom... Mom had loved him completely. She missed him completely, and right now it looked like that was too much for her to bear. Lauren could hardly bear watching her try.

"You look like him sometimes, you know," her mother said, "and you remind me of him."

That made Lauren push away. The thought of her father, stagnant, resentful, letting every scrap of happiness sour in his fist, and her like him... She needed to leave, right now. She'd leave the house, the town, the continent if necessary, to get away from the idea that she was like him.

"There's an opening at Green Mountain," she found herself saying. "A promotion that's up for grabs. I might be moving up in the world soon."

Onward and upward, like her father had wanted to go but never did.

Mom sighed. "He would be so proud of you."

Lauren darted past her and out the door.

* * *

A frantic shower and picnic basket scrub later, she was standing on Georgia's doorstep, watching the woman's face light up just the way she'd imagined.

"Oh, this is perfect! I can't believe you just had this. God, it's vintage! And it really held up, wow. Thank you so much for lending it to us. Come in, come in!"

Lauren checked that there were no kids in sight, then pulled Georgia down into a kiss. Georgia deepened it. Just when Lauren thought she couldn't take anymore of this without wanting to take it even further, Georgia wrenched herself away.

"Picnic," she panted.

They went into the kitchen, and Georgia went back to cutting and bagging a pan of brownies like nothing had happened. Lauren looked around the room like she'd never seen it before, unfocused, or maybe too focused on the wrong thing. When Hannah and Abby said hi, she tuned back in. The girls were standing on stools to reach the kitchen counter, making peanut butter and jelly sandwiches. Abby, clad in her karate gi like always, was watching her friend closely, trying to mimic her exact motions. Hannah looked like she was painting an American masterpiece, stroking her knife across the peanut butter so it spread across the entire slice of bread, all the way to the very edges. Her layer was even and smooth.

"Why are you making it so precise?" Lauren asked.

"So I can get the same amount of peanut butter and jelly in every bite. It's better this way."

"She's right," Georgia said. "I'd been eating sandwiches wrong for my whole life, but Hannah showed me the light. She also taught me to eat around the edges first so the filling doesn't ooze out as much." She sighed and gazed at her daughter with sticky-sweet, exaggerated affection. "I'm raising a sandwich genius."

Her peanut butter spreading complete, Hannah carefully aligned the edges of her two pieces of bread before patting them gently together. Abby's sandwich-sealing pat was more of a smack, and she lost a bit of jelly out one side. Lauren barely stopped her from licking it off the counter.

Georgia settled four sandwiches and the bag of brownies in the basket with a blanket and hoisted it onto her arm. Lauren blinked.

"That's all we're bringing?"

"The farmers market is open, so we can get fresh snacks there," Georgia said.

"Right. So...why did we need the basket?"

Hannah cocked her head. "It's a picnic."

The corners of Georgia's mouth lifted nervously, and Lauren realized she was ruining the fun. If Georgia wanted a picnic basket, that was reason enough.

"Mom likes bread from the Stensons' farm," she said. "I can fill the basket with that when I take it back."

"Like Little Red Riding Hood!" Abby said.

"Sure."

As long as no one asked her to skip through the woods, Lauren could play along with whatever the kids came up with. She was getting better at that. Georgia winked at her in approval and took her hand while they all walked to the car.

The Holderness farmers market was a cluster of tents, folding tables, and rolling carts in the park across from the old railroad depot. Dappled sunlight and falling apple blossoms brightened the shade, and a light breeze spread the smell of fresh bread, garlic, and the month-old calf the dairy farm had brought. Hannah and Abby made a beeline for the calf. Lauren darted three stalls down and snagged the last bunch of fiddleheads in the whole market. Ed Garritsen scowled from three steps behind her, too late. He was probably already planning his letter to the editor about the barbarism that had taken root among young people these days.

"Hey there!" the herb lady called.

Lauren didn't know her name, but she didn't know Lauren's either, so that was fine. She had the best parsley and rosemary in three counties, and that was all anyone needed to know.

Georgia and the kids rejoined her while she paid for more herbs than she probably needed and dreamed about getting into cooking again.

"The cow's name is Peaches!" Hannah said, catching Lauren by the hem of her shirt.

"You want to know a secret?" Lauren said. "The cow's name is Peaches every year. Different cow, same name."

Hannah laughed.

Someone waved, and Lauren nodded in reply. Then someone called Lauren's name, and a flushed woman in workout shorts jogged toward her. She looked like a person who jogged at all times.

"Excuse me, are you Lauren?" the woman asked.

Lauren shifted on her feet. "Probably. Why?"

"Dave Stenson said you can make computers behave. I need a hand, if you have a minute."

From behind a pile of rolls and scones, Dave Stenson gave Lauren a thumbs-up. Lauren followed the jogger at a leisurely stroll to a stationary bike that was rigged up to a blender. The jogger tapped a digital screen on the bike's handlebars.

"I'm trying to track the total miles everyone rides to make the smoothies," she said, "but the numbers keep going back to zero. It's plugged in, I've turned it on and off again, and Dave slapped it for good measure. I don't know what else to do."

"Does a pedometer count as a computer?" Georgia said.

"It stores multiple states and performs a function. Or it's supposed to," Lauren grumbled while she unclipped the machine. She restarted it, pressed the two buttons available to push, then pried the back off.

"There's a wire loose," she said. "It probably disconnects when the bike bounces around. You can take it to Dana at the hardware store on Monday, she'll fix it."

The jogger pouted. "There's nothing you can do about it today?"

Lauren sighed, then waved the kids over.

"See that lady in the big hat?"

Hannah and Abby looked at the woman, whose straw hat was held down with pins like sabers, leaning on an ancient wheelbarrow-like cart with a honeycomb pattern hand painted on all sides. She was hard to miss.

"That's Nell Martinez. Tell her I need some beeswax."

Hannah looked to Georgia before she made her way over, but Abby bolted. She was halfway back by the time Hannah caught up, with a clump of beeswax and a honey stick in her hand.

Lauren rolled the beeswax in her hand, then jammed it around the loose wire. Dana was gonna love cleaning that out later.

"If you hold it steady, that should get you through the day," she said, handing the machine back to the jogger.

Several people had noticed the activity by now, and they all held their breath while someone clambered onto the bike to test it. The blender whirred, the bike wobbled, and the pedometer kept counting. When the jogger cheered, the small crowd applauded. Lauren shouldered through them to the Stensons' booth to buy bread.

"Nice work!" Dave told her.

"Easy fix."

He grinned and shook his head. "Good to see you, Ms. Modest."

"Good to see you, too," Lauren admitted. "How are your barn cats?"

Nell Martinez, when they got to her cart, gave Hannah a honey stick, too, and refused Lauren's money.

"Your dad never let me pay him for painting my cart, and I'm happy to help you help people," she said.

"Did you hear Tracy's running the store now?" Lauren asked.

She had, of course. It was in the paper.

Two other people waved as they passed her. She waved back. Ironically, people hadn't been this friendly in Philly, because no one knew her. She hadn't realized until now that she'd missed it.

Georgia squeezed Lauren's hand, and her eyes were bright in the springtime sun.

"You're kind of wonderful, you know."

Lauren scuffed her toe in the grass, but she couldn't help but smile.

"Everyone knows you and you get free stuff," Abby said. "Are you famous?"

"Big fish in a small pond," Lauren said.

Both girls stared at her.

"It means I seem cool because there aren't a lot of people in Holderness to compare me to. In a big pond, like a city, there are lots of people who do what I do, so it's not impressive."

Hannah gnawed on her honey stick in thought, then said, "You have to have big fish, though. If all the fish were the same size, what would they eat?"

Lauren didn't have an answer for that. It did feel pretty good, though, to be a big, proud fish for a while.

"I think the question right now should be, what are we going to eat?" she said.

The four of them meandered through the market, gathering spinach, peas, and the first strawberries of the season to pair with their sandwiches, then spread the blanket on a patch of open space under a tree. The girls ate quickly and ran off to play. At first they practiced their karate, then Abby tried to teach Hannah how to do a cartwheel.

"Remember you promised your dad you'd keep you gi clean!" Georgia called.

Abby looked over and shrugged. "It's never clean. He won't know the difference."

Georgia sighed and said to Lauren, "I love that mudpuppy child. She's finally convincing Hannah to get dirty and have fun with it. I worried she'd miss out on that sort of thing."

"Dirt is a great part of childhood," Lauren agreed. She stretched out in the shade, enjoying the slight give and chill of the ground under her back.

"Yeah, and not getting dirty would make it hard to do field work as a biologist."

Lauren chuckled. "Or run a reptile rescue out of her kitchen like Jody Feinsod. Do you know her?"

There was no answer. When Lauren looked over at Georgia, she was frowning down at her.

"I never thought of that. I just sort of went biology: biologist."

Had the suggestion of another idea upset her? It wasn't impossible that Georgia had a rigid vision for her daughter, though the thought made Lauren squirm.

"Bio's good for all kinds of stuff," she said. "Park ranger, vet, technical illustrations if she likes art like you do."

Georgia leaned back against the tree, watching the kids play. "It's awesome, isn't it? Finding out who a person's going to be. I'm so glad I get to see it happen."

Lauren rolled onto her side and reached for Georgia's hand, her chest swelling with adoration like it had earlier with pride.

"It's awesome getting to know you."

Lauren fell asleep with her head against Georgia's thigh, soothed by the market murmur and the buzzing of honeybees. She didn't wake up until Georgia opened the Ziploc bag full of brownies and wafted the smell onto Lauren's face.

"You have to eat these, I made them," she said, and Lauren didn't disagree.

Crunch time at work meant all her good habits had fallen by the wayside, so meals hadn't been a top priority this week. The brownies were burnt around the edges, but hungry as she was, she didn't care. Georgia, she noticed, had taken a middle piece. Adorable.

The taste of charred chocolate was wonderful. Playing tag with Hannah and Abby until she dropped was wonderful. Even getting trapped in conversation with Kitty Bakerson for twenty minutes was wonderful, because she took home the rest of the burned brownies to feed to her pig. Mom was going to love hearing that Kitty Bakerson had a pet pig now.

At four, the girls allowed themselves to be rounded up and herded back into the car, both of them slightly grass-stained and sweaty. It was a look Lauren had never seen on Hannah, and it was wonderful, too.

"Can Hannah spend the night next weekend?" Abby asked while she was buckling her seat belt.

"Thank you for asking in advance!" Georgia said. "It would be okay with me. Have your dad text me if it's okay with him, too."

Abby and Hannah were satisfied with this, but it pinged wrong for Lauren. Why not talk to Ben when they dropped Abby off at her house? They were friends, weren't they? But when they pulled up to Abby's address, Georgia didn't even get out of the car, let alone greet Ben when he came out on the porch. He looked forlorn as Georgia pulled away from the curb without a glance. Lauren waved to him out of pity. She'd gotten a chilly reaction from Georgia before, and it had stung like ice in her gut.

"What did he do?" Lauren asked. She knew he'd been an ass at that dinner in Massachusetts, but the extent of Georgia's dismissal of him surprised her.

"What do you mean?" Georgia said.

Maybe she didn't want to talk about it in front of Hannah. Lauren shrugged it off for the time being. She enjoyed the rest of her day off before returning to another two days of grinding through the swamp of work that Felix had left behind, and the enjoyment made those days sail by. She also updated her résumé, because everything she looked at was cast in a brighter light, even Green Mountain Software. The frigid moment between Ben and Georgia settled in at the back of her mind, waiting for her to look at it in another light later.

CHAPTER TWENTY

Unlike Kelly, their eldest daughter, Marjorie and Preston Gray called at the same time on the same day every month, the first Thursday at eight o'clock. Kyle had always put the phone on speaker so he and Hannah could talk at the same time instead of handing the phone back and forth or leaving his parents hanging when Hannah was silent. Since Kyle died, Georgia sat on one end of the couch and pretended she wasn't listening to Hannah's half of the now private conversations. None of the Grays were interested in talking to her.

"Karate is going well," Hannah reported. "I got to use the makiwara this week. It's like a punching bag, except it's on the ground. You use it to practice your strikes and feel resistance to them. I'm just using the soft shuri makiwara for now, because that's for beginners, but once I move up a belt and get better at kicking, I can use the ude makiwara, which is…"

Georgia had heard about the makiwara many times now, because Hannah talked about it to anyone who'd sit still. They'd gotten several books from the library and researched them online together. Karate passion was taking root in Hannah, just like Kyle had thought it would.

On the phone, Hannah had moved on to discussing another passion of hers: planning her birthday party. "We should have a makiwara at the party, and everyone can strike it and feel the resistance and make sure their stance absorbs it properly. You'd be really good at it, Granny. I don't think Laine should try it because she's still a baby, but she can have a turn next year. Aunt Katherine and Uncle Brock should try, then Ashlyn, then Mommy and Lauren, then…"

It was like being electrocuted, hearing Hannah say that name. Georgia sat straight up, and so did the hair on the back of her neck. Hannah was continuing to list every member of the Gray family, but Georgia heard the question that interrupted her: "Who's Lauren?"

"Lauren is Mommy's girlfriend. I think. Hold on." Hannah turned to Georgia, her face as calm as Georgia's heart was calamitous. "Is Lauren your girlfriend or just your best friend?"

"Girl," Georgia croaked.

Hannah confirmed the facts for her grandparents, then continued describing her birthday party plans. She brooked no further questions, and the tinny protests Georgia could hear on the other end of the call ceased.

Georgia escaped to the kitchen, her fingers wound tightly in her hair. She had never intended to tell the Grays about Lauren. They didn't need to know. They probably didn't *want* to know. It wasn't that they were homophobic. It was just that no one she was with would ever be welcome in the role the Grays had reserved for Kyle. Lauren didn't deserve their judgment, but it would surely come.

At least Georgia didn't have to figure out how to invite her. Lauren wouldn't want to come anyway, and now she shouldn't.

When Hannah finished her call, she put the phone on the kitchen table where Georgia sat, saying, "You have a text message."

"Thank you, baby," Georgia said.

She squeezed her hands together to keep them out of her hair until Hannah left, so Hannah wouldn't notice her anxiety, then picked up the phone. The text was from Lauren.

What's your Saturday like?

Georgia took a deep breath and answered casually. *Unscheduled so far. Why?*

Do you wanna do something questionable in the Monument parking lot with me at 8ish? Probably have to wait around, would rather be with you.

How questionable?

Come and find out.

Well, that revved up some very dirty scenes in Georgia's mind. There was no way she'd opt out of parking with Lauren on a Saturday night after dark, even though that was almost definitely not what Lauren had meant to imply. She texted her sitter.

* * *

The Holderness Monument was a three hundred and two-foot obelisk commemorating a Revolutionary War battle that had happened elsewhere in the state. Georgia relied on it as a navigation landmark, but several businesses in Holderness relied on it for a sense of identity, building their names and logos around it and spending hard-earned marketing money on floats for the annual parade, which celebrated a battle that had not been fought in Holderness. The stone it was made of had fossils in it, though, which made it interesting enough.

Lauren parked beside the only other car in the lot. Georgia thought at first this was part of the night's illicit adventure, until a pair of older tourists climbed in almost immediately and drove away. It was too dark now for pictures or to linger under a monument one couldn't see.

"So what are we doing?"

"Waiting, for now," Lauren said. "Our guy got lost on the way, so he won't be here for a bit. I brought snacks, though."

She unbuckled herself and twisted around to reach into the back seat.

"What are we waiting for?" Georgia asked.

Halfway into the backseat now, still rummaging for the promised food, Lauren grinned. "Do you want to keep asking questions I'm not gonna answer, or is there some other way to entertain you?"

Georgia hooked her fingers in Lauren's belt loop, motivated by her fantasies of what this excursion could have been, even though it probably wasn't about that. "I can think of one entertaining thing to do."

Lauren abandoned her backseat quest and leaned forward. She unbuckled Georgia's seat belt.

"If you're thinking what I think you're thinking, I like the way you think."

That made Georgia laugh, which was a shame because she never knew how to transition from silly to sexy. Lauren didn't have that issue. She ran her thumb along Georgia's bottom lip, hooked her finger under Georgia's chin, and exerted such gentle pressure that Georgia tilted her head almost without noticing Lauren was coaxing her to do so. Giggles melted into a lustful sigh as naturally as day to starry night.

Lauren kissed with confidence, but when her hands started to wander, she was tentative. Georgia was running her palms up and down Lauren's back, sometimes petting her hair or gripping the back of her neck. Lauren hadn't settled on any one place to touch. Her fingers trailed down Georgia's arm, barely brushed her hair, then her knee, and failed to advance to any more erogenous area.

"You can touch me," Georgia finally said.

"I don't want to do it wrong."

"I'll tell you if I don't like something. Firmer is better, though. You're gonna tickle me if you keep doing what you're doing, and I don't think that's what you're going for."

"Not really," Lauren said.

She smiled when she kissed Georgia again. One of her hands wove into Georgia's hair to keep her close. The other slid, firmly and with assurance, up Georgia's thigh. She parted her lips and deepened the kiss to encourage Lauren further. How far would she be willing to take this in a car? Was there really someone coming, or had this been Lauren's entire plan?

A sudden knock made Georgia jump, and their teeth banged together. There was a weedy white boy with horn rim glasses standing by the driver side door.

"Are you Lauren?"

"Jesus, dude," Lauren said. "Don't tap on the window right next to my head! Pull up and flash your lights or something. What kind of covert operator are you?"

"I'm a grad student."

Lauren untangled herself and got out of the car, muttering, "You sure are, man."

Georgia caught her breath and joined Lauren and the boy in the parking lot.

Lauren said, "Georgia, this is Chuck. Chuck, Georgia. Also, seventy bucks."

Georgia stared at the wad of cash Lauren pulled out of her jeans pocket and handed to Chuck. Was this activity more illicit than she'd planned on?

"What are you paying this guy seventy dollars for?"

"Reptiles are expensive."

Chuck said, "They're amphibians," and opened the passenger door of his car. There was a glass fish tank buckled into the seat, half full of water. In the glare of the monument display lights, its pink occupants seemed ghostly white.

Axolotls. Chuck had two axolotls in a tank in his car.

Georgia could barely stop her hands from flapping long enough to hug Lauren, who stumbled under the force of it.

"Don't knock me over now, honey," she said. "We have to carry this thing."

In fact, Chuck helped Lauren carry the tank, because Georgia was too excited. She helped by sweeping the snacks and junk mail that littered the backseat onto the floorboards and babbled while the precious cargo was strapped in.

"I can get everyone who comes to the party to bring a different part for the habitat and we can put it together together!

There's a range of prices for—wait. Only seventy dollars?" The low price brought Georgia up short.

Chuck said, "I got a speeding charge while I was here during ski season. The court fee is seventy."

"Oh. Should I give you more than that?"

"I'll take your money."

Lauren took Georgia's hand and pulled her back toward the passenger side of her own car. "You'll take what we agreed to, Chuck. Drive slow while you're here, use your turn signal, all that. G'night, dude."

She helped Georgia into her seat, shut the door, and hurried to the other side so she could drive them away. Georgia didn't see how Chuck reacted to being dismissed. She was busy staring at the little swimming creatures in the back of the car.

A few blocks later, she realized they weren't driving to her house.

Lauren said, "I was gonna keep them a surprise until her actual birthday. Is that okay?"

"Probably, if you know how to feed them. And hey, speaking of what you know…"

"I know they're not reptiles, I promise."

Georgia settled into her seat and smiled at Lauren's easy-going profile. The temperature was dropping outside, and when they reached Lauren's apartment, Georgia wished she'd put on an extra layer. Lauren hauled the axolotl tank onto a handcart she'd borrowed from the art store.

"Thank god this place has an elevator," she said.

"I've never seen your place." Georgia had wondered about it, but she'd been very careful not to ask questions that could come across as inviting herself over.

Lauren pushed the button for the third floor. "It's not impressive. Turing will be happy to meet you, though."

Turing did run to the door when it opened, but he ran away again when Lauren knocked the edge of the aquarium into the doorframe. He leapt onto the top of the fridge and sneered down at them while they maneuvered the bulky tank through the tight spaces of the apartment and into a computer room that could be closed without disturbing Turing's routine.

It was dark in the apartment, and the overhead light Lauren turned on didn't make a dent in the atmosphere. The space was neat by virtue of being sparse more than by any visible effort at tidiness. Georgia was disappointed. A home should be a reflection of the person, not a storage container with windows.

"Are these walls even at right angles?"

"Nope," Lauren said. She dropped herself onto the couch, then held her hands out for Georgia. "I was thinking we could bring the axolotls over the night before the party. She'll be at her friend's house, right?"

Georgia intertwined their fingers and stood between Lauren's knees. "Are you going to let me pay you back?"

"I'll let you pay for one of them."

She pulled Georgia closer, until Georgia put her hands on Lauren's shoulders and leaned over her, one knee on the couch for balance. They both wanted to be doing other things, but the mention of the party reminded Georgia that the Grays existed.

"Hannah told her grandparents you're my girlfriend," she said.

Lauren's hands stopped toying with the edge of Georgia's light cardigan.

Georgia continued explaining, despite the fact that she was obviously killing the mood. "They're mad at me for not marrying Kyle, and they might take it out on you if you're at the party, which you probably didn't want to go to anyway. Hannah invited you, but I don't expect you to come. There's plenty of reasons not to."

Lauren frowned, but instead of pulling away from Georgia, she kissed her. "The only good reason for me to not go to the party is if you or Hannah don't want me there. What Kyle's family thinks isn't our problem. As for me being your girlfriend, I hadn't realized I was that lucky."

"Are we not girlfriends? We don't have to be, Hannah just assumed. I guess I assumed, too, but I shouldn't have. Should we talk about it? I don't want to move too fast or freak you out. I just like you."

"I like you, too," Lauren said.

She pulled on the lapels of Georgia's cardigan, and Georgia clambered onto the couch, careful of her weight until Lauren dragged her fully onto her lap and held her there. The eager press of lips against her neck made Georgia cast her worries aside.

CHAPTER TWENTY-ONE

Turing didn't appreciate being shut out of the computer room for almost a month. Lauren had to scoop him up before she opened the door, then toss him gently into the living room and slam the door behind her every time. Some days he sat on the fridge in a huff. Today he stuck his nose along the crack at the bottom and cried.

"Go watch birds, buddy," Lauren told him. He mrowled back but turned away.

Lauren tossed the frozen bloodworm cube from hand to hand as she carried it over to the axolotl tank. She'd been afraid at first that it'd stain her hands, but the red of the cube was only inside the worms, not in the liquid that held them together. A little rubber cone called a worm tube was attached to the tank, under the water. When she dropped the bloodworm cube into it, it thawed slowly, unfurling tendrils of worm bit by bit.

"Eat up, Wheel. Eat up, Axle."

The nearsighted creatures turned slowly in the water. The faint motion of the sinking worms drew their attention. Axle rose sharply when she inhaled, sucking up worms like a vacuum. Lauren had watched them do this every day, and she still wasn't tired of it. No wonder Hannah loved them so much.

Of course, having animals hidden in her house gave her extra tingles. She tried not to gloat like her mother, but she loved springing surprises on people. It made sense to her now why Tracy had tried to keep a secret pet rat in fifth grade, despite how obviously ill-fated that idea was.

A gust of wind rattled the tree outside her computer room window, and Lauren took a deep breath of the lightning-charged air that blew in through the screen before she shut it. It was a good day. Something pleasant was rolling in with this storm. Had she ever smelled a wind so great?

When she arrived at Tracy's house for breakfast, Tracy said, "Last time you grinned like that was when you got a spot on the volleyball team. What'd you win?"

"Nothing yet, but…" Lauren realized which sweet victory was within her grasp. "I'm gonna ask Len about taking over the FrogTalk project."

FrogTalk was a nice little company that made private instant messaging systems for offices ("collaborative team-based virtual workspaces," they called them) based on concepts developed by herpetologists studying the same species in different states. Given how many people worked from home nowadays, instant messaging was interesting stuff. Len had chosen not to replace Felix, so that promotion hope had vanished, but an impressive application programming interface, well built and well managed, might spark recruiting interest in an up-and-coming operation like FrogTalk. From there, Lauren could see plenty of other lily pads to hop to, all the way across the pond. Forward, upward. Up, up, and away.

The dark clouds that gathered in Lauren's mind as it wandered didn't matter right now, so she ignored them. The first step was to claim the project manager title.

"Can you help me practice my pitch?"

Tracy stared into the pancake batter she was stirring, unimpressed. "And here I thought you finally made it with Georgia or something. What's taking you so long with that?"

"I'm not on a schedule. No worries about the future, right?" Though a new job at FrogTalk in the future would put a schedule of sorts on her relationship. Worry snaked up her spine, but she warded it off and relaxed. Second-guessing and scrambling her priorities wouldn't get her where she needed to go.

"How's progress on the store?"

The question lit Tracy up like a flare, and it would keep her talking for hours instead of asking questions. Lauren could practice her pitch in the car.

* * *

She got to work exactly on time, rain-spattered and dripping, and slid into a chair at the conference table so quickly it spun. Jamar hid a smile in his coffee cup, but no one else looked amused.

"Okay, updates on the FrogTalk API. Lauren?"

Her update was sharp and concise, and the conversation moved on. She tried to focus on her coworkers' reports, noting who was ahead or behind, which areas were likely to need more attention as the project progressed, but she was too busy reciting her pitch in her head to keep track. She'd catch up when she got the job.

Len dismissed the group with bland encouragement, and everyone scattered to their preferred work habitat. Lauren followed Len to his office, knocking on the door as he closed it.

"Oh, come in," he said, reopening the door. "Good work on that lilipad bit, by the way."

Lauren tried to stand up straighter. "Thanks," she said. "I was hoping I could talk to you about another aspect of the FrogTalk project. The management? You said you'd manage it until you chose someone else to take over. I'd like to do that."

Len, who had been nodding encouragingly from behind his standing desk, stopped. "You'd like to do that?"

"Yes?" Lauren said, cursing the anxiety in her voice.

"The past couple months it seems like you barely want to do the job you have now. Your pace is the slowest in the office."

She hadn't noticed that. Her recent improvements, the ones she was going to list as qualifications, came out as justifications instead. "But the code I've been writing is cleaner, and I've never missed a deadline."

"The deadline is an absolute minimum. I expect better." Len turned to his computer like he was reviewing something. "I've also heard complaints that team meetings have to be delayed because you're not in the office—"

Lauren balked. Did he mean that one meeting someone tried to call her in for at ten o'clock at night?

"—and you're frequently not available for conferencing on evenings and weekends."

Phone calls and voice mails were being answered with texts these days, it was true, and she'd haggled on the scheduling of a few video calls. The manager position would be less flexible and more demanding, which would mean more calls then ever. Lauren imagined canceling dinner plans to join a call and eating cold leftovers alone, or letting Tracy take the full weight of store shelving while she answered a brief question, or turning on the bedside lamp in the middle of the night, her and Georgia wincing in the light while she whispered into her phone. She took a deep breath. Concessions had to be made.

"Of course I'd make myself available for the duration of the project. That's not an issue."

"You're also not very sociable these days. Where were you during the staff movie night last week?"

Making out on my girlfriend's living room rug. "I've never been very sociable," was the best answer Lauren could say out loud.

"And that behavior's affecting your teammates as well."

Surely he wasn't referring to the fact that Jamar was now using the time off he'd rightfully earned. No one had a right to complain about that.

Len huffed at her silence. "Look, you've done good work here, Lauren, especially with the architecture suite, but even then you weren't a team player."

"I managed the situation, and I worked extensively with Jamar to do so. I couldn't have done it without him." She hoped that was seen as a point in his favor rather than against him.

"Management's not about bossing people around," Len said. "It takes devotion, to your project and your team, and lately you've given the impression that this is just a job to you. Maybe you've gotten bored after the excitement of the architecture suite and managing a project would be the challenge you need to get in gear again, but I can't take a risk on that until you give me a reason to believe you'll rise to the occasion. I'm sorry. Ask again some other time."

He didn't see the rage that flashed across her face, and he didn't watch her flee. Jamar did see, but Lauren didn't break stride or meet his questioning eyes. When she was safely in the hallway, out of sight of everyone, she ran. Her momentum built as she crashed down the staircase, sometimes taking steps two at a time. On the last step, she slipped. Her stomach leapt into her ribcage and her heart rammed into her throat, her hands flung uselessly forward with nothing to grab. Physically, her foot slammed to the ground almost immediately, but her guts didn't rearrange—she felt like she was still falling, had felt that way since she left Len's office. Her heart throbbed where it didn't belong. Her chest was too full to draw in air. She had to get outside, away from here.

There was no one else in the parking lot, no one on the street passing by, but still Lauren refused to cry until she had reached her car. No one would have been able to tell even if they had seen her. The storm she'd smelled this morning was at full force. The rain poured down at an angle, fat drops that stung against her bare skin. Every inch of her was dripping wet by the time she flung herself into the driver's seat of her car and shut the door. There was nothing dry enough to wipe her glasses with, so she tossed them onto the dashboard while she heaved and sobbed. She didn't really cry, though. She never did, even when she wanted to. All she managed was the ragged breathing and the snot.

A text message arrived while she was catching her breath. *How'd it go?* Tracy wanted to know. Lauren hurled her phone into the backseat, wiped her glasses with a napkin from the passenger floorboard, and started the car. If she wasn't going to cry, she was going to drive for a while.

Rain smacked the windshield like bullets, which meant her wipers had their work cut out for them. Some of the smaller roads in the valley were probably already flooded, so Lauren drove toward the mountains. Up, up, and away.

CHAPTER TWENTY-TWO

Georgia sat on her couch with the lights off and quivered, much like the needle in her mind that swung between waiting at home and searching for Lauren. She'd texted in the afternoon, asking if they could push their plans back an hour because client meetings were taking longer than planned. When she didn't hear back, she texted again. Then she called. Now Lauren was almost thirty minutes late according to their original plans, and she hadn't answered a single message or call. Had Georgia said something wrong, or was something wrong with Lauren? Maybe she should go looking for her, but the rain hammering down had already washed out a large pothole in the driveway, which didn't bode well for road conditions, and what if she went out and Lauren came here while she was gone? On the other fidgeting hand, what if Lauren was out there somewhere, alone in a wreck of metal and downpour, waiting for someone to find her? What if it was already too late for finding her to be of any help? What if Georgia had been blissfully going about her day while something terrible happened, again?

Lightning cut a gash through the sky outside her window. The thunderclap vibrated painfully in her spine and echoed off the mountains. No one applauded the ruckus, like Kyle used to do.

Over and over, that last night with Kyle played in her head, holding over her all the things she hadn't noticed, hadn't done. It had all seemed so normal.

"Sorry about the rice," Kyle had said while Georgia and Hannah had crunched it between their teeth. "I'm expecting a rice cooker for Christmas next week."

"We got you a foolproof one, right, Hannah?" Georgia had said.

Hannah had worked through a particularly arduous bite, swallowed with a gulp, and nodded while she washed it down with water. She'd drummed her feet against her chair hard enough to scoot herself away from the little square dinner table in Kyle's kitchen. Georgia remembered looking at Kyle, both of them knowing their daughter wouldn't be able to stand sitting this way much longer.

Kyle had wiped his mouth with his paper towel napkin and said, "Before you go home, I wanted to let you know that Kelly's heading home from a conference in Albany tomorrow. She actually texted ahead to say she's going to stop by in the afternoon."

"For once," Georgia had grumbled.

"Does that mean we'll be staying here with Aunt Kelly instead of movie night at Mommy's?"

"No, it just means Aunt Kelly's going to join us for the movie. Is that okay?" Kyle had asked.

When Hannah had nodded, he'd reached out his hand to her. She'd taken it happily. Kyle had pulled her up and swung her onto his shoulders, ducking a little to avoid the hanging light over the table. Georgia had picked up the dinner plates and scraped them into the trash while Kyle and Hannah danced a circle around the kitchen. Kyle had put Hannah on the floor and given her a spin before he let her go. Georgia had caught him putting a hand to his chest as he turned to the sink again.

"Is she getting too big for that, or are you getting too old?" she'd teased.

"I've just been tired today, that's all. Sunset at four doesn't help. You'll be nice to Kelly tomorrow night, right?"

"I swear I won't pick a movie she has nightmares about this time. Although I still say *The Brothers Lionheart* is not that scary."

"The dragon is a little scary."

Georgia had rolled her eyes, but she'd patted Kyle's shoulder and promised, "I'll be nice. You get some sleep tonight."

Hannah had told her dad goodnight, and she and Georgia had gone back to the other side of the duplex, leaving Kyle to the dishes and his early bedtime. Georgia had never considered that anything might be wrong.

Even the next morning, when she'd come into the office after dropping Hannah off at school, Kyle's absence only gave her a second's pause.

"His sister probably showed up early," she'd told Gerald. "She does that."

Kelly had arrived earlier than planned, but not until ten thirty. She'd called Georgia at ten fifty, after the EMTs had delivered their verdict. The horrible calm that had fallen over her made the call confusing.

"Hello, Georgia," she'd said. "Kyle is dead."

"No, he's not, I saw him last night."

"I'm looking at him now. The coroner's on his way. He's dead, Georgia. Did you not check on him when he didn't show up for work?"

"I don't need to check on him, he's fine. He'll be here any minute."

The wall of Kelly's flat insistence hadn't given way. "He's not fine, Georgia. He's gone."

A third denial was forming when Gerald caught her eye.

"Are you okay?" he'd asked.

Georgia had managed to fall to her knees slowly, a controlled implosion. Once on the ground, though, she'd wailed, so sharp and keening that—

Georgia startled from her tortured memory. Outside in the summer rain now, someone was knocking on the door.

In her rush to answer, she tripped over the blanket that had been on her lap and landed elbow-first on the hardwood floor. The impact was loud, and Lauren opened the door calling Georgia's name. She rushed over when Georgia reached for her from where she'd fallen, feet still tangled in the blanket. Lauren wrapped her arms around Georgia's waist and heaved her fully off the ground and onto the couch again. Georgia felt like she weighed nothing.

Lauren looked as alarmed as Georgia felt when her hand covered Georgia's tear-wet cheek.

"What happened? Did you hurt yourself? Should I call someone?"

Georgia shook her head. Lauren's palm was damp when she squeezed it with her own hand.

"Where were you?" she asked.

"Rutland." Lauren winced. "I was upset, so I took off for a drive. I got your texts about coming later, though. Should I have been here earlier instead?"

"Why didn't you call back?"

"I was kind of ignoring my phone. I should have called, I'm sorry. God, I haven't done anything right today."

Lauren pulled her hand away from Georgia and scraped it through her hair. Her whole body was balled up tight, folded in, like it had been at the art store party. Something was wrong.

"Why were you upset?"

"It's stupid. Are you sure you're not hurt?"

Georgia extended her arm to squeeze Lauren's knee, and it did hurt to do that, but she didn't say anything about it. She glanced up and looked into Lauren's eyes for a moment, then followed the line of her face down her neck and over her shoulder, looking for the answer to her question somewhere in the tense lines of Lauren's body.

Lauren, wonderful Lauren who watched her so closely and spoke her language, gave her an answer.

"I asked for the project manager job and didn't get it."

"Oh. Why not?"

"Apparently my job is 'just a job' to me lately. I'm not devoted enough."

Devoted was one of the top descriptions Georgia would use for Lauren. The corners of her lips twisted in confusion. "Is it just a job?"

"It didn't used to be. I've been feeling good about it lately, and doing good. Or I thought I was. None of this is what I expected from my career, but I thought I could get back on track, or find another track, or…I don't know. What am I gonna do now?"

Georgia stood and took a box of tissues off the bookshelf, pulling some out before passing it to Lauren. She dried her eyes while Lauren kneaded her tissue in her hand. Then Georgia sat in front of Lauren on the coffee table. She almost tipped it over before she found the right balance.

"You're going to stay here and feel better now," she said, "because right now, you're okay. We're okay. And it's been a terrible day, but it's over. How do you want to end it, my love?"

When Lauren turned away, mumbling apologies, Georgia cradled her jaw and coaxed her gaze back. Lauren surged forward and kissed Georgia hard. Georgia grabbed her shoulders. The taste of salt from her own tears made the kiss harsher, more desperate, until Lauren pulled away.

"I need to use the bathroom, and we should unpack the axolotls," she said, "but um…do you like to dance?"

"The axolotls can wait in the car for a little while, that's fine. What kind of dancing?"

"Really simple dancing. Like, swaying mostly. It's something we've always done in my family after long days, even though Tracy's the only one who's any good."

Georgia tried to imagine the Ashburns she'd met, and the patriarch she knew so little about, being tender and clumsy together. It was so different from everything else Lauren had described about her family that Georgia struggled to picture it. It must have been wonderful.

"I love that," she said.

"I…" Lauren swallowed, then smiled back. "I love it, too."

She kissed Georgia's cheek and went upstairs to the bathroom. Georgia went to the kitchen to splash water from the sink on her face. That smile of Lauren's had been strange, bright as a full moon and almost as distant. Had she thought something different than what she'd said? Georgia dried her face and huffed in exasperation. She wished she knew how to read these kinds of things better. She wished Lauren had said she loved *her*, because Georgia was rapidly approaching that point in her own heart.

At least Lauren was here, and she wanted to dance with her. Georgia knelt in front of one of her bookshelves and started leafing through her old-fashioned vinyl collection.

When Lauren came back downstairs, she knelt down, too, and bumped shoulders with Georgia.

"Hipster," she joked.

Georgia bumped back and said, "That crackling sound you get with records is the best, okay? What do you want to dance to?"

Lauren picked out Etta James' first album, and Georgia set it up on the record player, handling it like a surgeon with someone's heart in her hands. She loved this album.

"Do you mind if I lead?" Lauren asked. "Tracy always made me lead so she could practice when she was in plays or ballroom club."

Georgia stepped into a comfortable frame. "Whatever works for you. I don't know much about it either way."

"This'll be really graceful then."

Lauren pulled Georgia a little closer and started a simple box step, murmuring gentle instructions when Georgia hesitated or lagged and chuckling when her toes got stepped on. Eventually they perfected the rhythm, and she started to turn them slightly and move through the small space the living room provided. They did a full rotation around the couch. Lauren caught Georgia gallantly when she tripped over the blanket on the floor again, and as they turned she let Georgia's hand go and settled both her own hands on Georgia's waist.

Georgia catalogued the sweet warmth of those hands through her thin shirt, along with other sensations that brought her back into this moment, where she so dearly wanted to be. The change from smooth hardwood to coarse rug under her feet made her curl her toes. Outside, the rain was still falling, but the sun was shining through the curtains, too, which meant there was probably a rainbow somewhere. The album crackled deliciously. Lauren's eyes were dark and sparkling.

They swayed, and Lauren pressed her forehead to Georgia's, brushing their noses together lightly. Her hands were still hot against Georgia's sides, and Georgia imagined that warmth under her shirt instead of on top of it. She ran her own hand up from Lauren's shoulder to her neck. Her thumb stroked the hinge of Lauren's jaw, then the sensitive skin behind her ear. Lauren's sigh broke across Georgia's lips, and Georgia kissed her. The gentle touch at Georgia's hips became tight clinging at her back as Lauren wrapped her up in her arms. She trembled, keeping the kiss slow even as it deepened.

The lights in the living room were still off, but her blood was singing and her heart was shining, so nothing seemed dark, or like it would ever be dark again.

CHAPTER TWENTY-THREE

Lauren didn't stop kissing Georgia until the music stopped. The vinyl shushed and whispered as it ended, and she understood why Georgia liked it so much. She could listen to just that sound for hours, as long as she could do it like this. Too bad there were other things to take care of.

"We should get the critters out of the car," she said, against Georgia's mouth because neither of them pulled far enough apart.

"Amphibians." Georgia's eyes were hazy, but she still had it in her to be precise.

"Amphibians can be critters. You got all the other parts in time?"

Georgia huffed and went to turn off the record player. Lauren missed her immediately and regretted changing the subject.

"Some of the Grays didn't think tank equipment was a good enough gift," Georgia grouched, "so I ordered a backup of everything the axolotls will need, and I'll send back what she gets."

Lauren sized up the pile of boxes stacked around the aquarium stand and guessed Georgia had ordered a few more things on top of that. Fish tanks—amphibian tanks—couldn't possibly need thirty different parts. It looked like a good eighth birthday haul.

"Shall we?" Georgia whispered in her ear, and Lauren let herself be led outside by the hand.

She had backed into the driveway and pulled up as close to the side door as she could, but the rain had doubled its force after a few minutes of calm, so they were both soaked before they'd even opened the passenger door. Lauren heaved the tank onto the woefully undersized handcart she'd borrowed from the store, setting it on one narrow side instead of the bottom and crouching to keep the water and amphibians from sloshing out. Georgia hunched with her arms on either side of the handcart, ready to grab hold in the event of a disaster, and shouted, "Run run run!" into the wind. It was impossible to move fast while squatting and balancing a load this size, though, especially when they reached the stairs. Lauren was blinded by the rainwater on her glasses by the time she made it over the threshold. Georgia pulled Lauren's glasses off so she could see her way to the aquarium stand.

"Should I try to wrap this water?" Georgia asked, blowing raindrops off the end of her nose.

Lauren inspected the plastic water jugs while she caught her breath. "Maybe just put some ribbons on the handle and bury them behind the other gifts? They'll blend in well enough to draw out the suspense."

Georgia went into the kitchen and came back with a dishtowel, which had done very little so far to help with the state of her hair. The parts she hadn't dried still clung to her neck and face, and the rest was a frizzy mass rolling down in every direction.

"I need to brush this," she announced.

She tossed the towel to Lauren and disappeared upstairs. Lauren dried her hair and glasses, then wiped down the aquarium.

"All right, Wheel and Axle, it's gonna get dark for a while, but Hannah's gonna be so happy when she sees you!" Lauren turned when she heard Georgia coming back down the stairs and asked, "You found a box big enough to go over the tank, right?"

"It's all wrapped up and ready to go. I hid it in my closet."

Normally Lauren would have a joke for that, but Georgia was staring at her in a way that made her skin prickle under the wet shirt that clung to it. Georgia stumbled a little trying to sit on the couch, because she wouldn't take her eyes off Lauren.

"Do you want to change your clothes?" Georgia asked.

Lauren didn't want Georgia to stop looking at her or to stop looking at Georgia, so she said, "Nah, I'm good," even though there were goose bumps on her arms now from the chill of being damp in an air-conditioned room.

"Do you want to come sit with me?"

If Lauren could have teleported to the couch, she would have. Georgia's erotic aura lapped at her skin before Georgia even touched her, and Lauren leaned forward like a hungry stray, begging to be touched. Kissing and dancing had been wonderful. She'd pulled away because she was desperate for a stretch of time when nothing could interrupt the building tension she hoped was as tight in Georgia's gut as it was in hers.

The way Georgia's fingers waved and wandered was promising. She kissed Georgia the way she had while they were dancing, firmly and with trembling restraint. Georgia parted her lips, and the restraint fell away. The taste of Georgia zinged through her. She could do this forever.

Georgia's passion was escalating, though, based on the way she nipped and panted and whined. She clutched the side of Lauren's leg and pulled her forward.

"Sit on my lap?" she suggested.

Lauren stood, and Georgia helped her settle with her knees on either side of Georgia's hips. Her legs were spread wide, which made her throb. Her enthusiasm rocketed up to Georgia's level in seconds. Georgia kissed the side of her neck once, and when Lauren let a sigh escape her lips, Georgia kissed her neck harder, again and again until Lauren had to tighten her abs to keep her hips from rolling. She turned her head, forcing Georgia away, and ran her tongue over the arch of her ear. She pulled Georgia's shirt up but only let her fingertips roam, not too lightly, underneath.

Georgia took Lauren's hand in hers and raised it to the side of her breast under her shirt. She shuddered when Lauren rubbed her thumb across the swell of it, not quite grazing her nipple but close enough for her to feel it tighten under the satin of her bra. Leaving Lauren where she'd placed her, Georgia let her own hand settle on Lauren's knee. Exploring fingers crept under the leg of Lauren's shorts, spreading high up her thigh and digging in.

"I don't think anyone's ever put their hand in my pants from that direction before," Lauren said.

"Good?" Georgia flexed her fingers.

Lauren groaned and nodded. She made a note to try it when she could. The girth of Georgia's thighs in her short shorts made Lauren salivate, and working her fingers under the hem, taking full advantage of the view and access afforded her, would bend her mind in permanent ways.

Lauren took the full weight of Georgia's breast in her hand, kneading it once the way Georgia was kneading her thighs.

Georgia's hips jumped up as she whimpered, "Yes," pressing her wonderful body between Lauren's spread legs. Lauren moaned and pressed back. She pulled the collar of Georgia's shirt aside so she could kiss and, when Georgia suggested it, bite her shoulder, but the way Georgia's body responded to her now made her want even more.

"Will you take your shirt off for me?"

She felt Georgia swallow hard under her mouth, so she pulled back to look at her face. The frown of indecision made Lauren want to back off, change tactics, but Georgia kissed her before she could panic.

"Will you come upstairs with me?" Georgia asked.

"Yes please."

"I'll take my shirt off first," Georgia said, pushing Lauren back so they could both stand. She pulled her shirt off over her head and handed it to Lauren, then turned toward the stairs. Lauren followed a step behind and took the time to stare at the planes of her back, the deep valley of her spine and the generous flow of her body toward her hips. So beautiful. Lauren stopped them for a moment so she could press her lips to the delicious curve of Georgia's shoulder. Unlike last time, Georgia didn't encourage her.

"I know this is supposed to be sexy, but I want to be in my bed now. Is that okay?"

Lauren groaned. "I want that too."

She didn't stop or slow Georgia as she charged ahead again. Lauren had never seen the bedroom, and she didn't notice anything about it now beyond the way the mattress bowed when Georgia sat on the edge of it. Twitchy, eager fingers hooked the top of Lauren's shorts.

"Can I?"

Lauren nodded, and Georgia unbuttoned her shorts. Just the slight vibration of the zipper as Georgia pulled it down made Lauren tremble. She pulled her own shirt over her head. Georgia growled in approval and kissed Lauren's stomach, which made Lauren trip over the shorts she was climbing out of.

"Mine too?" Georgia asked.

Lauren couldn't nod hard enough. She pulled the glorious short shorts down while Georgia shuffled toward the top of the bed. She dragged Lauren after her and hugged her, pressing Lauren's full weight down onto herself. Lauren kissed the side of her face and breathed in the wonderful smell of her hair. Georgia snuggled down under Lauren's body. Lauren let herself melt, thinking things might be slowing down for the moment, until Georgia's thigh pressed between her legs. She gasped and bucked against the force of it.

"Good?" Georgia asked.

"Yeah, god. Can I?"

The answer was Georgia's hand sliding over her ass and down the back of her thigh, pulling it forward. Lauren rose onto her elbows and responded exactly as she was guided, following instructions like the most devoted of students.

The familiar stroking of Georgia's hand down her back as they moved together turned to curious fingers working their way under the band of Lauren's bra.

"Is that in your way?" Lauren asked.

"Yes."

Lauren sat up and watched Georgia's beautiful, unreadable face as she pulled the bra off over her head. As always, Georgia's hands told the story of what she was thinking far better than her expression. She reached up immediately, running her hands up Lauren's sides, then cupping her breasts. Lauren leaned forward, but Georgia pushed her gently sideways. She laid Lauren out on her back and took one of her nipples in her mouth. Lauren moaned.

Georgia knew what she wanted to do with Lauren's body, and Lauren was happy to confirm that she wanted it too. Sweet questions were followed by decisive action. Georgia increased the pressure of her mouth on Lauren's breast, kneaded her hip, kissed down from her sternum to her stomach, and finally pulled her briefs off and dropped them on the floor by the bed.

Naked under Georgia, Lauren realized she had catching up to do. Georgia was eager to help her. They threw her bra and underwear aside as fast as they could, then came back together entirely bare. Both of them were more tentative now, hands running over the mountains and valleys of each other's curves. Lauren took the initiative, reaching between them toward the soft, open place between Georgia's thighs. Georgia followed her lead, and they both shivered at the simultaneous discovery of wetness and the shock of being touched. Lauren kissed Georgia and let her fingers move against her.

They fell into each other's rhythm just as easily as they'd danced. It wasn't graceful or well practiced, but it was warm and earnest and everything Lauren had wanted. When touching and being touched at once became too much for Georgia, Lauren pressed her back and devoted herself to the task of touching. In that moment, it was all she wanted to do.

A sweet wind blew in through the open bedroom window. The day was exactly as wonderful as Lauren had known it would be.

CHAPTER TWENTY-FOUR

Georgia had read about this feeling in books: sore in pleasant places, replaying the night before, humming to herself as she drifted through her morning routine. She had left Lauren in bed, happy to know that her lover was comfortable enough to stay asleep while she moved around. Hannah would be home at ten, the Grays would start circling at eleven or so, and Kelly might arrive at any moment. None of that hurried her. She stood barefoot in the kitchen with only a robe on and watched the coffee she was brewing especially for Lauren drip.

It was going to be a long day. Georgia had no idea what that was going to be like, and yet she felt ready to find out. The silence on the other side of the kitchen wall was noticeable as ever, but for once it didn't ring in her ears. She wasn't alone today. Maybe she'd never have to be alone again, if wonderful Lauren stayed by her side.

She was pondering what it would be like to live with both axolotls and a cat when her phone chimed. Kelly was less than an hour away, and she wanted to know if she should pick up ice.

Georgia told her yes, then went upstairs to wake Lauren and make sure they were both presentable.

When she entered her bedroom, Lauren was already sitting up on her elbows and rubbing sleep out of her eyes. Her hair stood up in spikes on one side, just like it had the night they first kissed, and Georgia hoped it always did that when Lauren slept so she could see it a thousand times more.

"Hey," Lauren said. "You got up?"

"It won't be a regular thing, trust me. We should get dressed. Kelly's in-bound already." Georgia pulled a dresser drawer open, dug out a shirt, then looked at the clothes still scattered on the floor.

"Where's my bra?"

Lauren reached behind herself, over the back of the headboard, and produced the missing underwear.

"I remember throwing it last night. Should I be more careful next time?"

Georgia shivered at the thought of next time. "Please don't."

The grin Lauren gave her was mischievous in the best way. She climbed out of bed and backed Georgia against the dresser, but she stopped her beautiful bare body just short of pressing against Georgia's.

"Have you showered?" she asked.

"We have…" Georgia looked over Lauren's shoulder at the clock. "Thirty-five minutes."

"Good."

* * *

When Kelly arrived, Georgia's knees were still wobbly, but she and Lauren were fully clothed and plausibly undebauched. Kelly walked straight into the kitchen and unloaded ice bags onto the counter, along with ugly paper plates and a half gallon of ice cream, which Georgia already had.

"She likes mint chocolate, right? I know she won't eat the wrong flavor."

"I got the right flavor yesterday," Georgia said. "You didn't need to bring more."

"It was on sale at Stewart's. You can never have too much ice cream."

"You can if it doesn't fit in the freezer," Lauren said.

Kelly looked up and stared at the stranger.

"Kelly, this is Lauren Ashburn, my girlfriend. Lauren, this is Kelly Gray."

Lauren held out her hand to shake, and Kelly put a package of paper napkins in it.

"You won't have to keep it in the freezer for long, right?" she continued. "How many kids are coming?"

"Two, Hannah and her friend."

Usually it was fun to watch Kelly stop in midstream and recalculate like a GPS. Right now, Georgia was distracted by the ice cream she was hefting.

"It's not green."

"What?" Kelly looked at the carton in her hand. "Oh. Well, it's still mint, so it doesn't matter."

The corner of Georgia's lips lifted in a frustrated smile. Dear god, there was so much ice cream. "It does matter. She won't eat it. She won't yell like she used to, but she still won't eat it."

"And whose fault is that?" Kelly demanded, finding a familiar track of conversation and charging down it. "You're the parent, you're supposed to cut that obnoxious picky eater stuff out before it gets like this! Our mother never—"

Out in the living room, the front door opened, and they all held their breath in anticipation of the Birthday Girl. Hannah appeared in the arched doorway, golden tangles framing her frowning, happy face. Abby stood behind her, only half a head shorter after a recent growth spurt and bouncing on the balls of her feet.

"Hello," Hannah said. "What ice cream is that?"

"Mint chocolate! Your favorite!" Kelly crowed.

Hannah squinted at it. "My favorite is green. Thank you anyway."

Lauren snickered. Kelly yanked open the tightly packed freezer and began trying to cram the ice cream in, muttering about how food dye is bad for you.

"What can we do to help, Mommy?"

Georgia held a hand out to her daughter, who squeezed it tightly. "It's your birthday, sweetie. You don't have to help. Go upstairs and take it easy until everyone's here."

Both girls left the kitchen, and Georgia listened to them whisper with each other in front of the pile of presents before heading to Hannah's room. Lauren pulled her head out of the freezer, where she'd been rearranging things as best she could, and asked what needed to be done.

The rain from last night had cleared into a humid, sunny midmorning, which was a mercy. Georgia hadn't felt confident in her indoor backup plan for eleven people. She and Lauren dragged two plastic folding tables out of the mudroom and into the backyard.

"I think this is the driest spot," Georgia said, scuffing the grass with her heel to test the mud under a tree. "It's not exactly flat, but I'd rather tilt a little than have people's chairs sink in. Right?"

"What do you usually do?"

Georgia put her full weight on a table to test its stability before she led Lauren back to the kitchen to gather chairs. "Usually we do this at Judge Gray's house, but they're renovating because both of them don't move around as well as they used to. Hannah said it'd be fine to have the party here. I have seven chairs, and the family's supposed to bring more."

Lauren hefted two kitchen chairs at once. "You call your mother-in-common-law 'Judge'?"

"She earned it." Georgia waited until Kelly was out of earshot to add, "In more ways than one."

It was Judge Gray who had reached the verdict that Georgia was only playing nice, that her politeness in the face of disagreement followed by a refusal to change her position was two-faced rather than attentive and steadfast. Luckily for Georgia, she didn't care what the judge thought.

By eleven, the presents, minus the massive aquarium and the gallons of water (hidden in the pantry for later), were stacked neatly on one table in the yard. Kelly was just laying out her hand-assembled cheese plate, on which the cheddar was sliced, not cubed, and it touched the Swiss, when the Gray family caravan pulled into the driveway. It was only immediate family, not the extended riot of aunts and cousins that gathered on holidays, but the sight of even these two cars full of people made Georgia tense.

Judge Marjorie Gray leaned heavily on her husband as she climbed out of their sedan, then strode slowly forward on her silver steel cane. Katherine's husband Brock tried to pull a highchair out of his trunk despite already being laden with both a diaper bag and baby Laine. Neither his wife nor his older daughter offered to help him, but Lauren rushed forward right away. The gesture warmed Georgia so much it almost melted the tension of seeing the Gray family swarm toward her.

"She didn't even say hello to Mother. Or anyone," Kelly observed, and the tension returned.

It escalated when Brock asked Lauren to hold Laine and she took a step back, saying, "I don't do babies."

Judge Gray reached the head of the plastic picnic table and settled with a groan.

"How was your trip, Judge?" Georgia asked.

"I travel about as well as a raspberry at the bottom of the pint," Judge Gray said. "Where's my girl of honor? Is she not helping you with all this?"

"I told her to play with her friend. She'll be out once everyone's settled," Georgia said. She'd seen Hannah look out her bedroom window when the cars pulled up.

Thankfully the Grays settled quickly, more willing than Georgia could ever be to sit down at a table after a three-hour car ride. Ashlyn was on her phone, which always seemed to bother other people in a way it didn't bother Georgia. Everyone hugged each other and made extended eye contact, interrupted by Katherine's insistence on taking posed portraits with her massive camera.

Preston Gray came to the table last, his orthopedic shoes leaving behind wide footprints in the wet yard. Georgia knew better than to try to take the three-tier birthday cake off his hands, but she walked by his elbow, chatting about the weather until he made it all the way to the table and set his creation down.

"You're an artist, sir," she said when he took the cover off and revealed a pink-striped tower of neatly spread frosting speckled with chocolate sprinkles. It was exactly what Hannah had asked for, thank god.

The birthday girl herself appeared moments later with Abby in tow and went to each of her family one by one to say hello. They all hugged her.

Lauren, sprawled now in one of the chairs from Kyle's apartment, leaned toward Georgia. "I thought Hannah wasn't much of a hugger."

"The Grays all are. If she does it up front, they don't bug her about it later."

"No one hugged you."

Georgia laid her arm along the back of Lauren's chair and ignored the observation. It was correct: the Grays rarely hugged her. She didn't want them to, though it might have felt less strange than being isolated from a family impulse that encircled the most precious people in her life. As each hug began, Georgia saw her daughter, who looked so much like her, pressed close to others who looked every bit like Kyle and his child. No matter how alike she and Hannah were, Hannah was a Gray. A Solomon-Gray. The hyphen felt a mile long without Kyle to bridge it.

"Glad the weather cleared up. This would have been a mess indoors," Brock said to her, trying for in-law camaraderie like he always did. "Is that chicken salad on the food table? Do you mind if I start it?"

Georgia looked at his left ear and eked out a smile. "The sooner the better."

He stood up, but Georgia felt like she was watching him from above. She was a helium balloon, tangled in the branches of the tree for now, but soon to shake loose and float away. The conversation around her didn't vibrate right in the light air inside her. She couldn't understand a thing. She tilted her chair back and squinted, trying to see which of Kyle's sisters (not hers) Hannah was sitting next to, but she couldn't make it out. There was too much to hear and see and feel at once, and she wasn't part of any of it, floating above and drifting away...

The jolt of her chair losing balance when she tipped it back too far hit her like lightning. Lauren's arm was like lightning, too. She grabbed the back and put Georgia's feet on solid ground.

"You okay?"

Georgia smiled. She could feel the way it cracked and knew it was the type of smile her parents had called creepy. "Not really."

"Do you want to eat something?" Lauren wrapped a curl of Georgia's hair around her fingers and tugged it, imitating Georgia's own comforting stim. "I can get it for you so you don't have to get up or make decisions. Unless you know what you want."

"No."

Lauren kissed Georgia's forehead and went to the food table. Georgia watched her, clear as day, and pressed her heels into the ground.

Lauren was here. She'd almost forgotten. Lauren was here, ready and willing to grate against the Grays because she wanted to be with Georgia and Hannah.

Everyone took the cue from Brock and Lauren and gathered their lunch. Georgia didn't notice what she was eating, but she ate what Lauren gave her as quickly as she could while also holding Lauren's hand under the table.

Being grounded again made it easy to hear Katherine say, "Who's your friend, Georgia?"

"Oh! We got so excited about the birthday girl, nobody got introduced. This is my girlfriend, Lauren." Georgia turned to Lauren, who looked like she was about to take an oral exam she hadn't studied for, then back at the crowd of Grays. She introduced them one at a time, and Lauren nodded.

"So at last there is a romantic lead in your life," Preston said. "I'd started to think there was no one who qualified."

"I don't know about 'romantic lead,' but I'm totally qualified," Lauren said.

Georgia laughed. No one else did.

"How long have you been dating?" Brock asked.

Lauren looked at Georgia sideways. "Not long. I mean, I wouldn't have said 'girlfriend' if she hadn't—I mean, I want to be…We met in February."

Judge Gray chewed and swallowed a sugar snap pea before she said, "That's not very long."

"That's how long I've been friends with Hannah," Abby announced, "and we're gonna be friends forever!" She punctuated the declaration with a primal roar and a karate chop that sent her fork flying into Ashlyn's hair.

Saved from the spotlight, Georgia leaned over and whispered to Lauren, "I'm glad you want to be my girlfriend."

Lauren squeezed her hand and kept quiet for the next half hour. Georgia waded through small talk until the lunch plates were cleared, then pulled Lauren's attention back to the party at the first mention of cake.

"You want to see a magic trick? Watch Hannah's hands."

She stood behind Hannah and gestured with one hand toward Preston's marvelous creation. "Judge Gray, if you would light the candles, please? I guess there's no way I can talk you out of singing this year?"

At the chorus of polite chuckles and eye rolls, Georgia reached down and took Hannah's hand in hers. Lauren watched intently, the only witness when Hannah accepted the most important birthday gift and hid them in her ears: earplugs.

The candles glowed on Preston Gray's beautiful cake, and everyone gathered closer to the smell of chocolate and smoke. The Grays took a deep breath and howled in unison. Lauren and Georgia stayed silent together.

CHAPTER TWENTY-FIVE

Lauren snuck off to use the bathroom the first chance she got, while cake was being passed around on paper plates that Georgia hated so much she refused to touch them. She took her time washing her hands. The bar soap was the same as in the shower, unscented but faintly sweet anyway. It wasn't strong enough to be part of Georgia's scent, but it made Lauren think of the warm woody smell that had filled her nose when she pressed close to Georgia's back in bed.

God, Lauren wanted to go back to bed. Preferably with Georgia, but she'd settle for the nice sheets that smelled like her. A bed was a good place to rest, to think. This party was not a good place to think.

"It's not like an eight-year-old's birthday was ever going to be fun," she told herself.

She splashed water on her face and pressed a damp hand to the back of her neck to cool down before she left the bathroom. Halfway down the stairs, she heard something she never had before: a creak from the other side of the duplex. When she pressed her ear against the wall, she heard voices. She couldn't tell what was being said, but there were at least two people over there, and no one had come knocking on Georgia's bathroom door, so it seemed unlikely that these guests were looking to use the unoccupied facilities.

If they even were guests. This was a nice enough neighborhood, but nowhere in Holderness was completely immune to theft. Lauren crept downstairs, grabbed a walking stick from the mudroom, and went out to the yard.

One, two, three… There were eight people at the table. The two in the other apartment were family. Even as Lauren relaxed, Georgia saw her and picked up the distress.

She came over to Lauren, eyes squinted with attention. "What's wrong?"

"Nothing. Heard somebody next door and got nervous."

Georgia didn't relax like Lauren had. She stomped over to the other back door and yanked it open, muttering that no one was supposed to be in there. This was going to get ugly, but Lauren followed Georgia anyway, loyalty outweighing her desire to mind her own business.

Georgia hadn't turned the lights on when they'd gathered chairs from the kitchen earlier today, so Lauren was surprised to find the living room lamps at full brightness. Why was the electricity still turned on in this place? The teenager and her mom were in the room.

"What are you doing, Katherine?" Georgia asked, saving Lauren from the fact that she didn't remember anyone's name.

"Ashlyn and I aren't big cake people, so we figured we'd take our turn to do the sticker thing." Katherine waved a sheet of green paper dots. The teen had some too.

"The sticker thing?" Georgia was confused.

"Yeah," Ashlyn said. "Putting stickers on stuff so you know where to send it."

Lauren looked at Georgia. Georgia's lips were twisted into a snarling smile, and her hands were clenched at her sides. This was about to go very wrong.

"Kelly told us to do it!" Katherine blurted, the younger-sibling instinct kicking in just like it did with Tracy.

"Told you to do what?" Georgia growled.

"I thought she asked you first! She acted like it was all rubber stamped!"

Ashlyn sat down on the couch like her exasperation was too heavy to stand up under. "Aunt Kelly sent everyone colored stickers and said we were supposed to go through Uncle Kyle's stuff while we're here and mark what we want to keep. She said it'd help you get it all done, because obviously you're struggling with it."

"Obviously?" Georgia said.

"Her words." Katherine held her hands up, but it didn't defend her from Georgia's icy glare.

"So you're just tromping through your brother's house and pawing through his things like it's a silent auction?" Georgia said.

"Kelly said if—"

"I don't care what Kelly said! This is my child's birthday party, not a fucking estate sale!"

Even Lauren took a step back. She'd never heard Georgia swear before. Katherine backed up all the way to the wall, and Georgia charged right up to her and snatched the stickers out of her hand. Ashlyn held hers out far in front of her, within Georgia's reach without her needing to come any closer. Georgia took a deep breath that looked like it could become a rant or an animal scream. Neither happened.

The door creaked open, and everyone turned.

"Mommy," Hannah said, "can we do presents now? I'm tired of eating."

Georgia's face twisted, her angry smile clashing with both the fake smile she forced for other people and the fake frown she needed to show Hannah. Lauren managed a hopefully reassuring wink when Hannah glanced at her, confused.

"Presents! Of course! Yes, let's do presents," Georgia said, at the same volume as when she'd first shouted at her in-laws.

Katherine and Ashlyn took the opportunity to scurry outside, and Hannah followed them.

When they were alone, Georgia turned to Lauren, hands clenching and unclenching in front of her. It twisted like a corkscrew in Lauren's chest.

"I'm so sorry, you shouldn't have to—" Georgia started to say.

Lauren stopped her, reaching out but not touching. "Don't worry," she said. "I've been to worse parties."

Georgia flung herself into Lauren's arms, and Lauren was glad she'd been working out again because she was strong enough to squeeze her extra tight.

Outside, it was unclear if anyone had heard Georgia's outburst. Ashlyn was on her phone again. Katherine was back behind her camera, and she didn't make eye contact when Lauren and Georgia approached the group. Everyone gathered around the table, watching Hannah choose a present from the pile with the care of a juror. She took a small one from the top and slid her fingers under the paper creases to slit the tape.

"C'mon, kiddo," the Judge said, "rip and tear!"

Brock muttered, "We're gonna be here all day."

Abby's body was vibrating with vicarious excitement. Lauren hoped eight-year-olds were mature enough to stop themselves from opening other kids' presents, or that girl was going to make a scene.

Hannah didn't notice any of that, or she didn't care. She folded the paper back gently, gently, and quietly read the box that she revealed.

"What is it?" the Judge shouted.

"It's a thermometer," Georgia told her. "From Ashlyn, right?"

Ashlyn nodded.

"Thank you," Hannah said.

"Hold it up and smile!" Katherine said.

Hannah complied with a huff. Georgia winced, but no one scolded the kid.

If she was confused about being given a thermometer, she didn't show it. She just deliberated again, then reached for a box with an envelope taped to it. When Lauren was young, she'd hated cards, skipped right past them and on to the good stuff, but Hannah opened the card and read it silently before setting it aside.

"What does it say?" the patriarch asked.

"Read it to us," Kelly said. When Hannah looked at her, she insisted. "Read it out loud. We all want to hear what your aunt and uncle wrote to you."

"Do we?" Lauren said.

It was really unfortunate that Kelly got so red and funny looking when she was steamed. It made it way harder for Lauren to feel guilty about being a smartass. The only thing that could stop her now was Georgia, and she looked like she was having fun, too.

"You can keep it private if you want to, baby. They wrote the card for you, not for anyone else," Georgia told Hannah.

Hannah peeled off the wrapping paper on a pack of blue and green ceramic tiles.

"Thank you!" she said.

It did take forever to open all the presents, especially since Hannah had to pose for photos with every single gift, but eventually she had a stack of unripped wrapping paper to one side of her and a full set of aquarium necessities, plus a few books and a plastic stegosaurus that Lauren was a little jealous of, in front of her. She was, at last, visibly baffled.

"Is this all?" she said. "I thought there was a big thing."

Abby was still vibrating with excitement, but Georgia was wound up enough to hit warp speeds. She held her arms to the house like a game show assistant and squealed, "There is a big thing! Too big to move, so come see!"

Hannah dashed across the yard to the backdoor. Katherine ran after her, yelling, "Wait! Don't open it until everyone's there to see! We need pictures!"

"We need video," Lauren said, hoping a recording would capture the magic moment without all the fuss over poses.

Katherine dutifully switched to recording mode on her camera. Georgia held Lauren's hand as they walked into the apartment together.

Ten people shuffled into the living room, ringed around Hannah and the great big paper-covered rectangle against the wall. Hannah gripped one end of the box, Abby the other, and they lifted it up together, inch by inch until their arms were over their heads to clear the top of the tank. When the whole tank was revealed, Hannah let her end of the box thump onto the floor.

The axolotls blinked and flicked their tails in the sudden light.

Hannah jumped once, then ran to her mother, shouting, "Thank you, thank you!"

Georgia pressed Hannah to her side, gleefully accepting the only hug that had been willingly given out so far today. "Thank Ms. Lauren, she helped me get them. They're from her, too."

Lauren was ready for a thank you, a forced smile, or maybe even a real frown. What she got was fifty pounds of eight-year-old slamming into her waist. Hannah was touching her.

The Grays released a collective "Aww!"

Once again, it was a gift to have such strong arms. For a kid's birthday party, this wasn't so bad after all.

CHAPTER TWENTY-SIX

Georgia turned down the invitation to dinner that Kelly extended. She wanted to get her house in order and watch Hannah and her friend construct the axolotl aquarium, not socialize until she croaked. Besides, she was still angry enough to choke an elephant. Lauren helped move the tables and chairs back inside, and when Georgia insisted she didn't need help with anything else, she fell asleep on the couch. Someday that poor woman was going to have a regular sleep schedule, if Georgia had to roll her up in bed sheets like a burrito to make it happen.

"Mommy," Hannah said, "can Abby spend the night?"

Georgia froze in the middle of washing the serving spoons. "You're not too worn out?"

"Not for Abby. It's different."

Besides her father, Hannah had never found someone who was different before, someone who wasn't exhausting. It was a special thing. Georgia snuck a glance at Lauren, whose shaggy hair was falling over her face. Someone different was a very special thing indeed.

"If it's okay with Ben, it's okay with me," she said.

Hannah hopped back to the living room. Georgia could hear her and Abby talking, to each other and then on the phone. The warm dishwater, soothing on her hands, lapped against the sides of the sink. Her analog clock ticked on the wall. Those were the only sounds, and for a few minutes it was comforting to have such blessed quiet. She had spent all day hearing things, and she was grateful to be finished. Inevitably, though, after the girls had gone upstairs and the clink of serving spoons being put back in their drawer and the gurgle of the sink drain had faded, Georgia heard the painful absence again, the silence where Kyle would have been.

Last year, at the Gray family house, Kyle had read all the cards aloud, held up presents for pictures, and kept things smooth, anticipating both his family's demands and his daughter's irritations without Georgia having to say anything. It was generally best when Georgia didn't say anything, because the Grays didn't like what she had to say. Everyone liked Kyle, though.

In the living room, Lauren twitched and snuffled awake. There was some satisfaction, Georgia supposed, in knowing that the Grays hadn't liked Lauren much, either. She filled a glass of water at the sink and brought it with her to the living room.

"You're not much of a people pleaser, are you?" she said, handing the glass to Lauren.

"People aren't usually pleased with me, no. Different priorities." Lauren drank half the water and set the rest aside. "Did I make it harder for you?"

Georgia put her head on Lauren's shoulder, and when that affection was met tenderly, she lay down in Lauren's lap. "It was going to be hard no matter what. I like that you're the way you are."

Lauren stroked her hair for a few minutes, and the silence was once again blessed. Then she said, "Can I ask about the apartment?"

Bile rose in Georgia's throat. She clenched her teeth and coached herself not to speak too loudly when she answered, but what poured out of her weren't wrathful words. They were tears.

"Oh, baby," Lauren whispered, and she petted Georgia while she tamped the weeping down.

"The lease on Kyle's apartment is running out soon. I don't know what I'm going to do, or what Hannah's going to do, or who's going to move in after. Kyle lived here the whole time I knew him. My home doesn't feel like home when he's not right next to it."

Admitting how you feel was supposed to make it seem lighter, but Georgia's fear, spoken, hung heavy as a thundercloud. Heavy as silence in a haunted house.

Lauren shifted under Georgia, but she put an arm on her waist to keep her from getting up. She drank the rest of her water. Georgia loved watching her chew the trouble over in her mind before she spoke, loved knowing that Lauren wouldn't tell her everything was going to be fine.

"Change happens fast," Lauren finally said, "but it takes a while to find out what it means. The biggest thing I was afraid of when Len turned me down for the job was the look my dad would give me when I told him. It's this frown that brings out all the lines in his face and makes his eyes squint up like..." Lauren contorted her face until it looked like something foul was stuck in her throat and poisoning her tongue. "But that's not going to happen. I don't know what's going to happen. I've never had to worry about everybody else being disappointed in me, 'cause my dad was disappointed enough for all of them."

"And his opinion mattered most."

"Yeah."

Georgia hugged Lauren's legs and burrowed into her lap. "What matters most now?" she asked.

Is it me? she wondered. *Is it us?*

"Now? Um," Lauren checked the time on her phone. "Dinner."

Georgia laughed. She'd been so emotional all day, she hadn't noticed she was hungry. Lauren knew exactly how to break the tension and put Georgia's feet on the ground. She'd come so far in taking care of herself, and that care extended to Georgia, too. It enveloped everything and everyone in Lauren's life, and

Georgia luxuriated in the privilege of being included while letting go of the desire to name how it made her feel. Lauren had her priorities in order. Love wasn't a concept they should confront on empty stomachs.

"Dinner sounds good," Georgia said.

CHAPTER TWENTY-SEVEN

Peak July weather had sucked the life out of the outfield in the middle school's baseball field. "Crunch grass season," the Ashburns all called it, but that phrase came from the clan that lived in South Carolina. It never used to get this hot in Holderness—as Lauren's dad had never failed to point out. Climate change and suffocating heat weren't distractions Lauren was entertaining now, though. She was so intent on keeping her eyes on Hannah that she didn't even wipe the sweat off her forehead.

Georgia's parents had sent Hannah's birthday present, ten days late and with apologies for not visiting this summer: a new bicycle. Georgia had called Lauren right away when it arrived, disassembled in a flat pack box, and Lauren had called Tracy. Between the three of them, they'd put the thing together. It looked like they'd done it correctly, but Lauren would never place bets on herself doing something right.

Abby held the bike upright and talked Hannah through it. Georgia had one hand tangled in her hair and one clenching

Lauren's bicep. The dirt of the baseball field would be more forgiving than pavement if Hannah fell again, but there were other kinds of injury to worry about.

"Faster is better," Abby explained. "Going forward makes it harder to fall over on your side."

Hannah smiled, which on her meant she was skeptical and nervous, but she pedaled when told and sped up as Abby walked, then jogged, behind her. Georgia squeaked and buried her face in Lauren's shoulder when Abby let go.

Hannah sped forward. She turned, rounded the bases, then braked so hard she almost threw herself over the handlebars.

"Mommy!" she yelled, wagging her tail as the bike tipped and she staggered to standing. "Mommy, I did it!"

Georgia ran across the field, hands waving. Lauren beamed at them both.

* * *

"By the way," Georgia said that night, while she and Lauren brushed their teeth side by side in the bathroom of the duplex, "Ben's friends, the Haydens, invited us to dinner with them when they're in town this weekend."

Lauren spit before asking, "The friends who thought you and Ben were dating?"

"They're nice," Georgia said blithely.

Lauren smiled. Of course befriending the people who'd ended her other friendship didn't strike Georgia as odd.

"So you and Hannah are getting dinner with them."

"And you. I talked about you and your architecture program a lot. Ava does computer programming, too, so she wants to meet you. They have two kids, and you haven't met them, so I understand if you don't want to come, but I was thinking maybe you could network. Find a job that appreciates you more than Green Mountain and doesn't have ridiculous expectations."

Wouldn't that be something? Lauren swished water in her mouth as she constructed her to-do list. She'd need to research Ava's company, make sure her good button-up was pressed, and brace herself for impact with the kids.

"It sounds doable. Thanks," she said.

Georgia met her reflection's eyes and winked.

They were in bed before it struck Lauren how different the proposal was from others. Her mother had set her up on blind networking dates before, handing her around to everyone she knew who did anything with computers and telling them Lauren was going to be the CEO of something-or-other someday. Tracy insisted that she could do better than Green Mountain, but she wanted her to do something wild and chancy like hook up with an app maker based in California. Her father always wanted to know what the next step was in a job, before Lauren had even taken the first one. Where would it get her? How far would she go? Georgia had presented a local opportunity that felt like fresh air, where other ideas had crushed like a cave-in. It made her want to work and to have work fill her with the same joy that hiking on a crisp autumn day or listening to Georgia sing while she dressed in the morning did. Everything else in life was good. Why not work, too?

Lauren rolled over in bed and kissed Georgia's shoulder. She brushed the hair away from the back of Georgia's neck and kissed there, then her ear and the hinge of her jaw.

"Are you asleep?" she asked.

"Not yet."

Georgia rolled over in Lauren's arms, blinking tired eyes that were nonetheless starting to blaze. Lauren pressed her lips to Georgia's like her mouth held all the answers to the future's mysteries. The way she talked and thought and kissed so perfectly, maybe it did.

* * *

The pub the Haydens wanted to eat at wasn't too nice, but Lauren wanted to make a good first impression for once in her life. She ironed her button-up and put it on fresh, despite how hot it was, because she had to move quickly if she didn't want to end up covered in cat hair. She was waiting outside when Georgia pulled up, exactly on time.

"I tried to be early," she said when Lauren got in the car, "but I couldn't find one of my shoes and then my earring fell out and I—"

Lauren kissed her cheek while she buckled her seat belt. "You're not late. It's fine."

Even if she had been late, Lauren would have forgiven her.

The Haydens were late, and they made an entrance. The two kids, one about Hannah's age and one a little older, according to Georgia, were screaming at each other about a video game.

"Meganic is the best one! She has the robots!"

"The robots are stupid! Weezil obviously beats her, he has teeth and a gun and his ultimate move is Poison Cannon!"

Ava looked less put together in person than in her company photo, but only by a hair. Her husband was trying to get one of the kids to take his iPad, but the argument was too far escalated to be settled easily.

Lauren settled it. "Weezil's attacks are stronger, but Meganic has healing abilities, so she has time to chip away at Weezil's HP. One on one, Meganic wins most of the time. Sorry, kid."

The Weezil fan snatched the iPad and slouched into a chair across from Hannah, whose light-up shoes started flashing when she kicked the table leg. The Meganic fan sat by Lauren.

At least I made a good impression on one of them, Lauren thought, smiling in the face of Evan Hayden's scowl.

"You must be Georgia's girlfriend," Ava said, extending her hand to shake before she sat. "She said you were decisive."

"That's a nice way of putting it. I'm Lauren Ashburn."

The Haydens ordered craft beer. Lauren declined, because while she could certainly use a beer, Georgia didn't like the smell. Two pints of it at the table would be bad enough without the risk of Lauren having the odor on her breath the next time she wanted a kiss.

"So what are you working on at your little company, Lauren?" Ava asked.

Lauren ignored the slight dig. Green Mountain was small; that was why she was interested in Ava's company.

"I'm part of the team working on an API for a private chat network called FrogTalk. There's a lot of thematic puns involved."

Ava tilted her head back when she laughed a little more than necessary.

"So you run Molecule," Lauren said, putting her research to work. "You're focused on edge colocation, right?"

The spark in Ava's eyes when Lauren mentioned edge colocation was bright and laser-focused, like the look in Georgia's eyes when she had studied every inch of the hand-sawn architectural ornamentation while they took in a visiting exhibit in the Holderness Museum. Lauren leaned toward that energy. Ava talked fast and changed subjects like a rabbit changed directions. She only half explained edge colocation before going in depth about the implications of interaction between 5G networks and meteorological equipment, and she expected Lauren to keep up without much space for questions. Thank god Lauren had done some reading before dinner—she was definitely being tested.

Ordering only slowed Ava down briefly, but she turned her attention to her kids, then to Georgia, once the entrees arrived. Lauren took the opportunity to catch her breath, then nodded along to the discussion of learning how to ride a bicycle.

Georgia said, "Your sister crashed into your dad's car, right? When she was learning?"

"Yeah, that was me, actually. I was just trying to be cool."

"You are cool," Hannah said. It was the only thing she said all night, and it inflated Lauren's confidence in a way no craft beer could have hoped to. Ava regarded her over a bite of tabouli as if the comment had improved her estimation of Lauren, too.

When dinner was done, just before they all sallied forth into the cloyingly humid night, Ava said, "There are job openings at Molecule. You should apply."

"I'll think about it," Lauren said, and she did for the rest of the night.

"It's not realistic," she told Georgia, "but I might get an interview, and that'll be good practice. She was really nice to offer."

"But why would she offer if she didn't think you could do the job?"

"She thinks I *might* be good for the job, but she hasn't seen my résumé yet."

"Well, I think you're cool," Georgia said. She winked, and Lauren felt, again, like she might just be able to do anything.

Molecule was located in Massachusetts, but it had satellite teams all along the Eastern seaboard. Most employees worked from home and traveled annually for conferences, development meetings, and other on-site requirements. Lauren liked to travel almost as much as she liked coming home, so that was fine with her. More than fine, even. It might just be exactly what she wanted.

Filling out job applications was like riding a bike. She had all the forms completed and sent in before she went to bed.

CHAPTER TWENTY-EIGHT

The Old Duchess Theater bubbled with the voices of people ordering popcorn, looking for their seats, and milling around before the opening night performance of *A Midsummer Night's Dream*. Georgia kept Hannah close, and Hannah cradled her reusable grocery bag full of flowers like a baby. Lauren swam through the crowd like a fish, unfazed by the way the concession stand's neon lights glared off the gold sconces on the opposite wall and the dusty crystal of the chandelier. She was familiar with this scene.

Georgia had passed the Old Duchess on Main Street many times over the years but had never been inside, despite all the times she saw the marquee and thought she'd like to see a show. If she had stopped in years before to see *Fiddler on the Roof* or *Steel Magnolias*, would Lauren have been there?

Tracy certainly would have been. Photos from previous productions going back decades hung in the concession area, and Lauren helped Hannah spot Tracy in a dozen of them before the show started. The usher knew both Lauren and her mother by name.

"Don't you think it would be nice to put your father's name on one of these seats?" Mrs. Ashburn asked when they were seated, rubbing her thumb over a gold leaf plaque on the back of the chair in front of her.

Lauren said to Georgia and Hannah, "There's a long tradition in our family of setting up honors and memorials in places the person being honored hates. Like the brick with my name on it by the fountain in town."

"You don't hate the fountain," Georgia said. She still didn't get the joke of Lauren pretending she was unhappy in Holderness.

"And your father didn't hate the theater. He just had high standards for productions. Besides, if we put the store name on it, it'd be good advertising."

"I hate good advertising," Lauren grumbled as the lights in the theater went down.

What she really hated, Georgia guessed, were empty gestures. Lauren was good at spotting them—like Georgia's forced smiles and the praise her boss had been heaping on everyone since Lauren's friend, Jamar, had resigned.

The curtain rose, and Lauren melted toward Georgia, comfortable as an old dog in the sun.

"You like theater a lot?"

Lauren hummed. "I like this theater and this play. *Midsummer* is one of my favorites, and the Old Duchess troupe can't go more than five years or so without trying some new take on it. One time they did the whole thing on roller blades. Tracy wiped out in front of everybody. It was great."

"Did it hurt?" Hannah asked.

"Nah, but she—"

"Shush!" Mrs. Ashburn scolded. "You're as bad as your father about running commentary."

"I started it, sorry," Georgia said, both because it was true and because Lauren had tensed up.

Mrs. Ashburn turned her attention back to the stage. Lauren put her arm around Georgia's shoulders and kept her close through the entire show.

When it ended, the audience flooded the brightly lit concession area, not orderly and at a trickle like when people had arrived, but all at once. Georgia's instinct was to huddle in a corner, but Mrs. Ashburn plunged through the thick of it, crunching dropped popcorn and at least one person's toes into the maroon carpet as she went. Lauren took Georgia's hand, and Georgia took Hannah's, and they weaved like a train of elephants in Mrs. Ashburn's path. The stage door was open, and the cast was fighting a traffic jam of their own trying to find their families in the crush. Tracy's crown of feathers made her easy to spot, but not easy to get to. She shoved her way through a group hug and stumbled into a sandwich board advertising season passes to reach her mother's outstretched arms.

"That was wonderful, honey!" Mrs. Ashburn shouted over the crowd.

"You didn't fall on your face," Lauren said, "so I hated it."

Tracy smacked Lauren's arm before she hugged her.

"You're wearing a lot of makeup," Hannah said.

"I know!" Tracy said, smiling. "It itches. Do you want to come backstage and see the counter where I put it on and take it off?"

Georgia did, but Hannah said, "No, thank you." Then Hannah pulled the bouquet of pink roses out of her bag and added, "We brought these for you because we knew you'd do a good job."

It was the thing to do when someone was in a play. There were at least five other actors being gifted with flowers, including one who had only been an extra, and they accepted the flowers with grace and joy before posing for pictures.

All three Ashburns froze. When Tracy took the flowers Hannah held, her hands twitched and her eyes were glazed with tears.

"Were we not supposed to bring these?" Georgia asked. Something was off, though she couldn't guess what. She should have cleared this with Lauren first. She should have known better.

Tracy sniffled, then asked Georgia, "Are we hugging friends?"

Georgia nodded, and Tracy engulfed her in a hug that reeked of sweat from the stage lights.

"Dad didn't believe in giving flowers after plays," Tracy explained. "He...well, he had opinions about art, as I'm sure you've heard."

Lauren scuffed her shoe against the fading carpet. Mrs. Ashburn asked if Tracy had eaten and started suggesting restaurants, because they always took their little star out to eat after a performance. She didn't seem to understand that that didn't make up for the lack of flowers. Georgia glanced at all the pictures on the wall, all the years of performances that hadn't smelled like roses.

"We'll meet you guys there," Lauren said to her mother. "I want to peek in the store windows on the way."

She laced her fingers with Georgia's and held her other hand out to Hannah so she could lead them through the still-tight crowd of people in the lobby. Georgia kept her elbows tight to herself so she wouldn't jab anyone by mistake. Once they wriggled out the front door, they all took a deep breath of the muggy air. It was somehow still fresher than what they'd been inhaling inside. They set out down the street in a clump, like the other groups of people who belonged together.

"I'm sorry we made Tracy cry," Georgia said, at the same time Hannah made her own pronouncement.

"Your dad was mean."

"And I'm sorry for that!" Georgia squealed. Several people on the sidewalk took the time to scowl at her.

They scowled even more when Lauren yelped with laughter. She stifled it quickly, choked on a breath, and went red. Georgia worried she was having an aneurism or a seizure, because it didn't seem at all like a typical response.

"Yeah," Lauren said, right as Georgia was resolving that she should get ready to call 911 just in case. "Yeah, Dad was hard to impress for sure. It made it hard for Tracy to feel like she was doing a good job."

"She did a good job tonight," Hannah said. "Just like you said she would."

"She always does. And hey, look at this place!"

They'd arrived at Ashburn's Art Supply Store (Grand Reopening September 21st!). Lauren pressed her face close to the window of the store, and Hannah copied her.

"What happened to the counter?"

Lauren pointed to one dark corner, where the counter had been moved. She laid out in detail Tracy's plan for the store, gesturing to show the scope, and Hannah nodded sagely. Georgia watched the two of them, heads bent close together as they shared a vision of the future.

"I'm sorry your dad was mean," Hannah said.

Georgia winced, not sure if she was more afraid of Lauren getting angry this time or laughing again. Instead, Lauren's proud shoulders just sagged.

"I'm sorry your dad isn't here to see you how great you are. You tell it like it is."

"Maybe our dads had to leave so we could be friends. Now you can tell me how great I am, and we can be nice to Tracy."

Lauren leaned against the shop window and gave Georgia a look she recognized: assessment. "Are you one of those 'everything happens for a reason' types?"

"No," Georgia said, "but I think finding the good in the bad is the best way forward."

That satisfied Lauren. She gave Georgia a crooked smile and returned to her side, declaring, "Mom and Tracy are probably wondering what happened to us. Let's have our Midsummer Night's Feast before we do the dreaming part, huh?"

Georgia thought about meeting Lauren years before now, in the Old Duchess or the art store or elsewhere. Lauren could have met Kyle, and Georgia could have had all her favorite people in one place. She and Lauren could have both been this happy sooner and spent a hundred other summer nights under the stars and the awnings of Main Street together. It could have been wonderful.

Then again, if things had been different in the past, they might not be here together now. It stung a little to admit it, but Georgia knew that here and now was exactly where she wanted to be.

CHAPTER TWENTY-NINE

Lauren needed a break from FrogTalk, so she checked her email with the casual air of someone who expected nothing more than a few political ads and bogus coupons. Sandwiched between those predictable things was one with the subject line "candidate interview schedule." It was from Ava Hayden.

"Dear Lauren," it read. "Congratulations! We're excited to offer you the opportunity to interview for the position of Newton, Massachusetts Team Manager at Molecule. Please call the number listed below as soon as possible to schedule your interview."

She called the number listed below immediately, hoping the secretary she spoke to would be able to answer a few questions. Excitement and anxiety were waiting in the wings, but confusion was center stage right now.

It did a graceful pirouette when Ava Hayden herself answered the phone.

"Hi, you sent me the wrong email," Lauren said. Then she corrected herself. "This is Lauren Ashburn. I got an email about interviewing for the Newton manager position."

"Yes! Jesus, you're prompt about calling back."

"Well, I wasn't sure the email was for me. I applied for the programmer position, not management."

Ava was quiet for so long that confusion and anxiety started a duet. Lauren imagined her going over her sent receipts and sighing in disappointment when she saw the mistake. "I'm so sorry," she'd say any second now. "Don't call again."

"Are you an ambitious woman?" Ava asked instead.

"Um, yes?" Lauren said. She had always intended to be, even if she hadn't quite managed it yet. "Yes, I'd call myself modestly ambitious."

"It's the modesty that's a problem," Ava said. "You applied for an entry level job that you're beyond qualified for. I want you to try for the manager job instead."

"I've never been a manager before."

"I've never run a company before. We all start somewhere."

"Inspiring," Lauren said, trying to laugh.

The sarcasm wasn't appropriate. She should be grateful, and she was flattered, but her skin prickled with trepidation more than anything. This wasn't what she'd asked for.

But if she could tell her dad this story, he'd never believe she'd gotten so lucky.

"Trust me," Ava said. "The management position is exactly what you want."

Lauren scheduled the interview and started planning for the three-hour drive to Newton, Massachusetts, ignoring the vertigo that had gripped her since she'd seen Ava's email. Onward and upward, at dizzying speed.

At six, she turned away from the half a dozen interview prep guides she had open on her laptop and went outside to meet Georgia and Hannah. Days were still hot lately, but the evenings cooled quickly, and the fresh air was soothing. She took deep breaths of it until Georgia's old Subaru rumbled into the parking lot.

"Thanks for inviting me to go back-to-school shopping," she said as she buckled herself into the passenger seat, which was still set to accommodate someone much taller than her. "I haven't been in ages. Have things changed?"

"Not a bit," Georgia said.

"Someday I'll get adult scissors," Hannah grumbled.

"Someday teachers will be able to afford their own scissors," Georgia said. "How was your day, love?"

Lauren blushed at the endearment and stared through the windshield. "Not bad, got a lot of work done. Nothing exciting."

That was technically true. Excitement hadn't arrived yet, only lingering nerves and a faint pulse of something like dread. She ignored it in favor of colorful folders, wide-ruled paper, and dull scissors. Hannah was excited about those things.

"Red is for English," she explained firmly as she put folders into the shopping cart. "Blue is for math, yellow is for science, and green is for history."

"I only ever had blue ones," Lauren said while she searched for a second yellow folder.

"But blue is just for math!"

"Sometimes you don't learn the important facts about life until it's way too late," Georgia said.

Hannah frowned and moved on with her shopping, but Georgia hung back.

"Should I not have said 'love' in the car?" she asked.

"What? No, that was fine."

Georgia's fingers were still scratching at her cardigan sleeves, so Lauren pushed herself to reassure her by sharing a little more. "I liked it."

"Then what's wrong?"

Lauren twined Georgia's nervous fingers with her own and kissed her cheek. "Nothing. Everything's good."

And for those last green and blazing weeks of August, everything was.

* * *

Lauren's interview was on the same day as Hannah's first day of school. She hadn't planned on getting together with Georgia until the end of the day, after the interview, but she woke up early sick with nerves and wanted nothing more than to see her girlfriend. She drove over after the school day had started.

The sound of Georgia's stereo drifted through the open windows of the duplex. It was ABBA, which probably meant a happy mood. Lauren swayed to the rhythm as she kicked off her shoes in the mudroom, then drew up short when she entered the living room.

Georgia was not in a happy mood. She was cocooned in her blanket on the couch, hunched over and ignoring what looked like a long-cold breakfast.

"What's this about, babe?" Lauren asked.

Georgia whined. The song started over, on repeat, and Lauren started to catch on—it was the one about kids growing up.

"How did Hannah's first school morning go?"

"It was fine, great. She got ready all by herself. She even has an alarm clock. She's so big!"

Georgia buried her nose under the blanket. Lauren sat down next to her, laying her arm along the back of the couch.

"Does this happen to you every year?"

Georgia nodded. She'd mentioned taking the day off from work; this must be why.

"What do you usually do? Just this?"

"Usually, um…" Georgia swallowed hard, and her eyes were so full of tears it was a miracle they hadn't started to fall. "Usually Kyle talks me out of it."

"Oh." Lauren shifted on the couch, wanting to wrap herself around Georgia but feeling far away from her. What could she possibly offer in this moment? This *family* moment?

"Do you want those eggs?" Georgia offered, nudging them with her socked foot.

"How long have they been sitting there?"

"Like two hours." Georgia finally looked directly at Lauren, a sheepish little frown on her face. "Poor eggs."

Lauren couldn't help it when a giggle escaped her in the face of this kind of sweetness. She tried to suck it back in with a deep breath, and she held it, waiting for Georgia's reaction.

Georgia snickered and leaned her head back onto Lauren's arm. They both relaxed at the contact.

More surefooted now that Georgia was touching her, Lauren had an idea. "What did Kyle used to say?" she asked.

"Oh, he'd remind me what it was like to change a diaper and the little snot suckers we had to use before Hannah could blow her own nose—all the gross stuff. I *hated* the really gross stuff. And I'd say she was going to be a teenager someday, and then she'd hate me because all teenagers hate their parents, and what was I going to do then? My days with my sweet little girl were numbered! Then he'd say that he never hated his parents, which was probably true. He has a freakishly good relationship with his parents. Had. But oh, even after the teenaged years, she was going to go to college and leave us! What then? And he'd say…"

Georgia caught her breath, and suddenly the tears that had been receding overflowed. "He'd say that we were a family, and we'd always be together in the end."

One selfish thought pierced the protective agony of seeing Georgia cry: if Lauren got the manager job, she'd have to move to Newton. The next time Georgia cried, would Lauren be able to hold her? Would they be together in the end? She pulled Georgia, blanket and all, into her lap and rocked her, turning thoughts of the future away.

"I'm sorry Kyle's not here," she said, "and I don't want to be a replacement for him, but I can be here. We can be together for a while."

Georgia tucked her head under Lauren's chin. She didn't ask how long "a while" would last, and Lauren didn't tell her it might be shorter than it seemed.

CHAPTER THIRTY

"Thank you again, Ms. Solomon," Mrs. Davis said, smiling fondly at the other Mrs. Davis. "Every time we think there's no solution, you find a way."

Georgia met each of the women's eyes for a few seconds and smiled, but not too widely. "There's always a way, Mrs. Davis, and I'm glad we finally found it. Corina should be in touch soon."

The Davises left Prysliak and Associates hand in hand, which was always the best sign. A couple could show up to Georgia's office hissing at each other like snakes, but they should leave as a united front.

Georgia was turning back to the stairs when Bev called her name. Bev and Gerald had just come out of his office, apparently engrossed in conversation, which had become common since they'd discovered a mutual fondness for reality shows and the mocking thereof. It made Georgia nervous to be invited into such a conversation. Had they been talking about her? What might Bev want to suck Georgia into? She approached the two of them with caution.

"Was that the crown molding couple?" Gerald asked, but he turned to Bev before Georgia could answer and said, "These women have serious crown molding in their dining room, and they want to expand their kitchen into the dining room but not get rid of the crown molding. We mocked it up on the 3D model, and it ruins the flow of the whole room! Two rooms! Did you talk them into getting rid of it?"

"They're going to extend it into the kitchen," Georgia said.

Gerald nodded knowingly, but Bev's nose wrinkled like she'd opened the forgotten takeout in the staff fridge.

"Whose idea was that?" she asked.

"Mine," Georgia said.

"I thought you wanted them to get rid of it?"

"I do." Georgia wrinkled her nose the way Bev had. "All crown molding does is build up spiderwebs."

"But now they're extending it. Because you said so?"

This was something people rarely understood, that Georgia could agree and disagree at the same time, could help someone along a path she never would have taken herself. Her parents had called it "people pleasing." Others, like the Grays, called it "lying." Time to find out what Bev called it.

Georgia forced her eyes up and stared at Bev's ear to make it look like she was standing firm and looking her in the eye. "It's their house. My job is to make something they like."

Bev reached out to pat Georgia's shoulder, then stopped and smiled more brightly when Gerald shook his head.

"Not everyone can have your good taste," she said, "but at least they have your talent on their side."

The breath puffing up Georgia's chest rushed out. She touched Bev's arm. "Thank you."

"Do you want to celebrate? First round of drinks is on me."

"Or we could get dessert," Gerald suggested. "Someplace quiet? Hannah could come, too."

Bev scored more points with Georgia by moaning, "Yes, I could murder some chocolate cake!"

Georgia wished she could. Even unscheduled outings sounded fun lately, but she had to decline and hope her new friend would forgive her.

"My daughter's aunt is coming over, so I have to be there and deal with her right after work. But thank you! We can do dessert next time you have something to celebrate."

"God save us from in-laws," Bev said, and she and Gerald wished her good luck when she left.

* * *

Kelly was already at the duplex when Georgia and Hannah got home. She had let herself in with her emergencies-only key and filled the house with smoke and smells.

"There you are!" she called from the kitchen. "I stopped at a farm stand on the way, and they had some great cuts of stir-fry beef, so I cooked dinner. You don't have any onions, though."

"Is something burning?" Georgia said.

The fan over the stove was blaring, and Kelly waved an oven mitt over a still smoking pot.

"Never did get the hang of cooking rice, but I found a rice cooker in the pantry, so no worries. Why had you never opened it? It's a nice one."

Georgia squeezed herself around the ribs. "It was Kyle's Christmas present."

"Oh."

"Why does it smell funny?" Hannah asked, tiptoeing up to the bubbling vat on the stove.

"It's green curry, your favorite color. I promise it's mild. It'd smell even better if there were onions."

"I hate onions," Georgia said. "We both do."

Kelly frowned and turned back to her curry. Hannah retreated to her room, away from the noise and smell, and Georgia turned the fan off and opened a window to clear the last of the smoke. When dinner was served, she and Hannah both had to pick out the bell peppers. Kelly chewed hers in stony silence.

Other than the peppers, it was good curry, but Georgia didn't say so.

After dinner, Kelly took Hannah to get ice cream while Georgia did the dishes. She'd been invited on the ice cream venture, but the time alone was necessary. Hannah should have fun with her aunt without Georgia's tension filling the room like smoke from burning rice.

Lauren gave her advice via text on how to salvage the pot Kelly had damaged, which brought on visions of the two of them doing dishes side by side, together every night. Lauren always washed the dishes she used while she was here, and Georgia let her because the gesture was kind and she liked the thorough, attentive motions of Lauren's hands while she scrubbed. Just the thought of how Lauren smelled when her hands had been soaking in soapy water was soothing. By the time Kelly was done reading Hannah a story and settling her into bed, Georgia's fantasies had made her almost calm again.

"Can we talk?" Kelly asked, motioning toward the porch, and the calm evaporated.

Georgia followed Kelly outside, leaving the door open so she could hear if Hannah called for her. Kelly sighed and leaned her elbows on the porch railing. Then she straightened her spine and tapped her fists on her thighs, like she always did when she wanted to smoke. Georgia pulled a necklace out of her pocket and offered it silently. She still wasn't sure why Kelly was here, but she never missed an opportunity to let non-autistic people stim.

"Mother would have lost her mind, watching you pick those peppers out," Kelly said.

She smiled when she said it, but Georgia wasn't sure it was a joke. It was just as likely to be a new way for the Grays to try to prod her toward their version of acceptable. She hedged with a half-joke of her own.

"Is there anything about me that doesn't make the Judge lose her mind?"

"She hasn't been fair to you," Kelly said while she wrapped the necklace chain around her fingers and tapped it against her chin. "I know it was Kyle who didn't want to get married—he just wasn't the type—but he never admitted that to the rest of the family. That wasn't fair of him."

Georgia clutched at her shirtsleeves and tried not to bring her hand up to her chin like Kelly was. The Grays didn't like her mirroring habits.

She said, "He would have told them, for me. I said he didn't have to. It wouldn't have helped."

"Why do you think that?" Kelly asked, staring.

"The word he wanted to say was 'aromantic,' but it just means he didn't have romantic relationships with people. You all already knew that, and it didn't change your expectations. You know Hannah and I are autistic, but knowing what it's called doesn't get you to listen to us or respect our boundaries, so why should knowing the name for what Kyle was make you understand him better?"

"So you told him to not let us try?"

"I told him he didn't have to."

The necklace chain dug deep into Kelly's knuckles when she clenched her fist. She stared off toward the street, and Georgia did, too, relieved to have a break from her intense eye contact.

After some thought, Kelly said, "We want to understand, Georgia, we do. But you have to understand us, too. We make suggestions because we care. We're family, and we want to be a part of raising Hannah with you."

"That's not your job," Georgia said. There were sirens going off in her mind again, warning her to guard her perimeter. "You're not her parents."

Kelly smacked her fist like a gavel against the porch railing. Georgia flinched.

"You don't hear a thing I say, do you?" Kelly spat.

Georgia wanted to say the feeling was mutual, but her tongue wouldn't move. Kelly unwrapped the necklace from her hand and left it tangled on the porch rail as she stomped across the porch toward Kyle's apartment.

"I tried to be nice about it," she muttered. "No one can say I didn't try."

The door to Kyle's apartment was unlocked, and Kelly had scattered papers all over the floor again. Georgia fumed. When had Kelly been in here? What had she been trying to be nice about? What was she going to try next?

Kelly picked up a book with pages marked and handed it to Georgia.

"These are the Vermont statutes regarding familial custody and visitation rights. As you'll see, based on the passages I've marked, grandparents do have rights in this state."

Georgia's blood froze into crystals that scraped inside her veins.

Kelly continued. "I think it would behoove us all to create an agreement to serve as a foundation, so that if something goes wrong we have rules to fall back on instead suing in court. Because we can sue in court if necessary. I bought Kyle that book and told him to make an agreement years ago, but he just said—"

"'Law is a hammer, and our relationship isn't a nail.'"

Kelly rolled her eyes. "I've tried to connect with you, Georgia, but this relationship, between you and my family, is still pretty nail-like from where I'm standing, so I'd like to get a firm grip on the hammer."

The book fell out of Georgia's shaking hands and hit the floor with a thump that made her recoil. Now was not a good time to go nonverbal, so she swallowed and gagged until she managed to force words out. Kelly watched her throat contort in silence.

"What do you think is going to go wrong?" Georgia said.

"What went wrong with that guy who was here last time I visited? Ben."

Georgia's mouth formed the word, "What?" but no sound came out.

"One minute you're going to dinner with him, and the next you won't even claim he's your friend. Have you spoken to him since?"

No, Georgia hadn't.

"You don't have any old friends from college or grad school. You burned bridges with the step-brother you supposedly loved so much, and you have no relationship whatsoever with your own parents. And what about your handsome new girlfriend?

How long is she going to last after the first time she pisses you off, huh?"

"Lauren," Georgia choked out. She couldn't explain right then that Lauren was different. That they understood each other.

"These are the people you like!" Kelly snapped. Her eye contact burned so badly Georgia had to look away, and her snarling left a bitter taste in Georgia's mouth. "So what happens to us? You never liked us. So what's stopping you from wadding us up and throwing us away like all the other people in your life? Why the hell should we trust you?"

The answer burst from Georgia's mouth so fast it felt like it'd skipped her clenched throat entirely and sprung directly from her heart. "Hannah!"

Kelly's face slackened, and her mouth hung open. Georgia cleared her throat and roared.

"Hannah loves you! I'd never take that away from her, no matter how much you piss me off or even how much you drive her crazy! God, who do you think I am?"

Georgia's outrage echoed off the walls of the apartment, because Kelly didn't reply. She stared at the floor for a long time, rolling and unrolling the curled corner of Kyle's rug with her foot.

Georgia took a moment to breathe before she concluded, "You don't need a hammer."

"Okay," Kelly whispered, not looking up from the floor. She walked out of the apartment and drove away.

CHAPTER THIRTY-ONE

The theme at the Healing House was regret. Sweater Vest Guy was on about his mom again, wishing she'd been better to him, wishing they'd had more time once things were good, and Lauren was slumped so far in her chair she was in danger of sliding onto the floor. It had been a while since Lauren had felt this disengaged.

"You look like you have something to say," Annabel told her.

It had also been a while since Annabel had felt the need to draw Lauren out, and Lauren didn't resist her. She said, "Are we going somewhere with this?"

"Where is it taking you?"

"In circles. Are we supposed to be perfect? If you got everything you wanted from your mom," Lauren glanced at the vest, "would that have been enough? Or would you want something else next? When are you satisfied?"

Georgia raised her hand. "Is it about the difference between need and want? You figure out what you need, and then you can be satisfied in pursuing that, even if it's not everything you want?"

"That's one way to look at it. What does regret tell us about what we need?"

"What we need is to let go and move on," Lauren said. "Isn't that what grief is? Saying goodbye to what's gone and readjusting to what's here?"

"Some things do need to be let go of," Annabel said. "Other things are worth holding on to. That's the decision we make, and sometimes regret. Mark, you had a thought?"

Lauren didn't listen to Mark or anyone else, not even Georgia, who was talking again about the epiphany she'd had with Kelly Gray. That story pinged something in the back of Lauren's mind, just outside her grasp. All the horrible lesbian custody stories, probably. She watched Georgia sketch a piece of elaborate crown molding until the meeting ended and they were released.

"Are you coming for dinner tomorrow?" Georgia asked while they waited for their order at the Catamount Café.

"I have dinner with Tracy and my mom. I could come over after, though. Spend the night?"

"Yes, please," Georgia said.

Her eyes lit up, even though her expression didn't change much. The tension that had brought Lauren's shoulders up to her ears relaxed at the sight. She did love to please Georgia.

She spent quite a bit of time on it that night, and she slept with her limbs thrown over Georgia despite the heat, too happy being close to her to let a little sweat separate them.

* * *

"I brought rolls," Lauren announced the next evening as she let herself into her mom's house. She kicked her shoes off and held the bag of frozen dinner rolls aloft for everyone to see.

"Pop 'em on that cookie sheet, the oven's preheated," Mom said, not looking up from the carrots on the cutting board.

Lauren stole a carrot slice. Tracy stole two more from Mom's other side while she scolded Lauren.

"This is why your father was all over me when I chopped vegetables," Mom whined. "He wasn't micromanaging. He was protecting me from you seagulls."

Her face only fell a little at the mention of Dad, and another joke had her spirits high again. Tracy forced her to sit at the table with a glass of wine, saying she'd finish salad prep. Lauren put the rolls in the oven and set a timer on her phone.

"When are you gonna bring your girlfriend to family dinner?" Tracy asked.

"Yes!" Mom yelled from the dining room. "Share Georgia with us!"

"Why would I want you contaminating her?" Lauren stuck her tongue out at Tracy and sat with Mom at the table.

"Maybe she'll be a good influence," Tracy said.

"She has been on you," Mom added. "I like that girl."

"I like her too," she said. Tracy laughed when Lauren's eyes lost focus, but she didn't care. "I'll ask if she and Hannah want to come next time we do this."

Mom clapped her hands and squealed. "Ooh, it's like I have my first grandbaby!"

"You had to make it weird," Tracy said.

Lauren was about to remind her mother that she shouldn't make sudden loud sounds around Hannah, which was more parental than she'd ever intended to be, when her phone rang.

"Rolls done already?" Tracy asked.

It wasn't the timer. It was Ava Hayden calling.

"Rolls need three more minutes. Hang on, I gotta take this."

The bathroom at the end of the hall was the traditional place for taking a call during family time. It was quiet and out of range of Dad's commentary about how cell phones were damaging the nuclear family. Lauren took a deep breath and answered the call. She hadn't expected one, but it made sense that after all the encouragement Ava had given, she'd call to explain why she was turning Lauren down. No reason to get excited or panicky.

"Hi! I'm sorry to call after hours," Ava said. "I just couldn't wait to tell you. You got the job!"

Lauren dropped her phone in the sink. Her reflection in the mirror was pale, shocked and shaking. Panicky.

She fished the phone out of the sink and dropped it on the tile floor with a horrible clatter before she managed to fumble it back up to her ear.

"Sorry, sorry!" she said.

Ava laughed. "No problem, I thought you'd be surprised. Not that you should be. So, the onboarding process..."

Lauren was going to have to call back tomorrow and ask Ava to repeat everything she was saying. Right now all she could do was say "yes ma'am" and "thank you" over and over. Tracy knocked on the door, asking what all the noise was about.

"I'm at dinner," Lauren managed to explain to Ava.

"Of course. I'll email you the details. I hope your dinner guests are proud of you!"

Lauren left the bathroom and brushed past Tracy, her questions like mosquitoes in her ear. She sat down at the table. The food was served but untouched.

"I have an announcement."

Tracy shut up. Mom set her wineglass down.

"I got a management level job in Newton, Massachusetts. I'm moving."

Mom clapped again, half drowning Tracy's protest that she hadn't heard anything about Lauren applying for jobs.

"I didn't want anyone to make a big deal about it because I wasn't going to get the job. But I...I did, I guess."

"I'm so proud of you!" Mom said. "Your father would be so proud of you. We knew you could do it."

"No one knows if I can do it yet," Lauren muttered.

No one had asked if she even wanted to. Then again, was that even a question? Of course she wanted to. She'd fought her father to study computer science, with the understanding that it was something she could finally be great at. She wanted to be great, to be appreciated. She just hadn't expected to be. That's why she felt like a sword was dangling over her head; it was too good to be true, and she was nervous about not deserving the gift Ava Hayden was offering.

She'd almost convinced herself of that when Tracy cut straight to the true heart of Lauren's rumination.

"Georgia doesn't know about this either, does she?"

For a second, there was utter quiet, inside Lauren's skull and outside of it.

Then Mom said, "Well, she'll be happy, too, won't she? If she doesn't support your ambitions—"

"Long distance might be tough for them. Her and Hannah."

Mom scoffed. "Lesbians do long distance all the time. After all, there are only so many of them in one—"

"Thank you for your brilliant insight into lesbian culture, Mother," Tracy said. "Let's eat in silence for a while, shall we?"

Lauren stuffed a bite of lasagna in her mouth and kept her head down. Conversation eventually flowed around her like a river around a rock, wearing at her from all sides. She didn't eat dessert or thank her mother for cooking. It was her turn to do dishes, but Tracy followed her to the kitchen and took the soap out of her hands.

"Why did you do this to yourself?" Tracy said.

"Do what? Work hard and finally get recognized for it? Gee, what a tragedy."

Tracy plugged the sink and let it fill. The kitchen overflowed with her silence.

Lauren finally relented. "I told you. I didn't think this would happen. I'm not trying to shoot myself in the foot."

"And yet, behold the limp."

"What am I supposed to do, turn the job down?"

"You could."

Sometimes, Lauren wondered if she and Tracy had been raised by different families. She'd dared to consider what Tracy was saying once before, when she'd been torn between the college with the best art program and the college her girlfriend was going to. Dad's message was clear and hard as diamonds: Don't you dare give up anything for a girl. Opportunity is rare and fleeting. There are always other girls.

She'd asked him if there would have been another girl for him if he'd left Mom to live in a bigger city, like he'd wanted to.

He hadn't answered. His regrets hung over Lauren's entire life, and she wasn't going to repeat his mistakes.

"No," she said. "I can't."

CHAPTER THIRTY-TWO

Hannah wanted company but not to be read to tonight, so Georgia sat next to her bed with her own book. She'd decided to finish *Journey to a Woman*, the book Lauren had picked up the first night she came here, but she wasn't making much progress. Her mind kept wandering to the idea of keeping the axolotls in Hannah's room, so they'd be safe from Turing if Lauren lived here.

How long did you have to date someone before it was appropriate to talk about moving in with them? Should she be thinking this way, or was she coming on too strong? Was she causing Lauren's odd, distant moments lately? Should she not have asked Lauren to come over tonight?

No. Lauren had asked to come over because she was happy here. Georgia knew that.

She was asking the Internet how long she should wait to mention the possibility of cohabitation when she got a text from Lauren saying she was here.

Door's open, she replied, then she kissed Hannah goodnight and went downstairs.

"We should get you a key so you can come in anytime," she said, because the Internet had suggested that as a solid first step. She hugged Lauren, eager to feel her powerful grip, but her arms only squeezed briefly.

Alarm bells rang. Should Georgia not have said what she had about the key?

"What's wrong?" she said.

"Nothing," Lauren said. "Can we have some tea? I know it's not your big thing anymore, but I could use some."

Lauren knew where everything in the kitchen was. She filled the electric kettle herself and pulled out two mugs at random. Georgia dug the raspberry tea out of the cabinet by the stove.

"Tell me about your day?" Lauren asked.

Georgia monologued while the kettle boiled, barely listening to herself. Lauren's hair was spiked in the way it got when she'd been running her fingers through it, which was a sign of stress. Her shoulders were rounded, and she kept her eyes off Georgia like she was afraid there was something in them Georgia would see.

"What's wrong?" Georgia asked again.

Lauren poured boiling water into her mug and bobbed the tea bag.

"You remember how Ava Hayden told me to apply for a job with her company? I got it."

"Congratulations!" Georgia hugged Lauren tight, but she didn't hug back. Maybe congratulations weren't in order. "Is there something wrong with the job?"

Lauren chuckled. "Even if there was, it can't be worse than the job I have. Hayden's offer is fantastic, with plenty of room to move up in her company or elsewhere."

Georgia squinted. "You'd take this job because you want a different one?"

"Not everyone gets their dream job right away, like you," Lauren said, smiling and warm with affection at last.

But she picked at a chip in the lip of her mug. It was the sort of thing people did when they had to tell Georgia something bad.

"The job's in Newton, Massachusetts. About three hours away from here."

"Oh." Ava had said there were local jobs, but they must have been filled. Georgia covered Lauren's hand with her own, trying to show sympathy for the disappointing news. "I'm sorry that's not going to work out."

Lauren turned her hand over and twined their fingers.

"No, I'm taking the job, and I want to talk about what that means for us. I want to talk about a long-distance relationship."

Georgia's brain short-circuited. She blinked slowly, as if that would change what she'd just heard.

"But you like living in Holderness. Why would you leave?"

"Holderness is a small pond. I want to have a big career."

Lauren's voice sounded like it was already three hours away. Georgia squeezed her hand.

"No, your dad wanted that. You always talk about your dad when you talk about leaving. I listen very carefully. I've learned how to listen."

"You're not listening now."

The life drained out of Georgia's fantasies about moving the axolotls, the visions turning inside out and stretching, a happy ending in reverse. The real world grew distant, too. Lauren's hand in Georgia's was neither warm nor cold, grasping tight nor letting go. Georgia watched her scratch at her own scalp on the other side of a thick pane of glass that had formed between them. Georgia thrashed in a tank of murky water, alone already, even though Lauren was still here. Why did everything always change?

"You're leaving," Georgia said.

"Yeah. But I'm not leaving you. We'll do long distance. People do it all the time."

The distance between them would only get longer, Georgia knew. Lauren wasn't leaving just for now. She was leaving for good.

"And it wouldn't have to be forever. Newton's a great place, with good schools and lots of old buildings, plus it's near Boston. Wouldn't that be great?"

"No."

It was the only clear thought in Georgia's head. A thousand others bubbled—Why was this happening? What would she tell Hannah? How could Lauren really want to leave Holderness, to leave everything she loved? She did love Georgia, right? And Hannah? And her family? Georgia had thought she'd understood Lauren, thought she knew what was happening between them. Had she really been so wrong? Of course she had. It was stupid to hope, hopeless to want. What would Hannah think? Why?— but above them all was the banshee scream of *No*.

Lauren's voice was a distant echo. "No?"

Georgia pulled her hand away and tangled her fingers in her hair. She yanked hard.

"I knew it," Lauren whispered. She backed away until her hip struck the opposite counter. "With Ben and Kelly, the way you acted when they did anything you didn't like, I knew you were gonna do this. I thought you'd understand. I thought you'd be proud of me, happy for me, but I goddamn knew you wouldn't. Why?"

What about your handsome new girlfriend? Kelly had asked. What happens after the first time she pisses you off?

Georgia wanted to answer Lauren's question, to explain that she didn't understand, that change was a yawning void of terror she didn't know how to bridge, but she couldn't. If she opened her mouth right now, only screams would come out. Georgia burrowed into her cardigan and rocked on her heels.

"Okay, Georgia," Lauren said. "If that's what you want."

She set her mug down on the counter so gently it didn't make a sound. She went to the door, put her shoes on, and walked away, which wasn't what Georgia wanted at all. Georgia didn't want any of this.

And now she didn't have it.

A few hours later, Lauren called. Georgia couldn't bear to answer, but she opened the voice mail. Lauren was a person who said "sorry," so maybe she would take it all back. Couldn't they both just take it all back?

"I know you're processing," the recording said, firm and final. "Take your time, and when you're ready to talk—"

Georgia deleted the message. There was nothing to talk about.

* * *

For the first few days, Georgia swam quietly in her tank, apart from the world she waded through. *I probably should have listened to the message*, she thought vaguely. Maybe Lauren would call again. Maybe Georgia would swim to the surface one morning and none of this would be real.

Lauren didn't call.

"Mommy," Hannah asked on day five, while she was eating breakfast at the table, "when is Lauren coming to visit us again?"

Georgia hadn't practiced how to talk to Hannah about this. She'd kept hoping she wouldn't have to, because she wasn't sure she could. Too late to plan now. What would Kyle say, if he'd been stupid enough to end up having to say it?

"You know how Granny and Gramps live far away, and we don't see them?" Georgia began, referring to her distant parents.

Hannah nodded.

"Lauren got a special job, so she lives far away now, too. She won't visit us anymore."

It took so long for Hannah to reply that anyone else would think the conversation was over. Georgia knew better. She watched her daughter chase the last bits of scrambled egg around the plate while the clock ticked like a bomb, and she tried to brace herself.

"Why didn't she say goodbye?"

That was most painful question she could have asked. Lauren would never have left without saying goodbye if Georgia hadn't melted down. Lauren would never have left at all if Georgia hadn't let her in. This was all Georgia's fault. How could she tell her daughter that?

"Lauren wanted to talk to you, but she was too sad," Georgia said. "I told her I'd do it for her."

"Will you tell her I said goodbye, too?"

"Yes, I will."

"Thank you," Hannah said. She abandoned the rest of her breakfast.

Georgia had never lied to Hannah before. Thank god she'd managed to pull it off.

* * *

At the Healing House that week, Annabel stopped her to ask why Lauren hadn't come.

"She's moving," Georgia said. "She isn't coming back."

"I'm sorry to hear that."

Georgia didn't know what the look on Annabel's face meant, and she didn't waste energy caring. Hannah was waiting for her in the corner, ear defenders on, sunk deep in a beanbag chair and drumming her heels against it.

"How was your session?" Georgia asked her.

Deb replied instead. "Hannah told me she was thinking about something and didn't want to be bothered, so we stayed in the corner tonight."

That was a vast improvement over past incidents, when Hannah had responded to interruptions by growling and snapping her jaws, so Georgia said, "Thank you for telling Ms. Deb what you needed. Are you ready to go to dinner, or do you want to think for a few more minutes?"

"I want to go home."

Georgia did a mental review of the pantry, but if Hannah wanted to disrupt her own routine, she probably wasn't going to eat. Deb helped her out of the beanbag chair, and she headed toward the car with Georgia trailing behind, her water-tank mind stormy with worry. She tried to give Hannah space, but she couldn't help glancing at her over and over again as she drove home, which made Hannah twist up like a pretzel in the corner of her seat, face turned toward the window.

What would Kyle have done now? Georgia had no idea. Kyle would have had better judgment than to date, break up, and put himself in this situation. Kyle wouldn't have fallen in love. Georgia wished he were here. She wished he'd never left.

The crunch of gravel under her car tires as she arrived home was comforting. The utter darkness of both sides of the house was not. She looked up, but it was too cloudy to see the stars.

Inside, Georgia asked, "What do you want for dinner?" in the vain hope that Hannah might have an answer.

Hannah picked up her stegosaurus and pressed the spines on its back under her fingernails. She rarely stimmed in harmful ways, but when her stress levels were critical, stomping and shouting simply wouldn't do. Georgia kept her hands at her sides to keep herself from yanking on her hair. Panicking now wouldn't help either of them. What would Kyle do?

Hannah said, "Abby's mom and dad divorced, so they live in different places."

"Yes, that's true."

"They're sad to not be a family, but they both see Abby, so they don't have to say goodbye."

Georgia's face tightened to hold back tears. "It's not the same with Lauren and me. We weren't married, and we weren't a family."

Hannah's eyes grew wide with rage. She crossed her arms and squeezed herself tightly, digging the stegosaurus into her ribs.

"I want to see Lauren," she said.

"I'm sorry, baby, you can't. What else do you want to do?"

"I want to see Lauren!"

Georgia took a cautious step forward, hands open in front of her. "I know you do, and I'm sorry. Lauren moved away."

"I want to see Lauren!" Hannah screamed. She spun. She raised the stegosaurus over her head.

Georgia leapt forward. One arm gripped Hannah's waist, and she snared the stegosaurus in her other hand. She turned Hannah around. If she'd thrown the toy, she would have hit the axolotl tank.

With Hannah facing her again, Georgia let go. She kept her hands ready, but Hannah's face was scrunched and red now, not dark and wide.

"I want to see Daddy," she sobbed.

"I know, baby," Georgia choked out. "I do too."

They clung to each other, crumpled on the floor, until Hannah cried herself to sleep. Georgia wasn't very strong, but she found it in herself to heave her daughter off the floor and carry her up the stairs to bed. Teeth hadn't been brushed, nor clothes changed, but she could do that if she woke up. It was a strange night, and no routine was strong enough to stabilize it anyway.

She left the front door open so she could hear if Hannah called for her, and she sat on Kyle's side of the porch. They'd been sitting here together when they decided to have Hannah. Kyle had been so calm, so brave, choosing a path with her that so few people understood. He would know what she needed to hear right now.

"What we need," said a voice from her memory, not Kyle's but no less precious, "is to let go and move on. Isn't that what grief is?"

Georgia stood. She had made a mistake, but she couldn't wallow in it. If she kept holding on to her grief, she'd have no hands free for Hannah to hold and none to reach out with.

Her phone weighed down the pocket of her cardigan. She pulled it out and clutched it tightly for a moment, then relaxed her fingers one by one and stared down her reflection in Kyle's apartment windows as she dialed. It was time to let go.

"Kelly, hi. Look, I need to deal with the apartment, and…"

Georgia took a deep breath and managed not to cry again. "I could use some help."

CHAPTER THIRTY-THREE

Ava Hayden wanted Lauren at work by October, so Lauren pulled her life apart at the seams with brutal efficiency. Ending her current lease early cost her dearly, so she settled on a beat-up apartment in Newton that rented month-to-month, planning to move again once her new and improved income replenished her savings.

Len seemed panicked when she handed in her notice, as if three resignations in as many months had finally clued him in that there might be something wrong at Green Mountain Software.

"Is there any way I can convince you to stay? A managerial position?"

"Too little too late," Lauren told him.

The day before she cut off her post office box subscription, she got a letter from the Healing House. Annabel was sorry to hear that Lauren would no longer be joining them, but hoped her new horizons were bright. There was also a survey about the program, because it was still new and Annabel wanted feedback to improve.

Under the section marked Additional Comments and Suggestions, Lauren almost wrote "Don't let your group members date," but Julie and Mark's tentative pseudo-courtship was going fine. This was Lauren's fault, not Annabel's. She threw the whole survey in the recycling bin.

"Are you sure you don't want help packing?" Tracy asked over the phone two days before Lauren was scheduled to depart.

Lauren winced at the twinge in her back when she lifted a box of books, but she said, "Yes, I'm sure. You have your hands full getting the store ready to open. I'm sorry I can't help you with that."

"Thank you for putting your move off for a day so you can be here."

"It's the grand opening," Lauren said as she filled another box. "How could I miss it? I'll see you tomorrow."

Tracy said goodbye, leaving Lauren to pack. When another box was full, she closed it and carried it toward the pile against the living room wall. Turing lashed out at her ankles as she passed his hiding spot under the couch. Lauren screeched, dropped her phone, and spilled the box of books. She swore as she washed out the deep scratch, but not at the cat. He had never moved before, so he was scared.

"You'll feel better when we're settled, buddy," she told him while she pressed a paper towel against the cut. She should put a bandage on it, but she'd already packed those.

When, she wondered, was she going to feel better?

Turing stayed hidden, burbling and spitting. She hadn't sworn at him, but he clearly had some choice words for her. Lauren spent a few precious minutes looking up ways to soothe an agitated cat. The effort set her back more than an hour, and the night had turned into a bruised morning before Lauren finished packing and went to bed.

* * *

Ashburn's Art Supply Store, always a gleaming star among the dusty and ever-changing storefronts of Main Street, dazzled like the sun on the first Saturday of autumn. The clean new awning shaded the textured marble ramp that had replaced the awkward tile steps up to the door. A friend of Mom's was handing out biodegradable paper cups of hot apple cider to everyone who passed, not just those who entered, and as the sun set, he plugged in fairy lights. The Lions Club popcorn cart was in attendance to celebrate the opening, and a few other stores had seized the opportunity and were advertising sales and extended hours, which turned a stretch of several blocks into an impromptu festival. A photographer from the newspaper was there to capture it all.

Lauren took her free cider, and when Mom's friend told her he didn't want to take a break, she made her way inside.

"Hey you!" Tracy said from the checkout counter, which was now right next to the door. She didn't have to shout across the whole store to be heard, and the displays lined up along the counter were in no danger of being blown away by a draft from the propped open entrance. "What do you think?"

A customer pulled Tracy's attention away, which was fine, because Lauren was still processing her answer.

The aisles were short and angled instead of running the length of the store back to front. Everything was visible, and there was more of it. Tracy had explained the flow of products, the way the inventory wound like a river from shelf to shelf, and how she'd surveyed a dozen other stores and interviewed countless customers to find the exact pattern that led from one art form to another. Lauren hadn't understood it, but looking at it made sense in a way that resonated in her eye and her gut.

Her mother waved from the back of the store. Lauren wound her way toward the new station, where Mom was going to make custom frames like she'd wanted to for years. Dad had always said they'd never compete with Walmart's plastic cheap-os, but Tracy was willing to take a chance that he was wrong. Mom, after all, had never bought plastic.

"I already have two orders!" Mom bragged. "People who can afford art can afford good frames. And don't you love the counter?"

Lauren did love the counter. It was made out of the salvaged wood from the staircase, which had been replaced by a small but accessible elevator with an old-fashioned golden grate.

"Have there ever been this many people here?" Lauren asked, counting heads.

"This many people wouldn't fit before," Mom confirmed.

Tracy waved from the checkout counter, so Lauren made her way back over to her, bumping into a woman in a wheelchair whose lap was filled with art supplies. Wheelchairs hadn't been able to get into the store before, so Lauren hadn't thought to watch out for them.

"Well?" Tracy asked.

Lauren slipped behind the counter and opened up the second register so she could help clear the crowd of customers in line. She didn't hesitate to do it, and she didn't think about all the sad summer days of before, when she'd frothed at the mouth at the sound of a cash register.

"I think it should have always been this way," she said.

It didn't cross her mind right then that it could keep on being this way, if that was what she wanted.

She worked side by side with her sister, too elated to be exhausted, for over an hour. Mom's friend brought them popcorn and second servings of cider, then sent Lauren outside for a break. The streetlights had come on, and the popcorn stand was packing up to leave. A quiet night was filling in the gaps where joyful locals had been. Lauren settled in the chair behind the cider table, filled a paper cup, and found herself handing it to Ben.

"Hi. Nice party," he said.

Seeing him was like a pin to the balloon of Lauren's mood. This happy beginning had made her forget, for a while, about everything that was over.

"Abby'll be sorry she missed seeing you. I was going to bring her, but tomorrow's the first time her mom is letting Hannah come over, on the condition that she finishes all her chores tonight. I'm sure you've heard all about it from Hannah. It's too important to reschedule."

Lauren ignored the implication that she'd heard anything at all from Hannah and tried to put the conversation to an end by saying, "Tell Abby I said hi."

And goodbye, she didn't add.

"Will do." Ben took a swallow of cider, flinched when it burnt his tongue, and continued. "I heard you got a job with Ava! I set her up with Georgia hoping she'd put in a good word for me when they hung out, but no such luck. I'm glad some good got done, though. Is Georgia happy for you?"

"Not remotely."

Ben paused in the act of blowing on his cider. "She's mad at you too? What'd you do?"

Lauren sighed and leaned back in the folding chair until it creaked. If he wanted a conversation, so be it. "The job's in Newton. Georgia doesn't want me to go."

"But you do?"

"You don't get many chances like this in life, right? Thanks for making it happen, even though it wasn't what you were planning."

"Sure," Ben said. He didn't point out, like Georgia would have, that her answer didn't address the question. "When are you leaving?"

"Tomorrow afternoon."

"Good luck, then."

Lauren nodded and filled a paper cup for another visitor. Ben hung around while his cider cooled, but when she didn't engage him any further, he walked away. Tracy came out shortly after to pack up the table and chair.

"Go get some rest," she said when Lauren offered to help close the store. "You have a long day tomorrow."

So Lauren left her family to their work and went home alone.

* * *

"Whose idea was it to get up this early?" Lauren grumbled as she tripped into her sneakers at six the next morning.

Turing growled from under the couch. Lauren slid his breakfast closer to him and tutted for a moment before she left.

It was a ten-minute drive to the Appalachian Trail and a two-hour hike to the cliff and back, so she needed to be quick to keep her day on schedule.

The trail was different than when she'd been here with Georgia and Hannah, dry and lush instead of muddy. She made good time up the steep hills. Being alone in the quiet, with only the earliest of birds, gave her more time to think than she should have allowed herself, so she needed this hike to be over quickly. Scientific names ticked off automatically as she went, barely interrupting her thoughts.

Pinus resinosa, red pine. (This job is exactly what I was working toward.)

Quercus velutina, black oak (So what if it isn't what I asked for? I earned it. It's mine.)

Catharus guttatus, hermit thrush (Long distance would be too hard on Georgia and Hannah. It's not realistic. Not practical.)

Ganoderma applanatum, artist's conk (Georgia made her decision, and I've made mine.)

Sorbaria sorbifolia, false spiraea (If she won't come with me, I'll go on without her. There are other girls.)

There were also other jobs. Mom had read her an article from the paper yesterday about Jamar's new business, a sweet little startup for farmers. He wasn't leaving Holderness anytime soon.

Lauren tripped on a root and scraped her hands on a lichen-covered rock (genus *Lepraria*). She needed to stay focused. She needed to be the driven go-getter everyone knew she could be, not a heartsick wimp who wanted to cry over dirty jeans and bleeding palms.

"Get up," she told herself. It sounded just like when Dad said it. He'd be so proud of her, wouldn't he?

At the peak of the trail, Lauren rinsed her hands off with her water bottle and refused to sit and rest. She had a schedule to keep today.

Looking out over the swell and sigh of the mountains slowed her down, though. A memory rose like the fog, one she kept wrapped around her heart so tightly the others couldn't pierce her too deeply. She'd been Hannah's age, and it was the first time she had ever completed this hike. She'd looked down on this valley for the first time, a river of red and yellow and fading green. Her father had sat beside her. The smell of him, mineral oil and aftershave on the autumn breeze, had wafted familiarly over the new scene. He'd put his arm around her, so gently she hadn't flinched. He'd kissed the top of her head.

"You know what I love most about you, Lauren?" he'd said. "Everything. Every little thing."

Now, Lauren smelled autumn and nothing else. She wiped her shirtsleeve across her eyes, and there were two tears, two streaks of damp, on the fabric. It was time to go.

"Goodbye, Daddy," she said.

She turned back to the trailhead and went home.

* * *

Tracy was late to help Lauren load the U-Haul van, but they made good time. Mom pulled up ten minutes before two and, instead of loading the last odds and ends into the van, she started transferring her essentials from her own car to Lauren's.

"Mom's riding in my car with you?" Lauren asked. She wasn't sure if liked the idea of being in the van alone.

"No, Mom's driving your car and I'm riding with you."

"Should Mom be driving that far?"

Tracy huffed and tossed her purse into the passenger seat of the van. "She doesn't want to ride in the big rig, and I don't want to listen to three hours of NPR podcasts. I assumed you'd rather avoid that fate too."

Lauren's eyes stung. Georgia loved NPR podcasts.

"Thank you."

She buckled Turing's cat carrier into the middle seat of the van, cooing at him while he cried, and climbed into the driver's seat. The Ashburn caravan set out for Massachusetts at two o'clock on the dot.

CHAPTER THIRTY-FOUR

When Kelly had said she'd bring packing boxes, Georgia had expected the brown ones they sold in stores, the kind that smelled inky and made her queasy, not the dented variety Kelly was piling on Kyle's porch now. Georgia read the label on one: 37.5 percent alcohol.

"Is this something I should be worried about?"

"Liquor store boxes are sturdy, small, and, most importantly, free. Best thing ever when you're moving." Kelly waited for Georgia to unlock Kyle's apartment door. "How'd it go at your group? Any good advice about how to handle this with Hannah?"

Georgia took a deep breath of the clean, vacant air in the apartment. She and Hannah had left the windows open when they locked up last night.

"Even better: Deb, one of the volunteers, came all the way out here on Friday afternoon to get us started on Hannah's bedroom, taking her clothes out of the closet here and hanging them up next door. We'd already brought a few toys and books over, so that wasn't too big a step. Hannah and I got through the rest of her room on our own yesterday."

There was a dent in the bedroom wall where Hannah had thrown a talking rabbit with dead batteries, because she had thought it was ruined for good, but that had been the only damage. A couple of AA batteries and a nap later, the meltdown moment had worked itself out. Georgia had worn steel-toe boots and earplugs all morning in preparation for much worse.

The fact that it hadn't been worse was a good sign, according to Annabel, though it didn't mean the healing was done. There would be more moments like those over time.

Annabel had said there'd be more moments like the one Georgia and Hannah had shared last night, too. They'd cooked dinner here and eaten at the table one last time, then danced while they washed the dishes. The air in the apartment had filled with the smell of rice, beans, and lightly fried tortillas. Finally, they had opened the windows, letting out the mild, delicious scent of their dinner along with the last of Kyle.

"We brought the cast iron skillet home with us, too," Georgia told Kelly. "I hope that's okay."

Kelly set the stack of boxes she'd gathered on the couch, nodding. "Dad bought each of us a skillet for our college graduation, so everyone else in the family has one already. You should have one too."

Everyone else in the family, Georgia thought to herself. Kelly probably just meant Hannah, if she meant anything particular at all, but it was a battle to stop herself from repeating the phrase aloud, over and over until her tongue could no longer pronounce these strange, sweet words.

"Did you bring the list of what everybody wants?" she said instead. "Should we put things aside if someone might want them? I have plastic tubs. That might be better than the boxes for stuff that's nice, right?"

"Good idea."

Kelly didn't smile, though. Georgia held eye contact with her as long as she could stand, waiting to hear what else was on Kelly's mind.

"And Hannah's sure she doesn't want to be here for the rest of it? We can wait," Kelly said.

Georgia picked up a box simply to have something to do with her hands. "She's sure. She said goodbye to all the rooms and closets except Kyle's bedroom last night, and now she's spending the day with her friend Abby. She'll be home in time to have dinner with us."

Kelly picked up a box of her own. "What about you, then? Do you know where you want to start?"

Both of them looked up the stairs, at the closed door to Kyle's bedroom. All Georgia knew about the state of that room was that Kelly had thrown away the bed sheets. No one had set foot in it since...

The thought left claw marks in Georgia's mind, but she had to think it. No one had been inside Kyle's room since the body had been taken away.

"Not looking forward to being in there again," Kelly said.

"Me neither."

Georgia did her best to smile so Kelly would know how glad she was that they were doing this together, so Kelly would know that she didn't have to be alone when she went in that room this time. Georgia hadn't thought about how awful that must have been until now. She hadn't thought about a lot of things Kelly must have been going through.

"There's a lot of books and papers?" she suggested, because it would get them both away from the staircase and the door above.

"Books and papers," Kelly agreed. "I usually play music while I work. Will that bother you?"

"I love music."

Kelly queued up a playlist on her phone. The apartment filled with joyful sounds again, the same as it had last night. It was almost like it used to be, even as it came apart, and the hair on the back of Georgia's neck settled down. They designated a plastic bin for family mementos, to be filled as they came upon things, then settled in to sort paperwork from the fireproof filing cabinets in the aired-out living room.

"You should keep these tax forms for seven years, then shred them," Kelly instructed when she came upon them. "Unless you want me to take them? I paid his taxes this year, so I have all those documents already."

"Oh. Thank you." Georgia had completely forgotten that Kyle was supposed to have paid taxes.

"Thanking me for something helpful I did without asking? You really have turned over a new leaf," Kelly said. She pulled a box toward her and wrote "Kyle Financial Documents" on the top and all four sides in marker. After what looked like a dramatic fight with her own throat, she added, "Thank you for inviting me to do this with you."

"Thank you for helping. I couldn't do it on my own. That's two thank-yous from me now, if you want to keep count."

Kelly reached up to shove her, like she used to do with Kyle, and stopped herself. Georgia bumped their shoulders together.

"I'm okay with you touching me, I think. I'll let you know if I need space. Are you hungry?"

"Pretty much always."

Sandwiches were easy to assemble to taste, so Georgia presented Kelly with an assortment of ingredients, including the leftover condiments from Hannah's birthday party, and put ham and cheese on wheat bread for herself. Kelly added a horrific number of pickles to hers.

"Let's eat on the porch," Georgia suggested, because the light breeze would blow the smell away from her.

The day was warming up quickly, like the weather had forgotten it was autumn now, but the trees were turning. Half the leaves on a grand black oak across the street were blazing red.

Georgia remembered Hannah chanting after their hike with Lauren, "Orange leaves and yellow leaves and leaves like blueberry guts!" The memory made her own guts curdle.

Kelly didn't comment on Georgia's unfinished sandwich. She made quick work of her own and dove right back into the last file cabinet. There was only one drawer left.

"Bingo!" she cheered when she opened it.

Four identical photo albums stood upright in the drawer. Kelly pulled the first one out and ran a loving hand over the cover.

"Katherine's going to make copies of all these photos for everyone. Do you want them too?"

Georgia nodded. She'd never been much for family albums, but she didn't want to be excluded, and Hannah might like to have them someday.

"I know Katherine makes you nuts with all her picture taking. Dad was the same way, and Mom is definitely sick of it. She loved it when your girlfriend told Katherine to take video instead. Oh, look at this one! We threw a party for Mom when she became a judge."

Kelly pointed to a photo of the three Gray children hanging their heads while Judge Gray wielded an inflatable gavel. The littlest kid was definitely Kyle, all leg then just like when Georgia knew him. Georgia would have loved to see it if she weren't so worried she had the same guilty look on her face.

"How is Lauren?" Kelly asked, like Georgia knew she would.

"She got a new job and moved away, so she's probably fine."

Kelly raised an eyebrow, like Kyle used to do. "Probably? You broke up with her?"

"I had to. She's not coming back to Holderness."

"You've never heard of long distance?"

Georgia rolled her eyes. "Long distance is for people who are going to end up in the same place eventually. People who want the same things. She's just going to move farther away because that's what she says she wants."

"And you, what? Grew roots?"

The world wobbled on its axis, and Georgia dug her fingers into the carpet to try to get a grip.

"I like Holderness."

"As much as you like Lauren?"

Georgia squeezed her eyes shut and said, "I don't want Hannah to move around all the time like I did. I want her to have a home."

Kelly nudged Georgia until she opened her eyes, then pointed at a finger painting on Kyle's wall that Hannah had made at school. It said, "Home is where the heart is."

"So you weren't planning to move," she said. "You weren't planning on Hannah either. Or Kyle. Do you regret it?"

Georgia took a deep breath and remembered the smell of baby wipes, birthday candles, and burnt rice. It was the smell of family, of home, gone but never to be forgotten. How could she regret that?

Her regrets were more recent. She doubled over, trying to hide the tears in her eyes.

"I already said no. And I really won't move."

"Okay, so find another option. You're both smart. Put your heads together and think of something."

Georgia groaned.

"How bad was it?" Kelly asked. "Will she not talk to you?"

"She called. I didn't answer," Georgia confessed.

She expected Kelly to snap, to hit her limit, and throw the book at Georgia like she had in the past. Her judgment would be righteous this time, because Georgia was so very guilty. Was burning metaphorical bridges still considered arson? Did the past few weeks of misery count as time served?

Judgment didn't come. Instead, Kelly set the photo album in her lap aside and patted Georgia's knee.

"Okay, take a breath," she said. "You have 'thank you' down. Now let's practice 'sorry.' We need to build a case for why she should talk to you. What's her favorite flower?"

Georgia looked up helplessly.

"Well, lilies are remorseful," Kelly said.

"No! Lilies are poisonous to cats! A lot of flowers are, actually." Georgia considered the question. "Could I give her catnip?"

Kelly cocked her head. "It's weird, but relevant to her interests. Probably a winner. Now, menu. What can you cook that all three of you are willing to eat? Hannah's cute factor is gonna be essential, so no picking things out like with the curry."

"Not steak, but maybe—"

Tires crunched the gravel outside. For a brief, ridiculous moment, Georgia hoped it might be Lauren, but Ben Lennox appeared at the open window.

"Can we talk?" he asked.

Changing gears set Georgia's teeth on edge, but talking to Ben might be good practice for rebuilding bridges—he'd settled things with his ex-wife so Hannah could be with Abby today, after all—so she went onto the porch. Kelly conspicuously edged closer to the window to listen.

"I know you don't think we're friends anymore, but I care about you, so I thought you should know I saw Lauren yesterday. She said something about not getting many chances in life. Your last chance with her is today. She's leaving this afternoon."

He stared at Georgia, but she took a moment to give him the reaction he seemed to be waiting for.

"It's afternoon now, Ben!" she wailed.

"Then go—ow!" Kelly stuck her head out the window so fast she smacked it on the frame. "Go now!"

"The case, the flowers…"

"Forget that!"

Georgia yanked her keys out of her pocket and dropped them. "Hannah needs to get picked up."

"I can do that," Ben and Kelly both said. Ben stepped back, letting Kelly take over.

"We got it covered," Kelly told her. "You do what you need to do."

Georgia leapt into her car and tore out of the driveway toward Lauren's apartment.

CHAPTER THIRTY-FIVE

Route Seven was a nice ride, south along the mountains. The U-Haul van sat higher than any car Lauren had driven before, and the weight of it created a lot of momentum on the downhill slopes, so she eased along the highway at slightly below the speed limit. Half a dozen cars passed her and zipped forward. Lauren didn't let them rush her. It was nice to do something that completely consumed her focus, but she adjusted quickly and felt her mind wandering toward the sad corners she'd been trying to avoid.

On the right they passed the crumbling house and sagging pool where Lauren's school friend Carrie's uncle had taught her how to swim. Lauren had been desperate to learn before her father got it in his head to teach her, because he kept saying he was just going to throw her in. Carrie's uncle trained dogs for a living, so he was patient and gentle. The way Georgia treated Hannah reminded Lauren of him.

Ten miles past that was the Apple Shack. Lauren ignored it as she approached, then glanced back in the rearview mirror at the last second. Cookie and Louise Crocker had run the Apple Shack together for as long as Lauren had been alive. They were sisters.

Lauren made eye contact with Tracy. That was a mistake, because it gave Tracy permission to talk.

"So Georgia never called you back? You didn't get a chance to say goodbye to Hannah?"

"No."

"Did you call again?"

"Why should I? I'm not the only one who has a phone."

Tracy leaned toward Lauren. Lauren leaned away.

"Her meltdown sounded pretty major. What if she's changed her mind, and she just needs you to take the first step before she can apologize?"

Lauren snorted derisively at that beautiful idea. "Georgia's not sorry, and she doesn't change her mind."

"She changed her mind about you."

Lauren stepped on the gas as if she could outrun this conversation.

"You don't want her to change her mind," Tracy said. "You don't want the temptation."

"Does everyone on planet Earth think they know what I goddamn want?" Lauren yelled.

It echoed in the tiny cabin, but Tracy wasn't chastened. She slumped back into her seat and swung her feet up on the dash. "Fine. You tell me what you want."

"I want my cleaning deposit back, so put your feet down." She shoved at Tracy's sneakers.

Tracy didn't budge. She said, "Look, I know what Dad always said about me. That I was superficial, going nowhere, not special like you…"

"You're special, Tracy," Lauren insisted. "You're wonderful."

"I know that too. My life might not be anything big or radical, but I'm happy. Are you?"

Lauren flexed her hands on the steering wheel. "I will be. I'm taking a step forward. That's important. I'm proud of that."

"A step toward what, though? And what are you walking away from?"

A farm stand along the highway was piled high with pumpkins. Lauren had been looking forward to carving pumpkins with Georgia and Hannah this year. Tracy was planning a carving contest at the store too. Dad would have hated the mess, but the idea was exciting.

Lauren's throat tightened, choked like the ditches along the highway that overflowed with still-blooming goldenrod and Queen Anne's lace. She drove past the dingy blue sign that marked the border of Massachusetts.

Tracy whispered, "You can't disappoint Dad anymore, Lauren. He's dead."

And that was all Lauren was missing, wasn't it? She could say goodbye all she wanted, but Dad would always be with her, unsatisfied. Did she need his ghostly approval on everything? She wanted it. She probably always would. But did she really want anything else she didn't already have?

Hadn't she been happy all this time?

For the first quarter mile into Massachusetts, the side of the road was nothing but a guardrail and a steep drop into the valley, but beyond that there was the barest sliver of weather-beaten shoulder. Lauren pulled over and slapped on the hazard lights.

"Ava Hayden's gonna kill me if I back out now."

"I know," Tracy said.

"I already signed a contract for an apartment."

"I know."

Lauren raked a hand through her hair, and it stood up in frazzled spikes.

"Georgia might not forgive me. She might not have changed her mind."

Tracy smoothed Lauren's hair back down.

"I know," she said.

Lauren flexed her hands on the steering wheel for one quiet moment, then stomped the brake pedal and wrenched the van into gear. She checked the mirrors, flicked her turn signal on, and revved the engine like a racecar driver. Then she slumped over the steering wheel with a groan.

"There's no way I can make a three-point turn in this van."

Tracy scrambled gleefully out of the passenger seat, yelling, "Betcha I can!"

CHAPTER THIRTY-SIX

"I'm sorry," the balding man behind the counter at the art store said. "Tammy's not answering her phone, either. Should I try Tracy?"

Georgia clenched her hands at her sides and forced herself not to hug herself or rock on the balls of her feet in public. Lauren's apartment had been dark and empty when she got there, and there was no answer when Georgia called. She'd come to Ashburn's Art Supply hoping to find help, but she was too late.

"No, thank you. You have a customer."

The man turned to the woman who'd been waiting. Georgia stared out the window at the Main Street traffic, cursing herself while a U-haul drove past, stopped with a squeal of rubber, and backed clumsily into a parking space. She wanted Lauren to be here so badly she imagined it was her jumping out of that U-haul.

Then the door to Ashburn's burst open, the sleigh bells clattering.

"Georgia! I knew that was your car out front. Are you looking for me?" Lauren asked.

Lauren was here. The fact of her, panting and dirty in the doorway to the art store, took Georgia so thoroughly by surprise that she skipped a few beats of conversation and launched straight into the script she'd been rehearsing in the car.

"I know you don't want to date me anymore, and that's okay, but I'd like us to be friends. Hannah misses you, I miss you, and I don't want you to just leave and never come back. I want you to be in our lives, even if it's not exactly the way I'd hoped. I needed you to know that before you leave because—"

"I'm not leaving."

Lauren's feet were planted and her eyes sharp and determined when she said it. Georgia's firm posture softened.

"You're not?"

"No," Lauren said. "I don't want to leave, so I'm not going to. I want to live here, and I want to be with you."

Georgia stared for a moment, even when it started to feel uncomfortable, because she didn't want to look away and let Lauren disappear.

"Okay," she said. Then, "Not as friends?"

One corner of Lauren's lips twitched, but she didn't smile when she said, "I'll take whatever you're offering."

The weight of this twist impressed itself on Georgia then. What was she offering?

"We should talk about that," she said.

Lauren nodded. A customer came in and pushed past her, not seeming to notice the atmosphere she was interrupting.

"Lauren, you girls are adorable," the man at the counter said, "but would you mind taking this outside?"

"That's a reasonable request, Ted," Lauren said.

Georgia felt her ears heat up and covered them with her hands. Lauren put an arm around her to lead her out of the store and down the street.

Downtown Holderness was active on a Monday afternoon, but a few blocks in the right direction took Lauren and Georgia through a residential neighborhood, then a short tract of woods.

On the other side of the trees, the town asserted itself again: the old courthouse, the fire department, and a little square with benches and a fountain. Yellow leaves floated in the fountain's basin and dotted the brick path around it. The sound of the water helped Georgia keep herself calm.

Lauren pushed a leaf aside and traced one of the bricks with her shoe. It was stamped, FOR LAUREN AND TRACY ASHBURN, FROM LUCAS ASHBURN, ASHBURN'S ART SUPPLIES.

"Do you think relationship drama is good advertising?" Lauren joked. She didn't look at Georgia to see her reaction, though. She stared at the top of the fountain, where the water bubbled up.

"How's Hannah?"

Then she looked at Georgia, her eyes so full of concern she looked like she might cry. Lauren never cried. Georgia's heart seized at how much all three of them were hurting.

"Hannah's not good. She'd have been better if I'd reached out and let you say goodbye. That would have been hard for me, though, so I didn't. That wasn't fair to any of us."

Lauren put her fingertips on Georgia's elbow, steering her toward a bench, and they sat on opposite ends.

"I wasn't fair, either," Lauren said. "I know what a meltdown is, and I knew better than to act the way I did when you had one. I shouldn't have dumped everything on you at once. I should have told you Ava Hayden had me interview for an out-of-town job instead of the one I applied for, then this whole mess wouldn't have come out of nowhere."

Georgia smiled, letting the cracks in her calm visage show. "That might have just made me really anxious, honestly. Although I was kind of anxious anyway, because you seemed off. I'm pretty attuned to that when I care about someone."

The way Lauren reached out to touch Georgia's shoulder was automatic. She wanted to comfort, to stroke and hold, always. She stopped herself now, her hand hanging in the air between them. They were both so uncertain. Georgia slid over on the bench and placed herself in Lauren's grasp as she continued talking.

"So you're right, telling me would have been better. We could have talked about—Wait." Something Lauren had said registered in Georgia's mind, and it changed the color of all her assumptions. "You didn't apply for an out-of-town job?"

"Of course not. I wasn't trying to sabotage us, I just…didn't stick up for myself, for us, like I should have, when one was offered. Jesus, I'm an idiot. I should have called twice."

Lauren took her hand off Georgia's shoulder and covered her face with it. Georgia stared at her. She thought she'd been a fool to put her faith in Lauren or that Lauren had lied about her intentions and ambitions, but this version of the story matched with the tender and tirelessly approval-seeking woman Georgia had adored. This made sense.

Georgia thumped her fist on her knee. This could have been worked out weeks ago, if she had been willing to try.

"I should have called you back, even though I didn't think we could work it out. I'm sorry I didn't. I guess I wasn't sure what to say or if you'd even answer. Did you want me to call?"

"More than anything."

Georgia glanced into Lauren's eyes, which were intense and watery again. She studied the line of Lauren's mouth, smiling but twisted under the pressure of so many emotions other than joy. Georgia wanted to take that pressure off. She wanted to kiss those lips until they only smiled. Would Lauren be truly happy if she did?

"Do you want us to be together again? For yourself, not just because of me or Hannah or somebody else? Because I want it, too, but I can't go through this again. It's all or nothing, in or out."

"I'm in. I always knew this was what I wanted, I just couldn't admit it. No way am I making that mistake again. I get that you don't want to repeat mistakes either, though. Do you want to take it slow, keep Hannah out of it until you're sure? Whatever you need, I can make it work. I don't want to make this hard for either of you."

Lauren was so earnest, and she was keeping her posture so rigidly upright it made her body quiver. Georgia put a hand on

Lauren's face and felt warm with pride when she relaxed. The decision wasn't hard at all. Lauren was here. What else could Georgia possibly need?

"We both need to answer our phones more," she said. "I did call you today, and you didn't pick up."

The practicality of the request seemed to give Lauren pause, but as always, she took Georgia's oddities in stride and gave her a serious response.

"I pulled a dramatic U-turn at the Massachusetts border, and my mom sent me a trillion texts asking what the hell I was doing. I guess your call came through in the middle of that. I'm sorry, I'll do better."

"We should get distinct ring tones so we know who's calling."

Lauren nodded. Her natural smile expanded into a wry grin. "A practical plan. Anything else?"

Georgia clutched and scratched at the sleeves of her sweater, suddenly anxious again. She'd called Lauren before she perfected the speech she'd given in the art store.

"Maybe delete the messages I left? I got a little dramatic. Not lying, just...I kind of said I love you."

Lauren eased Georgia's fingers away from their scratching and squeezed her hand. Georgia squeezed back and didn't let go.

"I kind of do love you," she repeated.

"I kind of love you, too."

Lauren leaned forward, tentative, testing, and Georgia kissed her. Their lips and hands were cold at first, but precious contact warmed them quickly. No fire could have done a better job.

When the heat between them started to rise from warm to steaming, Lauren pulled away. It took Georgia a moment to realize why Lauren wasn't sweeping them off to somewhere they could be alone: the entirety of her apartment was in the back of a moving van. Lauren had blown up an entire life to be here now. Georgia would have crawled out of her skin with anxiety about where to stay, where to work, but Lauren didn't seem afraid.

Georgia took a breath and tried to decide what to do. What would Kyle say now? Even better, what would Lauren offer, if Georgia were in her place?

"Do you want to go to my house?" she said. "Hannah will be home from Abby's soon, and she'll be happy to see you."

The smile that spread on Lauren's face was bright as the sun.

"Okay," she said. "Let's go home."

Bella Books, Inc.

Women. Books. Even Better Together.

P.O. Box 10543
Tallahassee, FL 32302

Phone: 800-729-4992
www.bellabooks.com